A

WICKED

LINE

Epertase Publishing
First American Edition

 Cover art by Steve Murphy

Visit Douglas R. Brown at epertasepublishing.com
Follow Douglas on Twitter @douglasrbrown22
Like Epertase on Facebook
Contact Douglas at epertase@gmail.com
ISBN 13: 978-1-7368820-4-7

DEDICATION

I dedicate this story to you, the reader. I tell stories in hopes of bringing entertainment to you. Thank you for being there.

ACKNOWLEDGEMENTS

I would like to thank my proofreaders. My work is always better from your input, and I greatly appreciate it. To Brian Baltz, Tana Lantry, Jeff Stanforth, Sean Wooten, and Bobbe Ecleberry, thank you.

I would also like to thank editor Rebecca Brown for putting up with my minor temper tantrums and always remembering that I'll get it right once I've tried everything else.

To Steve Murphy: Though I keep telling you I could do better if I only had the time, I'll continue seeking out your incredible skills in creating these wonderful covers. In the meantime, I'll remain in awe of your awesome work. You are a good man and a better friend.

To Sean and Helena Wooten, Dale Ullom, Darby and Hazel Blackstone, Bryan and Kara Young, Cory and Amiee Knight, my wife, Angie Brown, my son, Aiden Brown, my cousin Greg Ecleberry, Kelly McClellan, my mom, Lillian Dove, my dad, Dale Brown, my sister, Amie Dove, and brother, Brian Dove, my aunt Bobbe Ecleberry, Cindy Busi, Jeff Stanforth, Matt McNemar, the folks at Columbus Fire Station 22, and everyone who has supported me throughout this writing career, I love you all.

PROLOGUE
TWISTED METAL
April 22, 1994

The garbage truck came out of nowhere.

Jackson's ears popped. A flash of white seared his eyes as coarse nylon canvas raked across his face. It sounded like a bomb had gone off. His arm slammed against the underside of the dashboard, his brand-new Motorola beeper, still illuminated with his wife's last message to "pick up milk," tumbling to the floorboard. Metal twisted around him like warm taffy.

A second deafening crash chased the first, this time from the passenger's side. His head whipped toward the center column and then back against the driver's side window, shattering the glass with the sound of a blown-up paper bag popped by a prankster.

His lights went out for a second—or a year—he couldn't be sure which. An intense ringing in his ears followed. And then everything went quiet. *What happened?* he wondered. His head throbbed worse than the nastiest hangover, yet he hadn't been drinking. It was a deep, encompassing hurt, the kind where he just knew that something in his brain was broken. A cloud of chalky dust burned his eyes. He struggled to focus on the steering wheel in front of him. The vomited remains of a deflated balloon hung from a gash in the center. He gagged on his next breath of lingering airbag dust.

God, his head hurt.

The world calmed for the longest second before he could hear people talking, though he couldn't make out what they said at first. They sounded distant and deeply concerned.

"Did anyone call 9-1-1?" someone asked.

"I think so," someone else answered.

He heard far-off sirens, quiet at first, but growing louder than mating cats. He hoped they were for him because something was seriously wrong. They stopped somewhere behind his car, though he couldn't turn his head to see where. Red lights danced across his dashboard. He tried to blink away the haze. Blood ran down his face and his head felt like someone had torn his scalp apart.

"Hold on, buddy," someone shouted from behind.

Pushing past the pain in his head, he noticed a new pain in his chest that pierced from his sternum through to his spine. "Wh-wh-what happened?" he asked.

"You've been in a wreck," the stranger's voice answered, this time right beside him. "I'm with the Fire Department. I'm here to help."

Thank God.

The fireman shouted, "Working extrication, Lieu."

Just outside his door, a sound like a lawnmower engine choked to life. The motor rumbled and then revved to a shrill, relentless screech.

"Cover his face," another man shouted. "We're gonna cut the A-post."

What the Hell's an A-post? Maybe he should just climb out and get a ride home. Jenna was waiting for him. He tried to move his leg, but knives stabbed his ankle.

"Hold still," a woman shouted over the engine noise. Her voice carried a Southern twang. He wondered how she had climbed into the back seat without him noticing. She cupped gloved hands around his head. "Hold still, cowboy. You're trapped in your car and we're gonna cut you out. What's your name?"

"Jackson," he answered, gasping at the pain in his chest.

"Jackson what?"

"Foster … Am I dying?"

Her breath tickled his ear when she spoke again. "We're doing everything we can to keep that from happening, Jackson. Now stop moving your dang neck."

"My …" A muffled grunt interrupted him. A moment passed before he realized it was his own. "My leg hurts," he struggled to say.

"I know. We're gonna help you, but you need to stay calm."

He thought he *was* staying calm.

Someone else shouted, "Make sure the car's in park and kill the ignition." Jackson surmised they weren't talking to him.

He wanted to rub his burning eyes, but his arms wouldn't move, pinned to his sides by a straitjacket made of jagged metal. All he could do was blink until he could see clearer.

Through his smashed windshield he saw a tool that resembled a giant metal alligator clip with hoses protruding from all sides resting on the hood. It looked like something made for a Mad Max movie. A fireman lifted it with a grunt. It looked heavy.

Someone draped a white sheet over Jackson's head, which was quite alarming. As far as he knew, that's what they did when you were dead. Or dying, maybe. He took as deep a breath as he could.

"Jackson, my name's Jennifer," the woman behind him said. She was under the sheet with him.

He chuckled, making his chest hurt even more. "That's like my wife's name." He wasn't sure why he was telling her that, but felt like it was the right thing to say.

"Then it'll be easy for you to remember," she answered. "Now, you gotta hold still."

He had never heard metal being torn apart before, but it was a unique cacophony of squealing, grinding, and crinkling. Any glass that hadn't broken in the crash crackled and popped as the machine revved and ripped at the car door. The car jerked and rocked with each powerful crunch of the alligator jaws.

The jagged metal straitjacket pinning his left arm to his chest popped loose, though it didn't completely break free.

The car jolted again. Then the lawnmower engine sputtered and stopped.

"Is he dead?" a man asked.

"Back up to the curb," a stern voice snapped back.

The sheet lifted away from Jackson's face, revealing the crowd that had formed. He was embarrassed that everyone was looking at him and didn't want them seeing him carried away. *I should climb out now,* he thought.

"Hold still," Jennifer reminded him. "We're gonna lift you out, but let us do all the work. It's important not to move."

This was the first clear look he had gotten of the garbage truck. Flashing lights flickered across the side. Other than the front tire being flat, he couldn't see any damage. 1989 Chrysler LeBarons were obviously no match for garbage trucks. The driver stood hunched over, rubbing the back of his neck. A paramedic leaned over beside him, talking.

"Is he okay?" Jackson asked.

"Yeah," Jennifer answered. "Don't worry about him."

A police officer climbed out of the cab, waved a flask in the driver's face, and ordered him to put his hands behind his back.

Someone in the crowd yelled, "Holy shit, that garbage man's drunk."

Someone else answered, "Who gets drunk this early?"

A fireman shoved something hard, flat, and uncomfortable under Jackson's left hip. The fireman said, "All right. Pivot him." Gloved hands grabbed his arms and legs and pulled. He spun to face the passenger door.

The only thing worse than the pain in his leg was the pressure growing in his head. He hadn't thought it could hurt any worse, but it did. He slid onto a flat wooden board. The pain in his lower leg briefly eclipsed the pain in his chest and head. He gritted his teeth and groaned.

"Hold his leg together," one of the firemen said.

That didn't sound good.

As they carried him from his car, he saw a fireman hauling his door away. He started to panic.

"You've gotta control your breathing," Jennifer said in his ear and then leaned into his field of vision. He looked into her hazel eyes. She gave him a comforting smile. "There you go. Now focus. Just breathe."

He wanted to do as she asked, but it was too hard.

"We're gonna move you now," she said.

As he seemed to float from his car to the stretcher, he looked past her to the sky. It was a clear, chilly morning and he marveled at how nice a day it was for everyone not named Jackson. His eyelids suddenly dropped as if they wore weights. Maybe he could just sleep for a little while.

"Stay with us, buddy," one of the firemen said as he tightened a seatbelt across Jackson's already tight chest. It was nearly impossible to take a deep breath now. But Jackson was too tired to care. As they slid him into the back of the ambulance, his thoughts turned fuzzy. The paramedics were talking to him—he could see their lips moving—but their voices came from the other end of a long tunnel and didn't make any sense. They sounded like Charlie Brown's teacher. His body went numb. At least the pain had gone away.

He was so tired.

A

WICKED

LINE

There is a wicked line that vigilantes must never cross.

1
EVIL LURKS
October 12, 1994

Drew bounced from the bottom step of the school bus onto the gravel berm, his untied shoelace landing in a mud puddle. "Gross," he whispered. He knew he should probably tie it, but there was no way he was going to now and get his hands all yucky.

A rumble from above turned his attention to the darkened sky.

"Hurry inside, Drew," Mrs. Sanchez said from the driver's seat. "Looks like it's going to storm again."

"I will," Drew answered.

When he saw his empty driveway, his shoulders deflated. Mom worked a lot now that Dad was gone. Drew wondered what he had done so wrong to make his dad leave and not come back.

He knew he'd better hurry inside. Mom had very strict after-school rules for when she wasn't home. "Straight from the bus and into the house," she'd said. "No lollygaggin'." She always made him repeat it, even though he wasn't sure what lollygaggin' meant other than maybe "get your butt inside."

He walked around the front of the bus, looked both ways before crossing the street, and then waved to the bus driver from the other side.

"Bye, Drew," Mrs. Sanchez shouted.

"Bye, Mrs. Sanchez. See you tomorrow."

Drew's friend Phillip stuck his head out a window and shouted, "Bye, stinky-head."

Drew shouted back, "Bye …" He paused, searching for the most killer comeback before settling on, "Stinky-brain." Nailed it. He grinned.

Phillip giggled and sat back in his seat. Drew waved to the other kids as the bus passed, dark exhaust belching from the rear. A raindrop landed on his shoulder.

He turned toward his house, hesitating when he saw a man he didn't recognize coming toward him. Drew looked away, hoping the man wouldn't stop.

"Hi there," the man said. His voice was deep and kind of scary.

Drew wasn't supposed to talk to strangers, but he didn't want to be rude. "Hello," he answered without looking up. He started up his driveway.

The man said, "Wait a second. Your shoe's untied. Want me to tie that for you?" He looked around and then closed the distance and started to kneel by Drew.

Drew stepped backward, pulling his foot out of reach. "No, thank you."

The man stood up again and backed up to the mailbox, never taking his eyes off Drew. He opened it and reached in. "Here," he said as he pulled out an envelope and extended it toward Drew. "Don't forget your mail."

Drew hesitated. "I'm not supposed to talk to strangers."

"Oh. Yeah. Of course not. That's very good. That's very important." His hand hovered, the envelope dangling from his fingers. Drew's mom would be angry if he let someone take their mail.

The man looked around again. "I don't wanna get you in trouble …" His eyes moved to Drew's backpack where his name was written in black marker. "… Drew. Is that short for Andrew?"

Drew nodded. "That's my dad's name. I'm a junior." He knew he shouldn't keep talking, but the man seemed friendly enough. "I should probably get inside."

"I suppose so. Your mom'll be home soon, huh?" He shook the envelope and stepped closer. A car drove past.

Drew stared at the envelope for a second and then snatched it from the man's hand. It didn't occur to him to ask how the man knew his mom wasn't home. "Thanks. I'd better go now." Drew started for the house.

"Hey, Drew," the man called out. Drew turned back. The man smiled, but there was something about it that made Drew nervous. Maybe it was his missing front tooth.

"I forgot to ask. Do you like X-Men comic books?"

That got Drew's attention. He nodded. He *loooved* the X-Men.

"I thought you might. You seem like a pretty bright kid. I happen to have a few in my glovebox." He pointed to a van parked by the curb a few houses down. "You wanna see?"

Drew hesitated. He really wanted to see, but he knew he shouldn't. Still, his curiosity got the better of him. "Do any of them have Cyclops? He's my favorite."

"I think so. I've got the one where the redhead girl—"

"Jean Grey?" Drew interrupted.

"Yeah. I've got the one where she marries that Cyclops guy you like."

Drew's excitement hit a wall. His shoulders drooped. "Oh. You mean the *wedding issue*?" He stuck out his tongue and made a face.

"I've got three or four others, too. They're yours if you come take a look."

Maybe Drew could look for just a minute. What could it hurt? He was the fastest runner in his class and could probably get away if he needed to. Besides, where else was he going to get free X-Men comics?

The man bobbed his head toward the van. "Comin'?"

But even all the X-Men comic books in the world couldn't drown out his mom's voice repeating, "No lollygaggin'" in his head. There wasn't a superhero ever invented worth his mom getting mad and leaving him like his dad had done. He shook his head and backed away. "I'd like to see them. Really, I would. But I can't. I'm sorry."

The man's smile faded and darkness washed over his eyes. He reached out again and stepped forward. "Come 'ere," he snapped through clenched teeth. His snarl sent Drew running up the driveway, careful not to trip over his shoelace. Drew glanced back to make sure the man wasn't giving chase. To his relief, the man still stood at the end of the driveway. The raindrops started falling faster.

"I'll see you later, Drew," the man shouted.

Drew used his key on the door beside the garage and raced inside, closing and locking it behind him. He ran up the stairs to his bedroom and parted two slats of the mini blinds just enough to see out. The man still stood at the end of the driveway in the pouring rain, staring up at Drew's window as if he knew right where he would go. Drew yanked his fingers away, letting the blinds snap back into place. He sat under the windowsill with his back against the wall and his knees pulled up to his chest until he heard a car pull into the driveway an hour or so later.

A careful peek through the blinds confirmed that the man was gone and his mother was home. As Drew raced downstairs to meet his mom at the door, he decided not to tell her about the man. He didn't want to get in trouble for talking to a stranger.

2
SPYDERBITE
October 19, 1994

It had been six months since Jackson's car accident, and recovery had been a bitch. He was glad Friday had been his last day of rehab. In hindsight, if anyone had told him at the start that he could choose between six months of rehab or death by a thousand beestings, he would have covered himself in nectar and kicked every fucking hive he could find. There were few tortures comparable to stretching a surgically repaired knee ligament or reworking a replacement hip.

As much as he hated it, he didn't feel he was ready to be done. He figured it had more to do with his insurance reaching its limit. The physical therapist said she'd taught him all the techniques needed to keep his leg limber and his hip working well, and it was up to him to keep it up. When he complained that he still had pain, she said he was going to live with a certain amount of discomfort probably forever.

His mental rehab, on the other hand, was a different matter. The head shrink, Dr. Hurley, said he would need constant therapy to deal with his brain injury, but Jackson was sick of talking about his feelings and hadn't been back for weeks, despite his doctor's urging.

Sitting on his couch with his eyes fixated on the TV, he felt numb and empty. On the screen, some so-called political expert droned on and on. The national news was impossible to watch during any kind of election season. The host overanalyzed the latest poll and explained why President

Clinton needed the Dems to perform well to further his agenda. Jackson couldn't care less that one blowhard politician had gained two points over the projected frontrunner in some state he'd never visit.

He mumbled, "Losers. All of them."

At some point since he'd come home from the hospital, his ass had formed a divot in his couch cushion. The divot seemed to exert a gravitational pull on him if he tried to sit anywhere else. That included the kitchen where his wife, Jenna, was setting the table for dinner.

"Jack?" she called out. He ignored her. "Jackson," she snapped.

His answer was an amalgam of "What?" and a grunt.

"Are you coming to the table tonight or are you eating in there again?" she asked. He had gotten used to eating on a TV tray over the last six months. He could hear in her voice how any answer he gave would be received. He shrugged his shoulders, hoping it would be enough to end the inquisition.

"Fine. You can get your own food whenever you want." She had stopped serving him after he refused to go back to see Dr. Hurley.

Jackson wasn't hungry. Since the accident, he rarely was. He had lost weight, though not by choice, and his already lean physique now bordered on sickly. Whenever he looked in the mirror, he half-jokingly pictured himself in one of those Sally Struthers commercials. For seventy cents a day, one could save a person just like him. But knowing he needed to eat more wasn't enough when the desire to eat wasn't there. Especially when everything tasted like vomit.

He knew rain must be on the way because his hip throbbed like a cartoon thumb smashed by a hammer. And he was getting another headache. He got them quite often.

"Why doesn't Daddy eat with us?" his nine-year-old son, Garrett, asked as he sat at the kitchen table. "He doesn't even need his cane anymore."

"He still doesn't feel well, honey," Jenna answered. She always covered for him with Garrett, though her tone had grown colder recently. The way she emphasized the word "feel" revealed her growing resentment. "We have to give him time."

The nightly news led into a blank screen and a chorus of voices shouting, "Wheel. Of. Fortune." A graphic of the popular gameshow's prize wheel spun across the screen. As the announcer introduced Pat Sajak and the lovely Vanna White, the hosts sauntered past a shiny new white Pontiac Grand Prix. Seeing it reminded Jackson of his beloved LeBaron—which reminded him of the wreck. Everything seemed to remind him of the wreck in some way.

While his eyes stayed glued to the TV, he listened to his family talk about him as if he weren't there. What the hell was wrong with him that hearing Garrett's concern didn't thrust him from the couch to race over and squeeze his son in the biggest hug he could manage? Why was knowing he was failing his family not a catalyst for compassion, but instead only made him angrier? He would have never behaved like this before. The longer he stewed, the more he decided it was better if he could just be left alone. Or dead.

Deep down he wanted to be the person he was before the wreck, playing with Garrett and eating dinner with the family like a normal husband and father, but that took energy he couldn't seem to muster anymore. It wasn't fair that Jenna had to bear the financial burden of the whole family with her single nursing salary. He hated when she worked overtime on her nights off, but their savings were dwindling fast and he wasn't ready to work again. His physical therapist had said he could ease back into the workforce and do as much as his bad leg would allow, but he was a mechanic by trade and wasn't convinced the physical therapist knew what that entailed. His old job at the tire shop required a lot of maneuvering and lifting, and he didn't think his leg was up for it.

After Jenna and Garrett finished dinner, Garrett carried a plate of food to Jackson and set it on the TV tray beside the couch. Then he climbed onto Jackson's lap and wrapped his skinny arms around him. Jackson didn't hug him back. He wanted to, but his arms were anvils weighted by sadness. To his son it must have felt like hugging a warm corpse. In a way, he was.

Garrett kissed his cheek, whispered, "I love you, Daddy," and then climbed down. He stood quiet for a minute and then asked, "Do you like my new haircut?" He brushed his hand over the stubble. "I had Mom cut it like yours."

Jackson glanced out of the corner of his eye and then looked back to the TV. He didn't feel like answering, so he grunted instead.

As Garrett ran back to the kitchen to help clear the dinner table, something touched Jackson's cheek. He found the strength to lift his arm and wipe the tear away. It would have been better for everyone if he'd never woken up after the wreck.

A little after Garrett went to his room, Jenna marched over and stood between the TV and Jackson with her hands on her hips. The phrase "You'd make a better door than a window" came to mind, but he knew better than to say it. He didn't need to look up at her face to feel the tension in her.

He leaned to the side to see the TV behind her. Not knowing whether Susan won the grand prize would drive him nuts. The final puzzle was so easy.

Jenna leaned into his view. "Why do you act like this?" she snapped. "It's been six months since the accident."

Shit. Now he'd never know if Susan knew that M-_-S-T-A-R-_ was MUSTARD. By the time Jenna moved enough that he could catch a glimpse, Jeopardy had already started.

"Answer me, Jack. Don't you see what you're doing to this family?"

Of course he saw it. Did she think he liked being this way?

"Garrett begged me to give him that damn haircut. He thinks if he cuts his hair like yours, it'll make you want to spend time with him again."

Jackson's body deflated deeper into the worn-out cushion. He wanted to throw up.

Her shoulders relaxed as her hands dropped from her hips. Her voice softened. "Jack, honey. I know the accident did something to your head. I know you're depressed. Won't you please go back and see Dr. Hurly? He was helping you."

Jackson wanted to shout, "That guy's a quack." Instead, he stared silently at the wall beyond her hip.

"I love you, Jack."

He didn't look at her face, but the quiver in her voice let him know she was crying. She cried a lot nowadays.

"You're driving us away. I can't live like this forever. I won't. I don't want to abandon you, but you have to put some kind of effort into this family."

There was something infinitely wrong with him that the blackness eating his gut was so much stronger than his will to show his wife the compassion she deserved.

She stood silent, hoping—praying—he'd tell her it would be all right. Or even tell her to fuck off. Anything would be better than her being the only one talking. When he couldn't find it in himself to give her that comfort, she stormed out of the room. He listened to her march up the stairs before she slammed their bedroom door. He felt so weak.

Rather than let the *Jeopardy* contestants prove how stupid he was, he flipped off the tube and watched the blank screen.

The next time he saw his wife was after ten o'clock when she came downstairs wearing light blue scrubs. She grabbed her keys from the narrow countertop beside the fridge.

"Garrett's tucked in," she said without looking at him. "He's asleep. Maybe you can have him dressed for school when I get home in the morning." She paused as she opened the door leading to the garage, waiting for some sort of acknowledgement. A grunt even. When Jackson gave her nothing, she added, "Then again, I won't count on it." She slammed the door behind her.

She didn't deserve this. After everything the accident had stolen from him—his job, his future, his happiness—his wife and son were all he had left to keep him from wearing a rope necklace. And now he was losing them too.

An hour or so passed before Jackson pried himself from the couch, and even then he only got up because he needed to piss. Gravity seemed to have a vendetta against his legs. It had been one of the bad days, not that he had many good ones anymore. He pushed to his feet, limped down the hallway, and stood in front of the toilet with one hand against the wall.

Droplets of urine splattered his pajama pants and he couldn't care less. Maybe he would change them later, maybe not. He hadn't changed them in three days and he didn't know why that night should be any different. He rubbed his head as he looked into the mirror, only it wasn't his reflection that he saw. It was Garrett's. His son gazed back, eyes wet and soulless. A hideous scar matching Jackson's started at his son's temple and stretched across his forehead before darting ninety degrees upward. Jackson closed his eyes and felt for the light switch. That was enough visions for one day.

After a Vicodin with a Bud Light chaser, Jackson plopped back into his ass groove on the couch, flipped the TV back on, and gazed at the screen. Breaking news. A helicopter followed a car chase in some big city. The chyron said that the perp had robbed a convenience store and may have killed the clerk on his way out. It seemed every car chase made the news ever since that OJ thing. The car on TV slammed into a minivan at an intersection. Jackson flinched. Death and destruction everywhere.

"Prick will probably get off scot-free," he mumbled to himself. He didn't have much faith in the legal system after the drunk who had hit him got off with some classes, fines, and probation. The last Jackson had heard, the guy was fighting to get his job back. He'd probably get it, too.

Stewing in his dark thoughts, Jackson watched TV until he passed out.

The door to the garage opening startled him awake.

"Jackson?" Jenna shouted. "Is Garrett ready for school?"

Jackson rubbed his eyes. His neck was stiff and his hip hurt like hell. "Uh. No … What time is it? I …"

Jenna dropped her coat on the opposite end of the couch. "Damn it, Jack. It's 7:40. His bus just drove by. He's gotta be at school in twenty minutes." She grabbed Garrett's bookbag from beside the stairs and shouted for him to wake up. When she returned to the TV room, she said, "I had a horrible night at work and had to hold over this morning. Can't you help with anything around here?"

"Why didn't you call and wake me?"

"I tried. The phone's been ringing all morning. This'll be the third time he's been late in the last three weeks."

Jackson rubbed his forehead. "There goes Harvard," he mumbled.

"You're not funny, Jack."

"No, seriously, Jenna. It's the fourth grade."

"You know, I liked it better yesterday when you didn't talk." She hurried upstairs. Jackson rolled to his side facing the back of the couch and closed his eyes. Before he fell asleep again, he felt Garrett kiss his cheek.

I'm sorry I'm like this, Garrett.

Jenna didn't kiss him when she left.

When she returned fifteen minutes later, she didn't speak. Instead, she passed through the living room, spraying Lysol over him and the couch. The thick mist burned his nostrils and made him cough. She couldn't have better conveyed her message if she'd hit him over the head with a hammer made of soap. The disinfectant cloud continued to gag him, so he covered his head with a blanket.

"By the way," Jenna said as she left the room. "Dustin will be here in a couple hours."

Jackson whipped around and pulled the blanket from his face. "What?"

"He's taking you to a late breakfast or brunch or whatever the hell you two want to do."

"Wait. Why?"

"What do you mean why? He's your best friend and he wants to see you. All you do is lie around all day and stink. I don't care what you do just as long as you get out of the house for a while."

He scrambled for a way out. "I don't wanna go anywhere today. Call and tell him tomorrow would be better."

"Nope. You tell him. I'm going to bed." She headed upstairs.

Shit. The second to last thing Jackson wanted to do was go somewhere with Dustin. The only problem was that the *last* thing he wanted to do was tell his stubborn friend he wasn't going.

Jackson ran to the portable phone and pressed the first four digits of Dustin's number, mentally planning what he'd say. *Hey, brother, I'm not feeling well today. My hip is killing me and I can hardly walk.* It was at least half true. Now, all he needed to do was finish dialing the number. If he was lucky, he'd get the answering machine and not even have to talk to his friend. Then he could ignore the inevitable return calls and say he was stuck on the pot or something.

If only.

He had no doubt that the driving reason Jenna had called Dustin was because of Dustin's unyielding tenacity. Jackson's thumb hovered over the final digit, but deep down he knew that he'd never actually call. Leaving such a message would only bring Dustin to his house two minutes after. And worse, Dustin had a key. For a split second he considered staying in his pajama pants to force his friend to reschedule for another day, but Dustin was just as likely to physically drag him out in all his stink. Instead, he begrudgingly accepted his fate and shifted his focus to finding the energy to take a shower and get dressed.

While the shower water ran down his face, he pictured Jenna lying in bed in the next room and laughing to herself, knowing she had won that round. Despite how irritated he was, it made him grin.

Clean for the first time in a week, Jackson tiptoed from the bathroom into his bedroom where Jenna had fallen asleep. He gathered clean underwear, blue jeans, and an old AC/DC T-shirt.

When he returned to the TV room, Dustin was already sitting on the couch. He wore a black Jack Daniels ballcap to hide his receding hairline and a faded Class of '80 T-shirt.

"'Sup, home skillet?"

Jackson shook his head. "That makes no sense."

"Your couch smells like a locker room," Dustin said.

"Yeah, yeah. Good to see you, too. What, no knocking?"

"I didn't wanna wake Jenna." Dustin scanned Jackson from head to toe. "You look like hell."

"Thanks."

Dustin pushed to his feet with a groan.

"You know, it probably wouldn't be so hard to get up if you didn't weigh three hundred pounds. Jesus, what have you been eating?"

Dustin flashed him a middle finger. "Whatever. I'll have you know I'm down to 240. Which is still more than enough to whup your skinny ass. You ready to go?"

"Where we goin'?"

"Tee Jaye's."

"A little early for lunch, don't you think?"

"Then get pancakes. They have everything."

"Do I have to go?"

"Of course." Dustin led the way through the front door. Jackson considered, albeit briefly, slamming the door closed and locking him out. But it would have been yet another futile attempt at putting off the inevitable.

"You want me to drive?" Jackson asked.

"Not likely. I don't want you offing us by driving over any cliffs."

Jackson snorted. "Come on, Dustin. We live in Pataskala. Do you know how far I'd have to drive to find a cliff? Do we even have any in Ohio?"

Dustin chuckled and climbed into his 1980 rust-bucket Dodge truck, waiting patiently while Jackson struggled to haul himself into the passenger seat.

Dustin's tongue traced the inside of his lower lip. "I need to stop for some snuff."

Of course he did. Anytime Jackson went anywhere with Dustin it meant they had to stop for snuff. There were three things he could guarantee about his friend's habit. First, he was always almost out of snuff and needed to stop for more. Second, he always had a puffy lower lip. And third, drinking out of open soda cans without verifying that it wasn't

Dustin's spit can meant at least two minutes of the worse gagging and vomiting imaginable.

The rust-bucket roared to life and R.E.M. blared from the speakers. Jackson wasn't a fan. "You got any Pearl Jam?" he asked.

Dustin shook his head and backed out of the driveway while R.E.M. continued to ask Kenneth what the frequency was. Jackson sighed and put on his seatbelt, noting without surprise that Dustin hadn't bothered with his. He never wore a seatbelt and it annoyed the hell out of Jackson, especially after the accident. Anyone who would choose a broken nose or a windshield hat because they were too lazy to fasten their seatbelts was clearly not the sharpest tool in the shed. Even before the crash, he'd given Dustin shit over it, but Dustin always told the same anecdote about a friend of a cousin of his wife who had drowned when she couldn't get her seatbelt off after crashing into a lake. Or an ocean. Or something. The story changed a little every time. It wasn't worth the trouble anymore.

They were barely out of the driveway when Dustin lowered the volume on his dash-mounted CD player and took a deep breath like he was about to burst into song. *Oh great. Here it comes. Serious Dustin.*

Dustin kept his eyes on the road. "So, what's wrong with your head?"

Though Jackson loved Dustin like a brother, his friend wasn't the most compassionate communicator. "You wouldn't get it," Jackson answered.

"From the sound of things, you're screwing up your life."

Jackson turned away and looked through the passenger side window. He noticed a garbage can near the curb and thought about his accident. What could he say? How could Dustin possibly understand what he was feeling? Whenever Dustin felt down, he'd just go out and shoot a deer or something. He'd never understand how Jackson could consciously know he was screwing up his life yet continue to do so because he was in too deep a hole to climb out. It was like quicksand for his brain, and it was relentless.

"You need to snap out of it," Dustin added. "Jenna says you ain't showered for over a week."

"I took one today."

"Are you eating? You look like you're from Ethiopia. No offense."

Yeah, how could that be offensive? "Do you say this kind of stuff in front of just anyone?"

"What'd I say?"

"You can't make fun of things like starva—Oh, never mind. I'm just going through a bit of a rough patch right now. I'll be fine."

"You know I'm here for you, right?"

"Hmph. Yeah. I guess."

"If you're sad or something, just stop being sad. What's so bad in your life?"

Jackson would have a better chance of success explaining molecular biology to a Rottweiler. "You wouldn't understand."

"I understand you're being a dick to your family."

Okay, maybe he *did* understand. "You're not helping."

Dustin pulled into the gas station at the end of the street. He said, "You grab my snuff and I'll fill up the tank. Get the green can. You know, wintergreen?"

"Yeah, I know. Same as always."

"We'll talk about this depression shit later."

Jackson could hardly wait.

Dustin tossed thirty bucks to him. "Put twenty on pump five."

Before Jackson could open his door, an eighteen- or nineteen-year-old boy strutted past the truck. He was scrawny with blond hair that was long in the back and buzzed up top. Jackson thought those hairstyles had gone out in the '80s. He recognized the kid from somewhere, but couldn't quite place where. The kid slowed and gave Jackson a cocky glare through the windshield. Jackson felt an immediate twinge in his stomach like he was about to be in a schoolyard fight or something. Not one for confrontation, he looked away. Out of the corner of his eye, he saw the kid continue into the convenience store.

Jackson climbed out. He looked over the truck bed to Dustin and asked, "You see that punk go in the store?"

Dustin shook his head. "Wasn't paying attention."

"He looked like he wanted to start a fight or something."

"Aaand?"

"I don't know. I got a bad feeling about him."

"Are you saying you want me to go in and get the snuff?"

"No, no. I got it. I just … I mean … Don't worry about it. I'll be right back." Jackson headed toward the store. The glass door was plastered with sale flyers, making it next to impossible to see inside. He reached for the handle.

Someone shouted from inside, "Stop, you little prick," as the door blasted open, almost jamming Jackson's hand.

Jackson jumped back as the cocky kid raced out, clutching a cigarette carton in each hand. Jackson cowered as he barreled past. The kid dropped one of the cartons, snatched it from the ground, and feinted at Jackson before running off laughing.

"Stop that kid," the clerk shouted as he raced from the back, carrying a wooden baseball bat. The kid was long gone. The clerk shook his head as he looked Jackson up and down. "Never crossed your mind to help me, huh? Trip him or something?"

"Yeah, right. And get shot?"

"Seriously, man? He was just a punk kid. You could have helped a bit."

Jackson didn't know what else to say. Maybe he could have done something. Dustin would have.

Winded, the clerk returned to the counter. "Stop letting the heat out," he shouted. "Are you coming in or not?"

"Oh. Sorry." Jackson stepped inside and closed the door. A cardboard display had been knocked over, spilling cheap Halloween decorations across the floor. "Are you going to call the cops?"

"The cops? What're they gonna do about a couple cigarettes? They gots more important things to deal with." He shook the bat in his left hand. "But no worries. I'll see that punk again. He's been in here before."

"So that's it? He just gets away?"

"Well, he might not have gotten away if you hadn't wet your panties when you saw him running at you."

"I wouldn't call it wetting my panties."

"What would you call it, then?"

Jackson sighed. "Whatever." He felt like an unbelievable wimp.

He pointed at the snuff cans on the wall behind the counter. "One of those. Wintergreen. And twenty on pump five."

The clerk grabbed a can. "You believe in karma?" he asked as he set the can on the counter.

Jackson tossed a pack of peppermint gum beside the snuff. "Not really."

"Why not?"

Jackson shrugged as he handed over Dustin's money. "Seems like a convenient way for someone to feel better about the bad stuff they can't control. It's just a way for the helpless to feel less … you know, helpless."

The clerk shook his head again. "You're a real ray of sunshine, ain't ya? All's the same, that kid'll get his in the end. I'm sure of it."

"You mean like karma?"

"Here's your change." Under his breath he added something that sounded like, "Smartass."

After dropping two pennies in the "need one, take one" dish, Jackson headed back to the truck. Dustin finished pumping gas and climbed in.

"Did you see that guy steal those smokes?" Jackson asked.

"I saw some kid runnin' off. Figured he took something. Is that what it was? Smokes?"

"Yeah. Two cartons. That was the same guy I saw going in. Remember, I said I thought he was looking for trouble?"

"Piece of trash if you ask me."

"Yeah," Jackson agreed.

Dustin spit in a Mountain Dew can. "He had a sweet mullet, though."

Jackson frowned. "What's a mullet?"

"His haircut. Long in the back, short on top."

"I didn't know it was called a mullet."

"What do you mean you didn't know? You used to have one, remember?" He chuckled.

Jackson nodded. "Yeah, yeah." It wasn't like Jackson was a freak or anything. Everyone wore their hair that way back in the eighties. Well, everyone but Dustin. His wrestling coach didn't allow long hair. "Anyway, I told you there was something fishy about him." Jackson sat quietly while Dustin pulled out of the gas station before adding, "Do you think I'm a wimp?"

Dustin's face twisted slightly. "Why would you ask that?"

"I don't know. I could have helped that clerk stop that guy or something."

"It was none of your business. Why would you even get involved?"

"You would have."

"Oh, I don't know. Maybe just for fun. But it's not your place to be gas station security."

"Yeah, I guess not." It didn't feel good to stand on the sidelines while someone got away with stealing, even if it was just a few cigarettes. "You know something? I think I recognized the thief from the neighborhood next to mine. On my way home from the store a few weeks ago, I damn near hit him when he ran out in front of me. I had to slam on my brakes. The punk gave me the middle finger like it was my fault. You know what's funny? I swear I heard his friends yell, 'Look out, Spider.' What kind of douchebag calls himself Spider?"

"The thief kind. And he probably spells it with a 'y' too. You know, just to be special?"

Jackson laughed. "Yeah, probably."

After a short silence, Dustin added, "Maybe you should have, you know?"

"Should have what?"

"Hit him with your car."

"Oh, yeah. Right. Just hit the kid?" Jackson picked at one of his fingernails. Though Dustin was kidding, it wasn't the worst idea.

Dustin probably didn't remember, but they had had a similar conversation a couple of years back at a party, and it had stuck with Jackson ever since. The question on the table was who in the room would have killed baby Hitler to stop his future atrocities. The others in the group decided they couldn't kill a baby no matter who that baby might later become. Most of them agreed they'd like to help baby Hitler throughout his life so he wouldn't become a monster or something along those lines. But that wasn't *really* answering the question, and it annoyed Jackson. He had the only right answer, as far as he was concerned. "Hell yeah," he'd told them. "I'd kill that little bastard. And I wouldn't feel bad about doing it, either." The others, some of whom he had just met that night, assumed he didn't truly believe what he'd said. But it wasn't hyperbole. He'd meant every word.

But Spyder wasn't Hitler and Jackson didn't want to kill him. There was a big difference between stealing cigarettes and committing genocide.

"Did you tell the clerk where Spyder lived?" Dustin asked.

Jackson shook his head. Even if he'd recognized the punk right away, snitching wouldn't have occurred to him.

Dustin steered with his knees while he opened the snuff can, spit out his current pouch, and shoved a fresh wad against his gums. "It'd be nice if someone went to that punk's house and beat his ass."

"I remember a time when you'd be just the guy to do that."

"Heh. That was a long time ago. Age, beer, and marriage have made me too soft for that nonsense now."

They pulled into the parking lot of Tee Jaye's and went in. Jackson got pancakes like Dustin had suggested. They were good.

Dustin drank coffee without spitting out the wad of snuff under his lip. With his usual bluntness, he asked whether Jackson was depressed enough to off himself. Though some days the answer might be up in the air, Jackson rolled his eyes and brushed off his friend's concern. The last thing he wanted was Dustin pitying him even more and telling him what a great life he had again. Thankfully, Dustin didn't say much more about Jackson's depression, most likely because it had taken every bit of macho suppression he could manage to say as much as he had already.

While Jackson tried to stay engaged in Dustin's rambling conversation about everything from football to politics (neither of which they agreed on), Jackson couldn't get his mind off Spyder. More specifically, he couldn't forget what Dustin had said about hitting the kid with his car. Getting away scot-free wasn't right regardless of the scope of his crime.

When Dustin dropped him off at home, Jackson wouldn't go so far as to admit to enjoying his first morning out of the house in weeks, but he was glad he had gone. The two beers from Dustin's cooler that they drank in the driveway didn't hurt either.

Seeing his friend must have done some good because that night he found the energy to eat dinner at the table with his family. When Garrett sat across from him, Jackson winked.

"Pretty cool haircut, kid." He rubbed his own head. "Just like mine."

Garrett grinned and looked down at his plate.

After dinner, Jackson's ass found its way back to the couch where he sat until Jenna came down for work. It was a bit earlier than most nights.

"Leaving already?" he asked.

"I need to get in a little early to get a head start on the full moon crazies. Could you tuck Garrett in, please? He's in bed already."

He nodded.

She kissed his cheek and whispered, "I'm glad you had a better day today."

Jackson followed her to the door and closed it behind her. Then he made his way upstairs to his son's bedroom. Garrett pretended to be asleep. Jackson called his bluff and turned off the light, pretending to leave.

Garrett sat up with a start. "Dad? Did you think I was really asleep?"

"Yeah, kid. You fooled me." Jackson sat on the edge of the bed.

"Will you sing 'Puff the Magic Dragon' like Mom does?"

Ugh. Jackson knew less than half the words and his voice, as Garrett once put it, sounded like "crap," but he gave it a shot. Garrett helped him through. It was the first time Jackson had ever actually listened to the words and realized they were depressing as hell. Little Jackie Paper grows up and forgets about his best friend? What a terrible song. He might as well sing "Cat's in the Cradle" next and send himself right over the edge. Instead, he finished with "Twinkle, Twinkle, Little Star" and then sat with Garrett until his son drifted off. After Garrett was asleep, Jackson sat on the edge of the bed and quietly sobbed.

3
STEP OFF

October 22, 1994

Something as petty as shoplifting shouldn't have bothered Jackson so much, but that asshole getting away after the Great Gas Station Cigarette heist of '94 stuck in his craw for days. He'd felt like a sissy after the clerk had chastised him. And it wasn't fair that Spyder's prize for stealing was a week or two of free cigarettes and no repercussions. Maybe they'd give him cancer or emphysema. One could only hope. He found it funny that he was wishing for the very karma he had scoffed at a few days before. He pictured the clerk laughing at him.

Jenna had left for work without so much as a goodbye after another argument over his ass growing roots into the couch. He sat watching a commercial for an exercise device shaped like a large bowtie that would supposedly make your thighs stronger. The pretty blonde from *Three's Company* demonstrated how to use it, and for some strange reason it seemed like a good purchase for a few seconds.

Channel-surfing away from news coverage of a forest fire landed Jackson on a made-for-TV drama about an abused woman getting revenge on her estranged husband. Though he had missed the first half of the movie, it wasn't hard to get up to speed. He settled into his ass groove and stuck with it through the final three commercial breaks. The acting was subpar and the dialogue was as stilted as a junior high school play, but the revenge part was something Jackson could really sink his teeth into.

As Jackson watched the battered wife, Victoria, call the cops sobbing, he thought about all of Spyder's victims, both past and future. While the movie's 9-1-1 dispatcher pried information from Victoria, he wondered if Spyder was enjoying his free smokes. When the camera showed the estranged husband, Fred, lying bleeding on the floor with a fatal wound from Victoria's still smoking gun, Jackson fantasized about Spyder getting his just dues. Not that Spyder deserved to die or anything.

He started rooting for Victoria. He hoped she would get away with killing Fred. To Jackson, it wasn't important that she invited Fred over and intentionally pissed him off, knowing he'd raise his voice for the neighbors to hear. His punching Victoria in the eye when she told him he couldn't get it up anymore was icing on the cake. None of what she did that night, not breaking the front window before he arrived or shooting him a second time knowing the first shot had done the job, was worse than what ten years of marriage to a monster had done to her. Fred deserved everything he got, and Jackson hoped he suffered in those last few minutes of the show. Victoria secretly grinning at the camera while being consoled by the growing crowd of neighbors was the perfect ending as far as Jackson was concerned.

The movie left it for the viewer to decide whether Victoria had succeeded in getting away with what could only be considered premeditated murder. Jackson had no question what the answer was. Of course she had succeeded. That was the only fair ending.

He thought about Spyder again and how he had cowered from him at the gas station. It made him feel like even less of a man than his depression did. Maybe the clerk was right and he should have done something. His thoughts turned to the drunk hitting him and getting off with a slap on the wrist, and it sat like spoiled milk in his gut. There should be consequences for flouting the law, but the police couldn't do shit. The garbage man should be in prison for at least as long as Jackson had pain, which would probably be forever. And Spyder should pay for his damn cigarettes. But what could Jackson do? He was just an out of work mechanic who couldn't even get off the couch to save his marriage.

And then an idea crept into his mind. His hip might hurt sometimes, but he wasn't crippled. And he knew where Spyder lived …

A sudden wave of energy shot through him and pushed him to his feet. For the first time in he didn't know how long, he knew what he needed to do. It all seemed so simple. Spyder needed to face some kind of consequence for what he'd done. Why couldn't Jackson give it to him? Just the idea of doing something made his stomach feel tingly.

All he needed was a plan. But what punishment did stealing cigarettes merit? As he glanced around the kitchen, the refrigerator caught his eye and gave him a perfectly devious idea. He remembered Spyder's house had an old Camaro sitting in the driveway. He smiled and retrieved a carton of a half-dozen eggs from the fridge's top shelf. Sure, egging someone's car was a petty thing for a thirty-two-year-old to do, but it would be fun. And maybe he could finally get the Spyder incident out of his mind and feel more like a man.

He went to the hall closet next and slipped on a dark brown leather bomber jacket. Then he pulled down the disaster zone that was the hat and gloves basket from the closet shelf. He found a gray winter cap and his black leather gloves and slipped them on. The gloves were tight on his hands, and it made his fists feel strong.

As he shoveled the spilled hats, scarves, and winter gloves back into the basket, a black winter ski mask landed on the rim. He tilted his head and stared at it for a few seconds. At first, the mask reminded him of his 1991 skiing phase that had been dramatically cut short by a tree, a broken wrist, and several stitches. Jenna had said the mask made him look like a bank robber. He figured it couldn't hurt to have a disguise in case someone saw him. He'd hate to explain to the cops why a grown man was egging a teenager's car. He shoved the mask in his pocket. Just having it made his little adventure more exciting.

The only thing that gave him pause was leaving Garrett home alone. But he wouldn't be gone long and the chances of Garrett waking up were slim. The kid slept like a hibernating bear. He scribbled a note, just in case. "Garrett, Took a walk. Be back soon." Then he signed it and left it on the table.

Once outside with the door locked and his keys in his pocket, he started down the sidewalk. He quickly realized how exposed he was to the prying eyes of neighbors, so he opted to sneak through backyards where there weren't any streetlights. It only took him a couple of minutes—and one unfortunate encounter with a massive pile of crap left by the Henderson's Great Dane—to get out of his neighborhood. After dragging his shoe through the grass and then scrapping the sole along the edge of the sidewalk, he reached Spyder's street.

The slight tingle that had been building in his gut since leaving the house now grew into a herd of spooked buffalo. He didn't know if it was fear, adrenaline, or both, but whatever it was, it wasn't sitting on the couch while life marched along without him.

Spyder's house wasn't hard to find. Ninety-nine percent of the houses in the neighborhood were clean and well-maintained, while Spyder's house was a two-story shithole with a six-foot strip of missing siding under one of the upstairs windows. Bags of moldy mulch rested beside the porch in a flower bed nearly hidden by two-foot-high weeds. The house was dark except for a single light in a curtainless second floor window.

His target, a black 1980-something Camaro with a red driver's door and a fist-sized rust hole on the rear quarter panel sat on the blacktop driveway. Jackson stood on the sidewalk across the street and glared at the car. He hadn't noticed its terrible condition before. There wasn't much point to egging such a beat-up heap. The right thing to do would be to hurry home to Garrett, but that seemed too anticlimactic and unfulfilling.

He looked both ways, slipped on his ski mask, and jogged across the street. The buffalo in his gut rounded the bend and came back for another pass. He hurled all six eggs at the car, careful to get them more on the paint than the windows. It was more fun than he'd care to admit. He tossed the empty carton aside and gazed at his handiwork.

His shoulders drooped. The buffalo in his stomach had run themselves to sleep. It was a letdown of epic proportions. He wanted … no, he *needed* something more. At most, he'd given Spyder a minor car washing chore for the morning. If Spyder even cared about the eggs at all. All that build-up and he'd accomplished squat.

As he looked the car over, another idea came to mind. He dug in his pocket for the pocketknife he kept on his keyring. It was a cheap knife with a built-in screwdriver which he used more than the actual blade. Until tonight. The thought of puncturing Spyder's tires woke up one of the sleeping buffalo. Changing a tire was infinitely more difficult and costly than cleaning up a paintjob that one didn't care about in the first place.

He knelt beside the rear tire and scanned the street for witnesses. No one was watching. His rebuilt knee and hip throbbed, but for once he didn't mind the pain. The single buffalo had woken up the rest of the herd. His heart pumped with the force and speed of a snare drummer. His hands trembled. He kind of liked the feeling.

He took a deep, calming breath, and then jammed the little blade into the tire. The buffalo ran for their lives. He pulled out the knife as air hissed out of the tire. It was perfect.

He stood up and admired his work while the tire seemed to melt on the blacktop. His skin buzzed with hair-raising energy. The only thing tempering his excitement was his internal clock screaming at him to get back home. It was time he listened.

He shoved the ski mask back in his pocket and started for home. He was only two houses away from Spyder's when a set of headlights turned onto the street. Whoever was driving was going way too fast for a residential neighborhood. Jackson eyed the driver as the car neared. The passenger side window lowered and someone climbed out and sat on the door.

"Hey, asshole," the passenger shouted over the roof. He hurled a beer bottle that shattered next to Jackson's feet, and then the car veered toward the sidewalk. The passenger laughed and ducked back inside as the car jumped the curb, heading toward Jackson.

Jackson dove into someone's front yard. The car plowed past with two tires on the sidewalk before bouncing back onto the street, almost striking a mailbox. Jackson rolled to his rear and sat up. His hip wasn't happy.

The car slowed and turned into Spyder's driveway. Jackson worried they might be turning around. But then the passenger door swung open and someone got out.

The driver lowered his window and shouted, "Go sleep it off, Spyder. I'll see your drunk ass tomorrow morning." The car backed out of the driveway and dove away in the opposite direction.

Jackson stood up and dusted himself off, ready to leave, but the buffalo were stirring again. Why did everyone think drinking and driving was okay? He knew he really should go home, but that's what a wimp would do.

He pulled his ski mask out and slipped it back over his head. Cold sweat soaked into the knit fabric.

Heart pounding, Jackson swallowed hard and marched toward Spyder as the oblivious punk staggered drunkenly toward his porch.

When action was needed, there were some men who acted, some men who reacted, and some men who did nothing. Jackson had always been the man who did nothing. As his anger grew, he decided he'd become a man who acted. Overwhelmed by Batman-level righteousness, Jackson made a fist.

"Hey," he said, pitching his voice deep and harsh.

Spyder casually turned around. Seeing Jackson made him laugh out loud for some reason. "Who are you supposed to be?" he asked.

"Your worst nightmare," Jackson snarled. Before the words had finished leaving his mouth, he cringed at the silliness of them. The tension he had tried to build turned into warm cheese with those three stupid words.

"Are you robbing me, dude?"

Jackson shook his head in what he hoped was a menacing way. He thought that might be more dramatic than saying something else stupid.

"Whatever, dude. I ain't got nothin' to steal. You want my car? Take it. You'll have to push it though. It don't run."

Spyder wasn't reacting the way Jackson had hoped. He'd better do something else. He stepped into arm's reach.

Spyder swayed, drunk and unimpressed. He sniffed the air and then made a face. "Did you crap yourself, dude? Damn."

"What? No. I … I stepped in … I mean … Shut up." This wasn't working. Jackson didn't consciously decide to do what he did next. As if some outside force had taken control of his limbs, he watched himself make a fist and throw it at Spyder's face. The impact made a dull clunking sound when his fist connected with Spyder's cheekbone. Equally as much pain travelled from his knuckles, through his hand, and up his arm as he'd likely dished out to his prey.

Spyder grabbed his cheek. "Ouch, dude. What the hell?" He wobbled, probably more out of drunkenness than the force of Jackson's punch.

For the first time that night, Jackson was more afraid than he was excited. He'd half expected that blow to be the end of the fight, like in the movies. When it wasn't, he panicked. He'd never tackled anyone before, which made it all the more surprising when he charged at Spyder and wrapped his arms around his waist. Together they tumbled to the ground. By luck or magic, Jackson landed on top, straddling Spyder's midsection. He tried to ignore the increasing throbbing in his leg and ache in his hip. This was a bad idea, but it was too late to stop now. Spyder pushed with both hands against Jackson's chest, but Jackson didn't budge. His confidence grew light years in those few seconds. He made another fist and aimed for Spyder's face, but the little thief wouldn't stay still. In the struggle, he missed his mark and struck the ground. It hurt like fire.

Spyder tried to push him off again, and again Jackson held his position. He made a fist with his left hand this time and hammered Spyder's water balloon of a nose. Blood splattered across Jackson's glove and mask.

"Okay, okay," Spyder cried, blood streaming over his mouth and chin and down his cheeks. "I quit. I quit."

The neighbor's porch light flickered on and Jackson panicked again. He scrambled up, leaving Spyder to writhe on the ground with his hands covering his bloody face. The neighbor's front door opened, and an old lady looked through her screen door. "Lawrence? Is that you out there? What's going on?"

Spyder cried, "Mrs. White, help. Call the police."

Lawrence?

Spyder rolled to his side, moaning and still holding his gushing nose. Jackson leaned over him. In a deep, gravelly growl that even he didn't recognize, he said, "That's for stealing." He immediately felt like an idiot again. *Less talking next time,* he told himself. Then he hobbled past the old lady's house while she impotently shouted for him to stop.

Once out of sight, Jackson slowed and pressed a hand against his aching hip. He stuffed his ski mask back into his pocket and limped through backyards, more cautiously through the Henderson's, until he reached his house. He had never felt so excited and scared and fulfilled in his life. It had been the best night he'd had since long before the wreck.

After he got home, he washed his Nikes in the driveway, scrubbed his mask and gloves in the laundry room sink, made a bag of ice for his hand, took a Vicodin, and then crashed on the couch, almost giddy with excitement. The pain in his right hand matched the throbbing in his hip until the Vicodin kicked in. Luckily, he could still make a fist, so it probably wasn't broken. With the bag of ice on his hand, he sat and stared at the black screen of the TV. This time he didn't need to turn it on. Instead, he relived his greatest triumph over and over in his mind. He barely slept a wink.

Before Jenna arrived home from work, he had Garrett dressed, fed, and on the bus. He met her at the door with a kiss. "Good morning," he said.

She stepped back and stared at him like he was an old friend she hadn't seen in years. "Uhhh. Good morning?" she answered. A long night at the hospital played out in the dark shadows under her eyes. "Where's Garrett?"

"On the bus," he said, as if there was anywhere else he could have been.

She scrunched her brow and asked, "You got him ready this morning?"

"Yeah."

"Did you sleep?"

"Yeah."

She crossed her arms. "Okay. What's gotten into you today?"

"Nothing."

Without looking down, she took his swollen hand. He flinched and then caught himself, but it was too late.

"What happened to your hand?" she asked, examining it.

"It's nothing," he said, the gears turning in his head. "I shut the car door on it when I ran out to look for my OSU hat."

She seemed to accept his lame excuse and continued her examination more gently. "You need some ice," she said.

"I've had ice on it most of the night. Here, look. It's fine." He made a fist and tried not to grimace. "See, it's better already. It'll be fine by tomorrow."

"Okay. I'm having eggs for breakfast. Do you want anything?"

Jackson's head spun. "Um ... I think we're out of eggs."

"I don't think so. I just bought some a few days ago."

"Yeah, I made some the other night before bed."

"You?"

"Yeah."

"You don't like eggs."

"Sure I do ... Once in a while."

"I've never seen you eat eggs."

He cocked his head like she was crazy.

She rolled her eyes. "Whatever. If I find out you and Garrett have been making pancakes without me, you're dead."

He smiled, intent on changing the subject before she called him out on more of his bullshit. "I'm gonna take a shower." He started to pull away, but she stopped him. "What?"

"There's something different in your eyes this morning." She smiled, leaned up, and kissed his cheek.

Yeah, it's called badassness, he thought. It took everything he had not to laugh at his own silent joke.

4
IT CAN'T RAIN ALL THE TIME

October 25, 1994

Though only a few days had passed since the Spyder Beatdown, it felt like ages. The rush had lasted about as long as the soreness in Jackson's knuckles, but eventually his ass had found the couch again, to his wife's obvious dismay. That's where he slept as Garrett missed the bus once more. Jenna woke him when she got home, and she was furious. Maybe she had just had enough. Or maybe seeing that glimpse of the old Jackson disappear so quickly hurt too much. She rushed Garrett to school without a word. That's how he knew she was really mad.

To top it all off, he had a killer headache this morning, which reminded him of his damn wreck again. With no chance of going back to sleep, Jackson fixated on *The Jerry Springer Show* on TV. This one was about a woman named Amanda falling in love with her boyfriend Bill's best friend. Jackson wondered how Jerry always managed to seem pretty shocked by the chair-flipping developments.

Even something as silly as that made Jackson angry, yet he couldn't turn it off. At least anger was a feeling. Then Amanda revealed that she didn't want either of the men because her new lover was another woman.

"Garbage," he whispered, and turned the channel to breaking news of a frantic woman begging for her kids to be returned after a carjacker had driven off with them. Jackson hoped they'd find the kids safe and the asshole who took them would be sufficiently punished, though he doubted the second part.

The door to the garage swung open and then slammed shut. He felt Jenna's anger weigh down the room. Instead of standing in front of the TV, this time she grabbed the remote from the couch, pointed it at the TV like a ray gun, and then threw it back on the couch once the screen went black.

Here we go.

"Please, Jack. Search yourself. Find whatever it was that helped you the other day and grab it with everything you've got. It's our last chance. I want my husband back. I've been more than patient, but I'm afraid I'm losing you more and more every day. Do you want me to call Dustin again?"

"No," he snapped. "I'm fine. I'm just tired."

"You're always tired."

"I don't wanna fight, Jenna. I just wanna be left alone today."

"And what about tomorrow?"

"Maybe."

"Would you go back to church with me? We haven't been there in years. Maybe Pastor—"

"No."

Her shoulders slouched. "Why not?"

"We're leaves of a tree, Jenna."

Confusion twisted her face. "What?"

"There are forests all around the world full of trees with leaves dying every day. Do you mourn them?"

"I don't understand."

"It's a simple question. Do you mourn every leaf that falls from every tree?"

"So, if I don't care about every leaf, then God doesn't care about us?"

"Worse. He's indifferent. If he's even there at all. We're all running around down here hoping not to fall from the tree.

46

And when we do, the world doesn't miss a beat. Why would God care about us anymore than we do a leaf?"

Her mouth dropped open. "Wow." She stood quiet for a moment. "We really need to go back to church."

"Whatever." He lifted his feet onto the couch to lie down, but he could still feel her glaring at him.

She snapped, "You know, I'd like to burn that fucking couch. You have to get off your ass and get out of the house again. I feel like these walls are killing you. You have to *do* something."

"Like what?"

"I don't know. Go for a walk. Go to the store. Anything."

"Fine." Jackson stood up, surprising himself as much as Jenna.

"Fine, what?"

"Fine, I'll go to the store."

She cocked her head and squinted at him. "Ummm, okay?"

"You want me to go somewhere, I'll go somewhere. If that ends this argument."

Jackson marched upstairs, put on blue jeans and a sweatshirt, and returned to the living room where Jenna still stood.

He glared at her. "Are you happy? I'm going to the store. I don't know why I'm going to the store, but if it'll get you off my back, I'll go." Jackson yanked the door to the garage open. "Am I getting anything while I'm there?"

"You could get spaghetti sauce?"

"Are you asking or telling me?"

"We need some for dinner tonight."

"Fine. Sauce. Goodbye." He slammed the door behind him.

Going to the grocery store for one item was among his least favorite tasks because he had no idea where anything was. As he wandered down the first aisle and into the next, he wondered where he had been when the secret map of grocery stores had been handed out. His wife obviously had one. If she'd asked him to find toothpicks or bouillon cubes she'd have to send a search party after him.

There was no sauce in the first random aisle, but if he needed toilet paper he was in the right place. Eventually, he found an isle with pasta. He was getting warmer. Finally, with sauce and garlic bread (just in case), Jackson left the labyrinthine store and headed to his car. He didn't need to see the darkening clouds to know it was getting ready to rain. His leg had been throbbing for a while.

As he limped past the first row of cars, a loud bang made him jerk his head around. He saw an old, beat-up Ford pickup truck with its rear bumper nestled against the passenger door of a nice Ford Mustang. A person would have to be either drunk or stupid to back into a parked car in a parking lot.

The driver climbed out to survey the damage. Chunks of hardened drywall mud fell from his overalls. Seeing the dent in the Mustang's door, he winced and looked around furtively. His eyes met Jackson's. He had a full beard and long, stringy hair like a muscular Axl Rose.

The guy spit brown snuff onto the pavement and then dragged the back of his sleeve across his mouth. "Oh well. What're ya gonna do?" he said with a shrug. "These things happen."

These things happen?

The man held a finger to his mouth. "Shh. It'll be our little secret." Then he hopped into his truck, turned over the ignition twice before it fired up with a puff of smoke from the exhaust, and pulled away. He gave Jackson a dickish wave as he sped by.

Jackson stood stunned. He watched the guy leave the parking lot, cross the main road, and then pull into the McDonald's across the street. Seconds later, a kid no more than nineteen or twenty years old crossed the parking lot heading directly toward the Mustang.

The kid oozed the cockiness of a boy given a fancy sportscar by his daddy. He was tall and lanky like a praying mantis, and his gangly arms bounced with each step. He didn't have a care in the world.

He said, "Hi there," in a chipper voice as he approached. Noticing Jackson looking at his car, he asked, "Like the ride?"

His overtly friendly demeanor took Jackson off guard. "Oh. Yeah. Sure. Real nice."

The kid clicked his keyless entry fob with an over exaggerated flick of his wrist. Privileged or not, the kid didn't deserve such a bruise on his baby. The kid climbed in and the sweet-sounding engine purred to life.

The Mustang backed out of the parking spot. Jackson glanced across the street to the offending pick-up truck and then back to the kid. It killed him to do nothing.

Just like Spyder and his stolen smokes, that son of a bitch across the street was downing a burger or something without facing consequences for what he had done. It was too much for Jackson to bear. He'd never forgive himself if he didn't say something, and it was now or never.

"Hey, kid," he shouted and stepped in front of the Mustang before the kid could pull away.

The kid lowered his window. "'Sup, man?"

Jackson nodded toward the passenger side. "You should take a look at this."

"What?"

"Come 'ere."

The kid dropped the stick into neutral, yanked his emergency brake, and then climbed out. He was all smiles as Jackson led him around his car.

The kid's materialistic world shattered. He clapped his hands to his temples and nearly collapsed to his knees. "Oh man, oh man." He caressed the dented door. "What did you do, man?"

"It wasn't me, kid." Jackson pointed across the street. "See that beat-up Ford over there at McDonalds?"

The kid squinted. "Yeah, I see it."

"It was the guy driving that."

The kid scowled. "And you were just going to stand there and say nothing," he said, though there wasn't much venom behind his words.

Jackson still winced. "No one really wants to get involved in these things, you know?"

"Did you at least get his license plate or something?"

Damn it. That would have been a great idea. "No. I'm sorry. I didn't think of it."

The kid went back to the driver's side.

"Where you going?"

"I'm parking my car and calling my dad."

"You don't have time to wait for your dad. Go confront that guy. Or … Or go get his plate number yourself. Or something."

The kid thought hard about it. Then he shook his head. "Nah. I don't wanna make anyone mad. Not without my dad here. It's best I call him."

"At least call the police first."

"You think they'll come out for this?"

"Maybe. Tell them it was a hit and run or something. Do whatever you want. I've done my part. I've gotta go."

"Well, thanks, man. I'll call the police."

Jackson threw his hand in the air as he walked away. "Better hurry." Even as he hoped he'd feel better now that he'd taken action, he didn't. He knew the cops would never get there in time to catch the offender. If they came at all.

Jackson sat in his car, but didn't start it right away. The guy getting away with such a dick move gnawed at him. He was no better than Spyder. Or the drunk garbage man. There was only one reason that guy was getting away and that was Jackson's reluctance to get involved. How could he go home to Jenna and Garrett knowing he had stood by and let some hillbilly screw over some nice kid? The old Jackson wouldn't have thought twice about letting it slide, but this Jackson—the one sitting on his scrawny ass in a parking lot—still had a chance to set things right.

There really was no other choice. Once he made the decision, the only doubt he had left was whether or not he'd get across the street in time. With his foot smashing the gas pedal, he zipped through the parking lot, across the street, and into the McDonald's lot. His heart raced as the nerves set in, just like they had when he'd beaten up Spyder. With shaky hands he pulled into the space next to the truck.

The door-denting dirtball sat at a window seat inside the burger joint shoving an Egg McMuffin or some shit in his mouth. Jackson wanted to go in and punch him in the syrupy face, but this guy wasn't some punk kid like Spyder. He looked like he could handle himself. Jackson considered jotting down the plate number and taking it back to the kid, but that's what pussies would do. He needed a solution between snitching and taking a butt-whoopin'. He thought about Spyder's car and got an idea. He opened the knife on his keyring. While Spyder might not have cared about a flat tire, this guy didn't have the same luxury. Not if he wanted to get home without walking. Maybe it would even keep him there until the kid got the police involved.

A quick glance around assured everyone coming or going was too self-absorbed to pay attention to him. Jackson dropped his keys next to the truck's rear tire, knelt to pick them up, and then jammed the blade into the tire. It hissed like a cobra when he pulled it out. A rush of nervous excitement surged through his blood. It felt so good he considered doing a second tire, but decided that might be too risky.

There was only one other thing that could make this more satisfying, and that was watching the game play out from afar. He climbed into his car, drove to the Olive Garden next door, and parked with a clear view of the truck. Then he waited.

After another fifteen minutes, the hillbilly walked out and crossed the lot toward his truck. Jackson rubbed his hands together. This was too good. The hillbilly opened his door and then hesitated before climbing in. Jackson giggled to himself. The guy was too far away for Jackson to hear what he said, but when he slammed his door shut and kicked the side of his truck, he spoke the international language of pissed off. Jackson burst out laughing, pounding his steering wheel with his palms. This was the greatest.

Then the rain that had been dogging Jackson's leg all morning began to land on his windshield, just a few drops at first, and then in a downpour that forced Jackson to turn on his wipers to see. He almost wet himself with laughter. The hillbilly grabbed a plastic tarp from the back of his truck, held it over his head, and proceeded to change his tire. He looked miserable. Tarp or no tarp, the guy had to be soaked.

Just as the guy lowered the jack and tightened the last lug nut, a police cruiser pulled up to the front of his truck and turned on its blue lightbar. The officer motioned the guy over to his window. Jackson's sides ached from laughter. If anyone could have seen him then, they'd think he was a loon.

And perhaps he was. If having so much fun while distributing justice meant he was crazy, then bring on the padded walls.

He backed out of his spot and took a leisurely drive home, barely able to contain his laughter. He still wore a smile when he got home, which didn't go unnoticed by Jenna.

"Well, that's a rare sight," she said.

"What is?"

"Your smile."

"Oh." He subconsciously covered his mouth with his fingers. "Something struck me as funny at the store is all."

"Yeah? Tell me about it. I'd love a good laugh."

"This guy at the store—this real jerk—was leaving and he …" Jackson trailed off. A part of him wanted to tell her what he had done, but he decided it should probably remain a secret for now. She wouldn't understand.

"And?" she asked, hanging on his words.

"He hit some kid's nice Mustang and then drove off like it was nothing. The funny thing was he got a flat tire before getting very far right as it started raining. I mean, not just raining, but pooouuring."

"Sounds like he got what he deserved, huh?"

"Yeah. But that's not all." Jackson started laughing as he thought about the man's face when the police car had pulled up. Jenna grinned in anticipation.

"Just as he finished changing his tire, a cop pulled up."

She playfully swatted his arm. "No way."

Jackson was openly laughing, and it was contagious.

"And you watched the whole thing."

"I couldn't look away."

"I wish I was there."

"Me too. It was great. By the end that hillbilly had a wrecked tire, waterlogged clothes, and a meeting with the Five-O."

Jenna shook her head. "I love it when assholes get what's coming to them."

"Me too." Jackson set the grocery bag on the island and gathered his composure. Jenna's eyes met his and lingered. She smiled.

He felt something he hadn't felt in a while.

"What?" she asked playfully.

"What, what?"

"Why are you looking at me like that?"

"I don't know. I'm thinking about taking a shower. Thought maybe you'd like to join me?"

"Jack, what's gotten into you? Are you suddenly schizophrenic or something?"

Jackson shook his head. "I don't think so." Then he asked, "Do you?" Before she could answer, he answered himself. "No. Not at all." He took her hand. "See? We think we're fine."

"Ha. Ha. You two are a real hoot."

Jackson grinned and led her upstairs.

5
EVERYTHING IS NOT ZEN
October 25, 1994

Jenna, wearing blue scrubs with her hair in a ponytail, met Jackson in the upstairs hallway as he headed for the bedroom. She whispered, "Garrett's asleep. I gotta get to work, but we need to discuss his game time on school nights again soon. He's getting out of control. He needs to play outside more."

This argument again? Jackson followed her down the stairs. "And what do you want him to do outside?"

"Play like a normal kid."

"It's fifty degrees."

"So? I played outside in the cold when I was his age."

"By himself?"

"Sure."

Jackson felt his eyes roll. "You want him to play outside by himself while all his friends are inside playing the Nintendo games he wishes he was playing? How fun."

She groaned and stomped past him. "I've gotta go. I can't argue about it right now."

"Then why'd you start?"

"I didn't … Never mind." She ripped the door to the garage open.

"Why do you do that?" Jackson asked.

She turned back with a glare. "Do what?"

"Why do you start a fight and then leave?"

"I didn't start a fight." She took an annoyed breath. "I just brought it up."

"You know this always starts a fight."

"I didn't mean for it to start a fight. I love you, but I've got to go. I'm gonna be late." She pulled the door closed behind her.

Jackson fought the urge to chase her and make another unarguable point. Ultimately, he restrained himself for the greater good. After he heard the overhead garage door close, he turned his attention to the blank TV screen. He turned it on. The couch called to him. He felt the blackness tug at his soul, but for the first time in months he didn't immediately surrender to it.

His stomach grumbled. He was turning away to get something to eat when the program coming on caught his attention. He stood and watched. It was a nature show about bullet ants and the Sataré-Mawé tribe. Young boys in the Amazonian tribe had to endure massive amounts of pain from bullet ant bites as a rite of passage into manhood. The program was so fascinating, Jackson couldn't turn away until the credits rolled. Something about those kids going through such a painful ritual just to become men really struck a nerve. Knowing what you could make it through at such a young age could only help a person in life. Jackson envied those kids in a way.

He wondered if his car accident could have been his own bullet ant ritual, but quickly realized the wreck had made him weaker, not stronger. His ass groove on the couch was proof of that.

In high school, Dustin had been jumped by three guys who hurt him so badly they'd sent him to the hospital. He became a tougher, take-no-shit kind of guy after that. Everyone in school saw it. The rest of high school had seemed easier for him because he'd walked around with a chip on his shoulder, daring anyone to knock it off. No one even tried. Maybe if Jackson had faced his own bullet ant ritual like that when he was younger, he could have worked through his accident recovery with courage and strength instead of weakness and self-pity. He'd wager that those boys of the Sataré-Mawé could face a similar recovery with ease.

Jackson sighed and went to the pantry for something to eat. A box of Frosted Flakes on the top shelf called his name. He was as close to being a cereal junkie as one could get. After filling a bowl with sugary flakes, he opened the fridge to find an empty shelf where the milk should have been. His shoulders slumped. He could have something else, but his heart was set on Frosted Flakes and nothing short of a nuclear war was going to stop him.

Since Garrett had been fine alone during the Spyder Beatdown, Jackson saw no reason his son wouldn't be fine if he went to the store. It was only a twenty-minute walk there and back. He could use the fresh air. After grabbing his bomber jacket and his keys and quickly scribbling a note to Garrett in case he woke up, Jackson was out the front door. His breath hung in a cloud like a puff of cigarette smoke.

The night was peaceful at such a late hour, and he enjoyed his walk. Even his bad hip seemed to tolerate it. His lingering headache wasn't as forgiving. As he walked, he thought back to the bullet ants, wondering if it was too late for him to find his own challenge that could harden him like Dustin and the Sataré-Mawé boys. For a fleeting moment, he pondered flying to the Amazon and doing the bullet ant ritual himself, but quickly realized that was wholly unrealistic.

The grocery store was a ghost town. Between the entrance and the refrigerator aisle, two different employees asked if he needed any help. One even cautioned him to not slip on the giant slug trails—Jackson's words, not his—that the guy on the ride-on floor cleaner was leaving behind. Where were all these helpers when he needed sauce? Late night grocery shopping might just be the way to go from here on out.

As Jackson continued on his way to the refrigerators, he stumbled upon a shelf full of toothpicks. "Well, I'll be," he whispered. He made a mental note of the aisle number (six) just in case Jenna ever sent him for toothpicks, and moved on to the coolers looking for one-percent milk.

Immersed in his own thoughts, he didn't notice another man approach until the door of the cooler next to him opened. Startled, he almost dropped his keys. He looked the guy up and down. Something about him gave Jackson a strange feeling. Maybe it was how the guy had crept up on him. Or how he completely ignored Jackson looking him over. He was tall and fit and wore a suit with a blue striped tie pulled loose at the knot. He had a pack of cigarettes in his basket and Jackson immediately thought of Spyder. As he continued studying the guy through the open cooler door, he wondered what the guy was doing out so late.

Jackson peeked into the man's shopping basket for clues. Shaving cream. A dozen eggs. A jar of bouillon cubes. Jackson was tempted to ask where in the world he'd found them. A box of condoms. And a six-pack of Zima. An odd assortment for a late-night shopping spree, but nothing truly suspicious. The man finally selected a carton of orange juice and shut the cooler door.

"How's it going?" Jackson asked with a nod, expecting to be ignored.

The man glanced over, gave him a half-smile, and nodded in return. He had a mole beside his nose. That would come in handy for describing him to the authorities later. The man turned and walked toward the front, his fancy shoes clicking on the tile floor.

Jackson sighed. This was ridiculous. What was he thinking? The guy was simply shopping. Who cared if he gave off bad vibes? That didn't mean anything.

… Did it?

It had meant something with Spyder.

Jackson grabbed a gallon of milk and hurried to the registers, getting in line behind the guy.

The cashier was already stuffing bouillon and condoms into brown paper grocery bags. A heavy gold wedding band flashed on the man's hand as he passed the cashier a credit card. She smiled and thanked the guy for shopping. Then she turned to Jackson. "Find everything all right?"

Jackson nodded.

She rang up his purchase, swiped his credit card, and handed it back. Jackson snatched it, grabbed his milk without a bag, and hurried out, leaving his receipt behind. He heard the cashier call after him, but he ignored her. He had to follow the man close.

Make him uncomfortable. Make him panic. Forcing him to make a mistake was the only way Jackson would figure out what was shady about him. It was kind of exciting.

At the first handicap parking space, the man slowed. Maybe it was working. *Here it comes.* The man stopped. Then he spun like lightning and grabbed Jackson's coat with his free hand. He was strong. Jackson flinched and his heart jumped.

The uninterested look in the man's eyes was replaced by anger. "Why are you following me?" he snapped. He had a speck of white spittle on the corner of his mouth and his breath smelled of peppermint gum.

Jackson's eyes went wide. "I … I wasn't following you."

"Yes, you were."

"No, really. I was just walking to my car."

The man shoved him away. "Where is it, then?"

"What do you mean?"

"Your car, asshole. Where's your car?"

Jackson scanned the mostly empty parking lot. "It's … uh …"

The man sneered. "Just stay the hell away from me." As he walked away, he muttered, "Fucking racist."

Racist? Jackson's heart dropped. *He thinks I'm racist? Why? Because he's black?* The man's skin color had never even crossed Jackson's mind. Racist was the last way he'd describe himself. He considered himself a full-blown liberal minus the gun control and weak on crime parts. He called after him, "Hey, buddy. I'm sorry. I didn't mean …"

The man kept walking. Without looking back, he raised his middle finger. Jackson stood frozen while the man climbed into a red Jaguar. His vanity license plate read "DOC B."

Stunned, Jackson tried to wrap his mind around what had just happened. If that guy wasn't up to no good, what the hell had Jackson been thinking? Could his bad feelings have been racially motivated? Jesus, he hoped not. That's not who he was. His hands trembled. Embarrassed, he scoured the lot in hopes that no one else had seen him make an ass of himself. A kid wearing a reflective vest and pushing a line of carts was watching on his way to the store entrance. Jackson threw up an "everything's okay" wave.

He turned around just as Doc B backed out of his parking spot. And that's when Jackson saw him lift a bottle of Zima to his lips as he pulled away. It all suddenly made sense. Jackson subtly pumped his fist and whispered, "I knew it." Doc B *was* up to no good and Jackson had been right to follow him. Whether it was instinct or intuition or whatever, something had told Jackson Doc B was trouble, and it wasn't racism.

Vindicated, he started for home, mentally kicking himself for letting Doc B off so easily. Imagine how different his life would have been if someone had intervened with the garbage truck driver's drinking before he'd made Jackson wear his LeBaron like a twisted metal suit. The more he thought about it, the more his blood started to boil. He hoped Doc B didn't cause someone else to go through that.

Now the only question was how had he known Doc B was up to no good simply from a strange feeling? He'd seen a show on TV once that said a small percentage of people actually gained unbelievable talents after receiving head injuries or having a stroke. The people featured on that program had developed incredible skills, like one lady who suddenly could speak a foreign language she'd never studied before. Or a guy who could play the piano like a virtuoso with zero previous training. It was amazing. Maybe Jackson was one of those people. Maybe that odd feeling he'd gotten from Doc B and Spyder was a gift developed from his brain injury.

Wasn't it possible that his accident had exposed a secret talent hidden in his own brain? He'd suspected he had some psychic abilities since he was a young boy and his grandma had appeared at the foot of his bed on the night after she'd died. She had said, "Everything will be all right, Jack." When he had woken up the next morning, he'd felt an incredible sense of relief and calm. The answer was simple. It was absolutely possible.

As he walked home, he fantasized about his burgeoning talent and how he could use it for good. What if drinking and driving wasn't the biggest crime Doc B planned to commit that night? What if he was going to get rid of Mrs. B so he and his mistress could be together at last? A celebration with his mistress afterward could call for a clean shave and condoms. And a few Zimas on the way home could give him the courage to go through with it. That might sound crazy, but Jackson had seen crazier stories on the news.

By the time he got home, he had fully convinced himself he must be on to something.

"Good game, Doc B," he whispered. "I only hope you reconsider killing your wife tonight. Otherwise, we *will* meet again one day, and I will give you justice." Then he shook his head in disgust. Why did things that sounded so good in his head sound so stupid out loud?

6
CREEP
November 5, 1994

Seven-year-old Dylan woke with a start. A powerful hand covered his mouth and nose. He couldn't breathe.

"Keep quiet, Dylan," a strange man whispered. The man pressed so hard against Dylan's nose and mouth that his teeth stung the inside of his lips. "If you cry and wake up your family, I'll kill them all. Nod if you understand."

Dylan nodded. His Mighty Morphin' Power Rangers blanket was wrapped so tightly around him that he couldn't move his arms. His eyes blurred with tears. The man slowly pulled his hand away. Dylan found the courage to whisper, "Are you going to hurt me?"

The man shook his head. "You're going to help me watch for them."

"Who?"

"Shh," the man hissed, and loosened the blanket so Dylan could sit up. "Come on."

Dylan's toes touched the cold hardwood floor. A warped floorboard creaked near the door. The man's head spun toward it and his hand shot to his waistband. Dylan hoped to see his dad walk in until he saw a knife handle protruding from the man's belt. Then he hoped his dad stayed in his room where he was safe.

When no one entered, the man whispered, "Come on. We need to hurry." He leaned into the beam of a flashlight that was sitting on Dylan's dresser and Dylan got a look at his face. He recognized him. He'd seen this man with the missing front tooth a few days before in a toy aisle at Walmart. The man had asked him his name and given him a Matchbox fire truck. When Dylan had gone to find his mom to introduce them, the man had disappeared.

The man led Dylan by the hand from the bedroom, down the hall, and to the back door. The wood along the edge of the door was splintered and the extended bolt lock protruded from the broken wood. The man grabbed a crowbar from next to the door.

Dylan said, "It's cold out here. Can I get my coat and tell my mom I'm leaving?"

"No. I'll let your mom know you're staying with me for a while."

The man led him out into the cold evening air. Dylan, dressed only in his Power Rangers onesie, shivered and wiped his eyes with his sleeve. He wondered if his sister was okay and if he'd ever see her again. The man scooped him up and ran through the back yard toward a white van.

7
JACKED UP
November 10, 1994

Dustin called to invite the Fosters out to dinner with the whole family. Though Jackson didn't feel like being sociable (he rarely did), Jenna really wanted to go. He figured it would be seen as a good gesture to oblige. Considering their current marital troubles, he needed all the wins he could get.

They met Dustin, his wife, Karen, and their two boys at Dustin's favorite Italian restaurant, Marciano's. Jackson wasn't looking forward to watching Dustin eat spaghetti, and he imagined neither was Dustin's shirt.

Dustin sat at the end of the table like he was the king. Jackson sat next to Dustin with Karen across from him. Jenna sat beside Jackson with Garrett beside her and Dustin's two kids across from them. Sitting the kids so close together quickly proved to be a mistake. Jackson was just starting to hope the rambunctious boys would get them kicked out of the restaurant when Jenna gave Garrett an elbow jab to the ribs, reminding him of his manners.

Jackson sighed in regret and glanced past Karen to the restaurant bar behind her. Staring back from a bar stool was a Grand-Canyon-sized plumber's crack on some hefty guy. Disgusted, he nudged Dustin and nodded toward the man.

Jenna caught his gesture and followed their eyes. When she saw, she looked away with a jolt. She gasped, "Oh my God, Karen. Look." She nodded toward the bar without any attempt at being discreet.

Jackson put his hand over his eyes and tilted his head away. Jenna's outburst had gotten the boys' attention, which was exactly what Jackson was trying to avoid. They gaped and giggled like someone had farted at the table. So much for subtlety.

Once everyone calmed down and the server took their orders, Karen and Jenna returned to their conversation about the boys' school while Dustin started bragging about the Cleveland Browns' rare 7-2 start to the football season as if he was a part of the organization.

When the server brought their meals, Jackson paused to thank her and then continued scoffing at Dustin's take on the football season. "They'll still never beat the Steelers."

Dustin dug into his spaghetti. "That last game was luck. We'll meet again at the end of the season, and then we'll see." He looked down and mumbled, "Shit."

Jackson glanced up from his chicken pesto as Dustin reached for his napkin. Not even two bites in and he'd already had an accident. The marinara sauce on his chest heralded another battle lost between His Majesty King Shirt and Sir Meatball of the House of Marciano's. Dustin dabbed at the red splotch on his white button-down. If the meatball had been a bullet, it would have hit him right in the heart.

"Not. A. Word," he said.

"I got nothing," Jackson answered.

Karen looked over and groaned.

Dustin shrugged. "You know, I guess stupid is as stupid does."

Jackson cocked his head. "What the hell does that mean?"

"You've never heard that saying?"

Jackson shook his head. "Should I have?"

"It's from that movie where Tom Hanks is … how can I put this sensitively … developmentally slow."

Jackson's eyes widened in pleasant surprise. "Look at you, Dustin. Maybe you can learn to fit in with society someday."

"Well, I almost said retarded, but I knew it would get me into trouble."

Without interrupting her conversation with Jenna, Karen reached over and smacked his shoulder.

"What?" he groaned. "I was saying that I didn't say it."

Karen continued talking without looking over.

Dustin threw his hands up. "I can't win. So, you haven't seen it?"

Jackson shook his head again. "Nope. I haven't seen any movies since the accident."

"You should. It's going to win an Oscar."

Jackson shrugged. He couldn't care less about the Oscars.

Waiting for Jenna to finish eating at a restaurant was always an exercise in patience. Everyone else was long finished and ready for the check while she took her time picking at her salad. She refused to eat the pieces that were even slightly wilted. Finally, she placed her napkin on her plate and she and Karen excused themselves to the restroom. This was Jackson's chance to tell Dustin what he'd been wanting to tell him all night.

He leaned closer to Dustin and whispered, "I did it."

"Did what?" Dustin slurped from his water glass.

Jackson looked around to make sure no one was listening. He waited for a waitress to pass by before saying, "Remember Spyder?"

"What spider?" Dustin wiped his mouth.

"The kid with the mullet. You know, the one who stole the cigarettes?"

"Oh, yeah. What about him?"

"I beat his ass."

Dustin cocked his head. "You what?"

"I beat his ass. I went to his house one night, waited for him to come home, and broke his nose." Jackson didn't know for sure he had broken Spyder's nose, but it made for a better story.

Dustin gave him a look like he'd just told him he had walked on the moon. "You?"

"Yeah, man. You should have seen it. I hit him and then tackled him and hit him some more. It was awesome. Oh, and I egged his car and flattened his tire, too."

"You're full of shit."

"No. I really did."

Dustin stared at him.

Jenna and Karen returned from the restroom. Jackson grabbed Dustin's forearm. "Don't say anything in front of the girls. You're the only one who knows. Jenna would kill me."

Jenna squeezed into her seat. "What's all the hush-hush about?" she asked.

Jackson scrambled. "Uh … Nothing. I was just telling Dustin what I got you for Christmas."

"Oh, yeah? So soon? And what'd he say, Dustin?"

With two after dinner mints crammed in his mouth, Dustin answered, "A Lexus."

"Yeah, right."

"No, really. Mike Tyson here beat up the salesman and got a real sweet deal."

Jackson gave him a look.

Jenna brushed her hand at him and said he was full of crap.

Jackson's eyes drifted back to the man at the bar with the exposed ass-crack. He was leaning heavily to one side and threatening to dent the floor. Seeing what was about to happen, Jackson gestured for the others to watch. Everyone at the table looked over just in time to see the drunk lean too far to one side and then crash to the ground, his glass shattering on the floor. Everyone in the restaurant turned toward him.

Garrett laughed out loud, and Jackson shushed him. "That's rude," Jackson snapped. Though once he thought about it, it wasn't any ruder than him telling everyone to watch before it happened.

The drunk pushed to his feet, tugged his drooping drawers up, and staggered against the bar. He shook his left hand like he had touched a hot stove. Then, seeing he had gained an audience, he flicked a hand at them and shouted, "Bugger off."

Most of the crowd turned back to their dinner conversations, figuring the show was over.

The bartender reached a hand across the bar to help steady him, but the drunk gave the bartender a death stare and slurred, "Whatareyoulookingat?"

The bartender turned away and shook his head. He shouted toward the back, "Hey, Jill. Brody's had too much to drink again."

A woman wearing a pants suit rushed from the kitchen. Jackson assumed she was the manager. "Are you okay, Brody?" she asked as she touched his shoulder. Brody jerked away, almost falling again in the process. A teenaged busboy hurried over with a broom and a handful of towels and started working on the mess. The manager righted the barstool, but Brody shoved it back over.

"I want it to stay there," he shouted.

Jackson glared daggers at him.

While the manager talked to Brody too softly for Jackson to hear, Jackson's waitress returned with their receipt. "I'm sorry you had to see that, folks," she said.

Jackson sat up straighter and puffed out his chest. "Do you need me to go over and escort that man out?" he asked. Jenna and Dustin shot stunned looks his way.

"No. That's okay, sir. That's just Brody. He'll leave on his own."

"You mean he does this all the time?"

"Nah. Just once in a while. He'll go home and sleep it off. Tomorrow, he'll come back and apologize and the manager will give him one more chance. Again."

"Who'll drive him home?" Jackson asked.

"We used to call him a cab, but he just leaves on his own before it can get here."

"So he just drives home drunk?"

"I know it's terrible, but there's nothing we can do."

"You can call the cops, is what you can do. He could kill someone."

"The cops would take longer to get here than a taxi. He only lives a few miles away. He'll be fine."

Jackson steamed.

The waitress thanked them for coming and apologized once more before moving to another table.

Brody grabbed his coat from the floor, threw three wadded up bills on the counter, and staggered toward the front with the anxious manager trailing him.

Jackson couldn't stand it. The old Jackson would have been content to simply let it go, but the Jackson who beat up Spyder for stealing cigarettes wouldn't mind taking a crack at a drunk driver. He could pretend it was the garbage man. He stood up with a start, catching everyone at the table off guard. "It's time to go," he blurted.

Jenna gave him a surprised look. "Maybe Dustin and Karen aren't ready to go yet."

Jackson kept an eye on Brody at the front door. He wasn't trying to be rude, but the drunk was about to endanger countless lives by driving.

"No, it's okay," Karen answered, not appearing at all offended. "It's a school night and all."

Jackson led the way toward the front, hardly waiting for his family to put on their jackets. He heard Garrett say, "I gotta pee."

Jackson snapped, "You can wait till we get home."

Jenna cocked her head. "Excuse me? Why can't he go now? What's your hurry all of a sudden?"

Jackson leaned in close and whispered, "Something didn't sit right. I don't know if I'll make it home if we don't go now."

"Can't you use the bathroom here?"

"I'd rather not."

She sighed and turned to Garrett. "Honey, you'll have to hold it until we get home. It'll only be a few minutes. You think you can do that?"

Garrett nodded, and Jackson rushed outside without holding the door for anyone else.

Brody was beside a blue Ford Taurus with a dent above the driver's side front tire. Probably from a drunken fender bender, Jackson imagined. Luckily, it took Brody forever to find the right key, drop it, pick it up, and then climb in. He looked like he might fall asleep right there.

Jenna and the rest of the crew joined Jackson outside. While he hugged Karen goodbye and fist-bumped Dustin, he continued to keep a sly eye on Brody.

As soon as the two families parted ways, Jackson practically ran to the car. Jenna and Garrett couldn't get in fast enough to suit him. Once in the car, Jackson rubbed his gut, groaned, and gave Jenna a pained look for effect.

"Should we put the windows down?" she asked.

"Ha. Ha. No."

Brody pulled out of the parking lot, almost clipping the "Enter" sign. Jackson dropped his shifter into drive before Jenna's door was even closed. He sped out of the lot and quickly caught up to Brody's car.

Jenna clutched the armrest. "Hey, slow down," she complained.

"Sorry, hon. Just trying to hurry." He slowed down, but not by much.

"Are you going to make it?" she asked with a grin.

"You'd better hope so."

"Toilet emergency or not, you were pretty rude back there, don't you think?"

"Not as rude as if I woulda shit all over everyone."

Brody changed lanes and Jackson trailed him.

"I'm sorry," he started again. "I didn't mean to be rude. My stomach is upset, and you know how I feel about public bathrooms."

She touched his shoulder. "I know. Thanks for going tonight."

Jackson gave her a smile, but never took his focus from Brody's Taurus drifting between the painted lines in front of him.

Jenna said, "Honey, don't get too close to that guy. He might be drunk."

"No worries. I'm keeping my eye on him."

"Between him and the guy at the restaurant, I wonder if there's anyone sober on the streets tonight."

"Yeah, no kiddin'."

She rubbed his shoulder again. "I hope your belly feels better."

Without signaling, Brody's brake lights flashed and he swerved into a residential neighborhood, almost taking out the stop sign in the process. Jackson wanted to follow, but just knowing the neighborhood where Brody lived should be enough to track him down later.

A quiet excitement carried Jackson the rest of the way home. Jenna talked almost incessantly about how nice it had been to see Karen and all the gossip she'd picked up from her, but Jackson barely heard a word she said. He nodded and smiled as he envisioned breaking Brody's arm in the very near future. Just the idea of what he might do started a nervous quiver in his leg. He hoped Jenna wouldn't notice.

Once they pulled into their driveway, he jumped out and raced into the house. He hung out in the bathroom for a while just to keep up appearances. It gave him the chance to read through his new Sports Illustrated NBA edition.

"Feel better?" Jenna asked when he finally emerged, his magazine in the wastebasket.

He fanned his hand toward the door. "I wouldn't go in there for a while."

"Did you turn on the fan?"

He scoffed. She knew he had hated bathroom fans ever since reading that the motors sometimes went bad and started house fires, but that never stopped her from asking.

"Feel like taking a little walk?" she asked.

"It's kinda chilly out."

"It's not that bad. We haven't taken a family walk around the neighborhood in a while. Have you seen the progress of the new houses they're building behind the Stephensons' lately?"

Jackson shook his head. "We can take a little walk, I suppose. Not far, though. My hip's aching a bit."

Jenna told Garrett to get ready while Jackson did some of the light stretching he had learned in rehab. Once he was loosened up, the three of them went for a short walk to the Porters' house and back. The walk was a quarter mile at best. Jenna leaned her head against Jackson's shoulder just like she had when they were first dating. It felt nice, but he couldn't stop thinking about Brody.

"Are you somewhere else?" she finally asked.

"What do you mean?"

"You seem like you've got something on your mind."

There was no way he could tell her he was preoccupied by all the things he wanted to do to a miserable drunk. Instead, he shook his head and gave her a weak smile.

She let it rest, but she obviously wasn't satisfied.

Two houses from home, Garrett shouted, "I'll beat you," and took off running.

Jackson had no doubt his son would win because he sure as hell wasn't running. Jenna took his hand.

"This is nice," she said.

He agreed.

That night, he helped her tuck Garrett into bed. It felt good to be a family again. He wondered if it was beating up Spyder, flattening the hillbilly's tire, or the thought of what he wanted to do to Brody that held the darkness at bay. Whatever it was, he felt something he hadn't felt in a long time. He felt happy.

After Garrett fell asleep, Jenna whispered, "Isn't this so much nicer than sitting on the couch all day and turning off the world?"

Jackson nodded. Her words further demonstrated how little she understood what he was truly going through. He wanted to tell her what he had done and how the adrenaline rush was what helped him. But he couldn't. Not only would she be horrified if she knew, but keeping it a secret added to its allure.

He ended up back on the couch after that. An episode of *ER* played on TV, but he wasn't really watching. He couldn't wait for Jenna to leave for work. When she came downstairs and saw what was on, she huffed.

"What are you doing?"

"What?"

"Why are you watching *ER*? I thought you didn't want to watch it."

"I don't."

"Are you at least taping it for me like I asked?"

He glanced at the VCR to make sure. "Yeah, but I don't get why *you* watch it. You're a nurse, aren't you?"

"And?"

"And isn't this a show about nurses and doctors working?"

"So?"

He sighed. "Do you think plumbers go home and watch dramas about plumbers? I mean, I was a mechanic. I've never once watched a show about fixing cars that didn't have some kind of educational value."

"Because fixing cars is boring."

"Whatever."

Her eyes locked on the screen where Dr. Doug Ross, played by the remarkably handsome George Clooney, desperately tried to stick an intubation tube down the throat of a young boy. Jackson didn't know what hospital the show was supposed to portray, but he'd never seen so many gorgeous people in one place.

Almost hypnotized by the scene playing out, Jenna practically floated to the seat beside him. She put her hand on his leg. "You know, I haven't called off in a while. Maybe I could take tonight off, and we can start this episode from the beginning. If you'll watch it with me." She smiled and squeezed his leg. "Wouldn't that be nice?"

Oh shit. Oh shit. Any night but tonight. He imagined trying to sneak out after she went to sleep, but that would be far too risky. "Uh … Yeah. That'd be great." He hoped his disappointment didn't leak into his tone. "Though, I don't really wanna watch this show, if I'm being honest."

Her hand slid from his leg. "Oh. Well, I shouldn't call off anyway. Val called off last night and I think she's off again tonight. Jackie will be swamped if I'm AWOL, too. She'd kill me."

Just let her keep talking herself out of it.

"How about we just spend tomorrow night together since I'm off?"

"Whatever works best for you, babe. Tonight. Friday night. Whatever. Maybe I'll even give this dumb show a try tomorrow night."

She slapped the inside of his thigh and popped to her feet. "That'd be great. I know you're going to love it if you just give it a try. It's soooo good." She moved slowly toward the door, her eyes still fixed on the screen. "See her?" she asked.

A nurse with dark curly hair hurried across the screen in pink scrubs.

"That's Carol. She tried to kill herself after Doug broke off their relationship. She—"

Jackson stood up and gently nudged her toward the door. "Okay, okay. You're going to be late. You'd better get moving."

She pushed back slightly. "Are you trying to get rid of me?"

"Of course not." He chuckled nervously. "I just don't want you to be late."

"Yeah, sure. You got a date coming over or something?"

"Actually, yes. You caught me. Her name's Carol."

"Carol?"

With an ornery grin, he nodded toward the TV. "She's a nurse. She took off from Hollywood to be here tonight and you're screwing everything up. Now, beat it." He gave her another playful nudge toward the door.

"All right, I'm going. I'm sure you and *Carol* will be very happy together. Make sure you tell her how much you fart in your sleep because I'm sure she's really going to love that. Or how—"

He grabbed her hand and kissed it. Her sense of humor was one of the things he loved most about her. "I'll see you in the morning. I'll get Garrett on the bus if you're running late."

Luckily, a commercial break came on or she might have never left. As she grabbed her purse, she asked, "You promise you'll have him ready?"

If it would get her to leave, he'd promise to hand-dig a swimming pool out back. He bobbed his head in agreement. He walked her to the door and kissed her goodbye.

Once her car was out of the driveway, he raced upstairs to check on Garrett. His boy was sound asleep, one leg dangling off the edge of the bed. Perfect.

Jackson rushed to his bedroom closet and searched through his hanging shirts until he found a black hooded sweatshirt. He pulled it on and ran downstairs to the closet. His black gloves still hugged his hands as nicely as when he'd destroyed Spyder. He searched his coat pockets until he found where he'd hidden his ski mask and stuffed it into the sweatshirt's front pouch. That Brody son of a bitch was going to get the rudest awakening he'd ever had. Jackson was so excited he forgot to leave Garrett a note.

On the short drive to Brody's neighborhood, Jackson repeatedly played out the coming beating in his mind, almost feeling sorry for Brody.

Almost.

Unlike with Spyder, Jackson wouldn't hesitate this time. Brody would open the front door and *blam!* Jackson would smash his face. If that didn't end things, then punch two, three, and, if necessary, four would surely do the trick. It was going to be legendary. That drunk slob would never want to drink and drive again.

It wasn't ideal that he had to drive his own car, but he didn't have much choice. Brody's neighborhood was too far to walk and there was no way Jackson was waiting until another night. He decided not to worry about it and just enjoy the quiet calm before the storm. It was going to be epic, like forty-five-year-old George Foreman regaining the heavyweight title by dropping Michael Moorer epic. The anticipation winded him before he even reached Brody's neighborhood.

He drove the streets until he saw Brody's Taurus parked half on the driveway and half on the front yard of a brick-front, one-story house. The driver's door was open and the dome light was very dim. Jackson smiled at the thought of Brody having a dead battery in the morning.

Jackson continued slowly past Brody's house to a twenty-four-hour convenience store at the end of the street. He pulled into a parking space beside a tire fill station. Parked with his lights off, he sat and concentrated on slowing his breathing. Keeping calm and focused was the key. This was it. This was what he'd been practicing for. This was real crime where innocents were at risk. With a final deep breath, he climbed out.

The chilliness of the night kept him sharp. Once he was out of sight of the store, he sneaked through several backyards, setting off a Doberman behind a fence that nearly gave him a heart attack. After catching his breath again, he crept onto Brody's street. He scanned the other houses for any signs of movement and found none. It didn't appear that the Doberman's barking had drawn any attention. He checked his watch. 11:17. He pulled his ski mask over his face and marched toward Brody's car. He felt strong, invigorated. He hardly noticed the dull ache in his hip.

There was no one around except him, Brody, and God. No one to help the cowardly drunk when shit got real. No one to interfere. As long as Brody answered the door.

Stalking toward Brody's house, he caught sight of movement inside the Taurus. He froze, watching Brody's car like a gazelle watched the trees for lions. Or, more accurately, like a lion watching the brush for gazelles. It couldn't be this easy. He moved closer for a better view. It was too good to be true. It was impossible. Of all nights, Brody chose this night to pass out in his car. It was as if the justice gods had been pulling for Jackson all along.

Jackson moved in. Groggy, Brody sat up and looked around. He was probably surprised to have made it home, the bastard. Jackson hurried to the driver's door, approaching from the rear so Brody wouldn't see him. Brody heaved one leg out with a grunt and looked up into Jackson's cold stare.

He rubbed his forehead. "Who the hell are you?" His voice was deep and intimidating. He belched and his breath smelled of vomit. He pulled on the doorframe and climbed out. Jackson stepped backward to give him room. Face to face, Brody was bigger than he'd appeared from across the restaurant. That didn't matter. He might be bigger, but he was still drunk.

Jackson puffed up his chest and glared into Brody's bloodshot eyes. Brody didn't wilt like Jackson expected. He just sort of swayed slightly. Undeterred, Jackson drew back and heaved a giant-killing punch at Brody's nose. His fist struck Brody's forehead instead, nearly breaking his hand.

If there was any hesitation in Brody's reaction it could only be measured in microseconds. He sprang forward, engulfing Jackson in powerful arms. Jackson's back hit the ground with a thud and the wind gushed from his lungs as Brody's full weight landed on top of him.

Jackson's keys fell from his pocket onto the driveway. Brody sat up, straddling Jackson. "I don't know who you are, buddy, but you done messed up," he said.

Jackson struggled beneath Brody's weight, but it was like wrestling a bear. Brody ripped off Jackson's ski mask.

Jackson saw a ball of flesh and knuckles an instant before his vision flashed white. His cheek exploded with pain.

Jackson saw the next punch coming, but his body reacted too slowly to do anything about it. "Okay, okay," he cried after the fourth punch. "I give up. Stop." He sounded as pathetic as Spyder had. He covered his face with his arms as best he could.

But Brody didn't relent and hit him again, breaking through the small gap between Jackson's forearms. Jackson panicked. "Heeelp," he screamed. Brody's narrow, angry eyes were that of the devil. Jackson covered his face with his arms again and struggled to roll to his side under Brody's mass. This was it. Brody was going to kill him and he was helpless to do anything about it. Brody blasted through his feeble guard again, and again the clap of flesh on flesh echoed in Jackson's ears, followed by ungodly pain in his forearms and face. The beating wouldn't end. Another punch slammed against his ear. The earlier quiet of the night was shattered by a ringing bell.

Just as Jackson resigned himself to death by intoxicated bear, Brody stood up and braced his hands on his knees, gasping for breath. His lack of stamina had likely saved Jackson's life. Jackson looked up through one good eye and one rapidly swelling slit. He was helpless at the mercy of the man who should have been his prey.

Brody laughed. "Thanks, bud. I haven't had a good scrap in years." He stepped over Jackson then turned back and kicked Jackson in the side for good measure.

Jackson's knees met his chest and he dry-heaved.

A shit grin crossed Brody's lips and he reached down. Jackson shied away from him and then heard keys jingling. "You need these?" Brody asked between labored breaths.

Still curled in a ball, Jackson could only nod. He couldn't get enough air in his lungs to speak. Brody heaved the keys toward the road. Jackson followed them as they hit the ground and slid into a sewer grate. Brody couldn't stop laughing.

"That's at least a three-pointer," he said, and then stumbled up the porch steps and into his house.

Jackson choked on a mouthful of blood from his split upper lip. His ear was on fire and still ringing. His forehead felt like a softball had been shoved under the skin. He panicked, unable to find the strength to get up and worried the police would arrive soon. Or worse, Brody would return for another round.

After what felt like eternity, he cautiously rolled to his hands and knees, amazed that he could. He tried to push to his feet, but his stomach cinched up. After the wave of pain subsided enough to move again, he crawled through the grass toward the sewer grate.

It took all his strength, but he made it. His keys glistened at the bottom. He reached in, pressing his shoulder against the cold iron, and stretched his arm as far as he could. He wasn't even close. He rolled to his back to gather his composure. His stomach kinked twice more before he could finally get to his feet.

Defeated, keyless, and stuck miles away from home, Jackson made the long, agonizing walk back to the convenience store. Once he reached his car, he sat on the curb beside it under a payphone and bowed his head.

Someone at one of the gas pumps shouted, "Hey, buddy. You okay?" Without looking, Jackson nodded with a polite wave.

He used the metal-coated flexicord of the payphone to pull himself up. Leaning against the booth, he wedged the phone between his shoulder and his good ear and dialed 1-800-COLLECT.

The automated operator rattled off instructions. Jackson dialed Dustin's number, said his name after the tone, and waited. If he had a choice, he'd keep what he was doing a secret forever, but he needed help, and Dustin was the kind of friend who'd help you bury a body at three in the morning.

After a few rings, Karen answered in a sleepy, raspy voice and accepted the call.

"Karen?" Jackson gasped. It still hurt to talk. He grunted with each breath. "I'm sorry … ugh … it's so late. I need Dustin."

"What's wrong, Jack? Are you all right?"

"Yeah," he lied. "I just … need Dustin for a minute."

"Okay. Hold on."

After a few seconds, Dustin's scratchy voice said, "What's up, Jack?"

"I need help, Dustin. I got into something … I shouldn't have. Can you bring me something?"

"What?"

"I need you to … go to my house … and get my spare car keys."

"Okay?"

"Then I need you to … bring them to the store at the end of Hazel Street. You know where that is?" Each breath was a monumental effort.

"Yeah. I'll be there in a few."

"Hurry."

Jackson let the phone drop and left it dangling off the hook. With his one good eye, he watched the road. What had he gotten himself into? Each fresh set of headlights sparked hope it was his friend and fear it was a cop. Finally, Dustin pulled up behind Jackson's car.

"What the hell, Jack?" he asked as he got out. "What'd you do?" He knelt and draped Jackson's arm over his shoulder to help him up. "What happened?" He propped

Jackson against the car door while he dug the keys from his pocket. Dustin's voice turned serious and angry. "Who did this, Jack? Where they at?" He pulled Jackson's car door open and looked around.

Jackson was glad to see Dustin still had some fight in him. "It was my fault, Dustin. I just gotta get home before the police come."

Dustin hesitated a moment before relenting. "All right. But you've got some explaining to do. Can you even drive?"

"Yeah," Jackson answered, though far from confidently. He could at least breathe now. "Can you just follow me home?"

"Sure. But then I want to know what the hell's going on."

Jackson nodded reluctantly. His hands trembled on the steering wheel. It was hard to focus with one of his eyes swollen almost shut. Dustin went back to his truck and looped around the parking lot until he stopped with enough room for Jackson to back out.

Brody's neighborhood soon faded in his rearview mirror. Jackson was almost home when he failed to notice the traffic light ahead changing to yellow. He was too close to stop and the light was clearly red as he drove through the intersection. He checked his rearview mirror. Dustin had stopped in time, but Jackson's luck had officially run out. A police cruiser shot out from a side street.

The night had just gotten infinitely worse. At least he wasn't speeding. Red and blue pulsating lights flickered across his rear-view mirror and the short whelp of a siren startled him. He'd never been pulled over before. It was scarier than he'd imagined.

He signaled to the right, checked his side mirror, and pulled over. He kept both hands on the wheel, cognizant to not appear to reach for anything. Dustin drove past, his eyes meeting Jackson's. He shook his head.

The officer approached, stopping to shine a flashlight into the back seat. Then he stepped forward and directed the beam at Jackson's lap. Jackson slowly lifted his left hand from the wheel and reached for the power window button.

"Do you know why I pulled you over?" the officer asked before the window was completely down.

"The traffic light, sir?" Jackson answered.

The officer stepped closer to the driver's window. "Yes. What's the hurry?"

"No hurry, officer. I just wasn't attention payi—I mean, paying attention." *Calm down, idiot. He's going to think you're drunk.*

"What happened to your face?"

"I got a little cocky at a bar earlier and a few guys followed me outside." He forced a chuckle. "As you can see, I lost."

"Were you drinking at that bar?"

He mentally kicked himself. "No, sir. I'm against drinking and driving."

"Hm. Do you need me to call you a medic? You look pretty rough."

"No, sir. It's not as bad as it looks. Thank you, though."

"Okay. License, registration, and proof of insurance."

Jackson handed over his insurance card and his license. He gestured toward the passenger side. "My registration's in my glovebox."

The cop nodded. "Go ahead."

Jackson lunged for the glovebox.

"Slowly," the officer snapped, taking a step backward, his hand moving slightly toward his hip holster.

Jackson nearly wet himself. "I'm sorry, officer," he stammered. "I've never been pulled over before and I'm a bit nervous." He slowly retrieved his registration and handed it over.

The cop said, "I'll be right back. Just sit tight." Before he turned away, Jackson caught a glimpse of his name tag. G Davis. George? Greg, maybe?

The officer returned with Jackson's information. "I'm letting you off with a warning today. Just pay better attention to the lights next time."

Jackson released the breath he'd been holding. He couldn't believe Officer Davis was so oblivious. He'd obviously just attacked some dude. But then he decided this cop was as inept at his job as all the other cops. It was no wonder Spyder could steal from the same store all the time and never get caught.

"Have a good night, sir. And get some ice on that eye."

"Sure thing. Thanks." He wanted to add, "Now go sit in your cruiser and wait for another crime to be committed that you won't do anything about," but of course he didn't.

Jackson crept home at ten MPH below the speed limit, much to the annoyance of the guy in the minivan stuck behind him for most of the way. As he drove, he thought back to the Sataré-Mawé tribe and wondered if Brody had just put him through his own bullet ant ritual like Dustin's. Other than every part of his body hurting and his face feeling twice as big as it should, he didn't feel much different. Besides, the pain from his car accident had been much worse. He decided it was unlikely. He would need something far more painful.

Dustin was waiting on the porch at his house. He was laughing when Jackson got out of his car. "This ain't your night, is it? Did you get a ticket?"

Jackson shook his head. "Just unlock the door, please."

Dustin complied, still laughing, and followed him inside. Jackson plopped onto the couch while Dustin grabbed a frozen bag of peas out of the freezer and tossed it to him.

Jackson held it to his swollen face and asked Dustin to check on Garrett.

"So?" Dustin asked when he returned. He didn't seem angry. Jackson would have been furious to be woken up in the middle of the night to go get his stupid friend who had started a fight he couldn't win.

Jackson weighed how much to tell Dustin and decided his friend deserved to know everything. Besides, keeping the secret was eating at him and Dustin's mouth was a steel trap.

"What I tell you now you have to swear on your kids that you won't tell anyone, no matter what. Okay?"

"Whatever."

"I'm serious, Dustin. You can't tell Jenna or Karen or anyone."

"All right. I get it. Are you secretly James Bond or something?"

He wished. He didn't remember 007 taking such a lopsided beating in the movies. "You know that drunk we saw at the restaurant tonight?"

"Yeah."

"You know he drove home that way?"

"And?"

"I followed him home after we left the restaurant and then went back tonight."

"He did this to you? That drunk slob?"

"Well, he'd probably sobered up a bit. Plus, he must have been a boxer or something in his day. He was a little more than I expected."

"A little?"

"It won't happen again. I promise that."

"It'd better not. You're lucky he didn't kill you."

"I guess."

"I don't get it. Why?"

"I thought I could … you know … fight some crime or something."

"Like fucking Batman?" Dustin's voice rose and Jackson shushed him.

"Don't wake up Garrett. And no, not like Batman." Though being Batman would be nice. Especially the billionaire part.

"And that Spyder kid you said you beat up? Was that part of this goofy new crimefighting idea too?"

Jackson didn't answer.

"Jesus, Jack. You keep this shit up and you're gonna make Jenna a widow. You've never been a fighter. I've had enough scraps to know these things can go south fast. Just like tonight. You were lucky. Don't push it."

As his entire body throbbed, Jackson didn't *feel* lucky. "I'm sick of people getting away with hurting other people. Especially drunk drivers. The police are worthless. All they do is clean up after the mess, but they can't do anything to prevent the crimes. I want to help people, man."

"Volunteer at a food pantry."

"No. I want to see some kind of justice in this world."

Dustin shook his head. "Your car wreck screwed up your head something fierce."

Jackson looked away.

"What are you holding back, Jack?"

"Nothing."

"We've been friends since the fifth grade. I know when you're hiding something."

Jackson couldn't look at him.

"Tell me, Jack."

"You won't believe me."

"I'll try."

"It's just … I don't know. Maybe that wreck wasn't such a bad thing."

"How so?"

"I think it gave me something."

"An uglier mug? We agree." He chuckled and went to the fridge to grab a soda.

"I'm serious, Dustin."

"All right. I'll be serious. What'd it give you?"

"You'll think I'm crazy."

"Too late." When Dustin didn't get the smile he was looking for in return, he added in a more sincere tone, "What'd it give you, man?"

Jackson held back for a second. Then he decided to blurt it out and let the pieces fall where they may. "Sometimes, around certain people, I get a strange feeling."

"We all get that. I get it when I pass a cop on the freeway when I'm speeding. It goes away after he doesn't turn around."

"I think it's something more than that."

"Like what?"

"I think it's a gift or something that lets me know when someone's a bad dude."

"You mean like a sixth sense kind of thing?"

"Yeah, kind of."

"What sense are you getting from me right now?"

"What do you mean?"

"Are you getting the sense that I'm about to knock the crazy outta you?"

"I knew you wouldn't take me seriously."

"All right. I'm sorry. Tell me one time when this so-called sixth sense told you something that turned out to be true."

"Um. Maybe look at my face."

"Besides someone beating up a crazy guy who shows up at his house to fight."

"Well, I'm still working on understanding it. But this guy at the grocery store the other night ... I could just tell he was a bad dude."

"Aaaand?"

"He got real defensive with me for no reason and then when he left, I saw him drinking at the wheel."

"Pop?"

"No. Zima."

Dustin's face twisted. "That's barely alcohol. What else did he do?"

"Well ... um ..."

Dustin leaned closer in anticipation. "Go on."

"I didn't actually see him do anything else, but I know he was going to. It's hard to explain."

Dustin sighed and rolled his eyes. "Come on, Jack. You've gotta admit that's a little out there. How 'bout you sleep off your beatdown and we'll talk about this nonsense later? This is too much and I'm too tired."

"Yeah. Fine." It wasn't nonsense, but Jackson didn't want to argue.

Dustin rubbed the back of his neck, a sure sign he was stressed. "You've got it out of your system now, right, buddy? You're not gonna go swinging from any Gotham skyscrapers?"

"No."

"Promise?"

Jackson nodded. What he wanted to say was, "Do I look like a quitter?" but if he did, Dustin would probably sit on him until Jenna got home.

"What are you going to tell Jenna about your mess of a face? And then what are you going to tell her about the injuries?"

Jackson grinned more out of courtesy than hilarity. There wasn't a lot of originality to Dustin's jokes. But his friend was trying to soften the tense mood, so Jackson figured the least he could do was to play along. "I don't know. I'll tell her I fell down the stairs or something. What are you going to tell Karen?"

"I guess that you fell down the stairs."

"But I called you collect."

"I don't know. I'll think of something." Dustin was a brilliant liar when he needed to be. He downed the rest of his soda and set the empty can on the table. "You good if I go back to bed now? Some of us work in the morning."

Jackson nodded. "Thanks for your help." As Dustin headed for the front door, Jackson grumbled, "I'll clean up your can."

Dustin blew him a kiss and left.

After a couple of Advil, Jackson went to the bottom of the basement stairs and lay down on the concrete. Then he pinched his swollen upper lip to make it bleed. The sting was intense but short lived. He smeared the blood on the floor. After he was satisfied with the effect, he went back upstairs, pressed a paper towel against his lip, and turned on the TV. He'd tell Jenna his bad leg gave out. He fell asleep to Letterman chatting with Tim Allen.

8
MONSTER
November 11, 1994

Dylan shivered, curled in a ball in a dog cage and wrapped only in a thin, ratty blanket. The cage had a small heater beside it, but it didn't help much. He was in a barn with several other kids in cages who he wasn't allowed to talk to or he'd get Todd's belt again.

It was colder than the night before and he could see his breath. The wind sounded like a ghost moaning through the gaps in the walls. Dylan needed to pee, but he knew to wait for Todd to take him to the bathroom. He shifted in the blanket slightly and the raw belt mark on his back stung when it touched his clothes.

The girl in the closest cage to his left shivered so loudly Dylan heard her teeth chatter. Her name was Samantha. She seemed to be Todd's favorite.

It was dark and the only light they had was the orange glow from the coils of the heaters. Dylan wished Todd would leave a light on at night. Maybe that would keep the rats and scary noises away. He thought about his mom and how much he missed her, which made him start crying again. He'd cried every night since Todd brought him to the barn.

"Be quiet," a boy named Drew whispered. "He'll get mad if he hears you."

Dylan was trying to be quiet, but he couldn't help it.

Todd kept a lock and chain on the barn doors and the rattle it made when he unlocked it was how the children knew when he was coming. He always stopped in before bedtime.

Dylan barely managed to control his sobs before the doors flew open. Todd stood silhouetted in moonlight like the devil. He wore a bulky coat and one of those hats with a fuzzy ball on top. He flipped on the dim, flickering light above.

Like he did every night, he glared into each cage, stopping with a death stare at Dylan. He was so scary to look at that Dylan kept his eyes on Todd's muddy work boots. Todd walked to a barrel beside the door, removed the top, and scooped out Cheerios with a metal scoop. He dumped them into the closest cage. The little boy inside scarfed every piece as fast as he could. Todd retrieved a dog leash and then unlocked the cage. The boy hurried to finish eating. Todd handed him one end of the leash and he fastened it to the dog collar around his neck.

Todd led him out of sight to the back of the barn. That's where he took them to use the bathroom. Only it wasn't really a bathroom. It was an old stinky portable toilet with a post next to it that Todd tied the leash to. At least he always went back into the barn and let them pee in private. While he waited, he scanned the barn from top to bottom. He kept looking at the loft like he thought someone was hiding up there in the hay. Once the boy finished, Todd took him back to his cage and locked him back up. Then he scooped up more Cheerios and moved to the next caged child in the line. Cage by cage, he got closer to Dylan.

He stopped at the cage of a girl who didn't look very well. She had been sleeping all day, curled in a ball on the cage floor.

"Jessica?" Todd called.

She didn't move.

Todd lightly kicked the cage. "Hey. Jessica."

She still didn't move.

Todd groaned, dumped the Cheerios over her, and then moved to Samantha's cage. After he brought her back from the bathroom, it was Dylan's turn.

"It's your night tonight, Dylan," Todd said while Dylan stuffed stale Cheerios into his mouth. "No more crying. It's time you toughened up."

Dylan nodded. He was doing everything he could to keep the tears in. Todd unlocked the cage and fastened the leash to Dylan's collar. "Come on." He gave the leash a firm tug.

Dylan didn't know what to do. He was too scared to go, but he didn't want to make Todd angry again, so he pretended to pee. Then Todd led him outside, closed the barn door, and put the lock and chain back on. Dylan looked to his right where a field stretched all the way to a forest surrounding the property. Todd led Dylan to the left toward a run-down trailer home. As they walked, a skinny dog burst from a hole in the skirting of the trailer and charged at them. He was big with black fur and white paws and a white snout.

Dylan crowded behind Todd's leg. The dog stopped and sniffed him. Then he growled and showed his teeth.

"Shut up, Blackie," Todd snapped, and gave the dog a swift kick in the side. Blackie yelped and limped to the trailer where he disappeared back into the hole.

Todd opened the back door and led Dylan up two stairs into the trailer. The floor was bare wood covered in dark stains. The kitchen sink overflowed with dirty dishes and roaches that scattered when he flipped on the light. Todd unhooked the leash and hung it by the door next to a longer restraint. He fastened that one to Dylan's collar.

Without looking back, he said, "Now you can walk around. Just don't try and take off that collar. Hand me that ax handle." He pointed to a piece of wood next to the door.

Dylan handed it to him. It was almost too heavy to lift. Todd jammed one end against the floor and the other end under the door handle. Then he slid a lock across the frame that was too high for Dylan to reach. "If you try to go outside, Blackie will eat you."

Todd took off his coat. He had fancy letters tattooed down his arm and a naughty picture of a girl with no shirt. Dylan looked away. Todd went to the fridge and made a sandwich while Dylan stood motionless at the door. Todd took a bite and then looked over.

"What're you doing?" He flicked his hand toward where the kitchen opened into a living room with a couch. "Go on. Make yourself at home. Your tiedown will reach."

Dylan still stood frozen.

"I suppose you're hungry?" Todd asked.

Dylan nodded. His stomach had been grumbling for days. The Cheerios were never enough.

Todd tossed him a piece of ham and it landed on the floor. Dylan snatched it up and wiped off the yucky dog hairs and dirt. The ham was cold and covered in fat, but Dylan devoured it and hoped for another piece.

Todd grabbed a beer bottle from the fridge and twisted off the lid. He took a swig and glanced at Dylan. "Want a drink?" He offered the bottle.

Dylan shook his head.

Just as he'd built up the courage to take a step toward the couch, some kind of monster groaned from behind a closet door. He whipped his head around. The groan faded into a sick rumble.

Todd sighed and then marched past Dylan. Dylan backed against the wall, terrified. He thought a werewolf might be hiding behind the door. He really had to pee now and wished he could have gone at the barn.

Todd yanked the door open. "Damn furnace," he grumbled, and gave something a hard smack. The beast belched and then quieted into a low hum.

Dylan's eyes drifted to Todd's sandwich still sitting on the counter. It had attracted some ants already, but it would still be so much better than Cheerios.

But Todd grabbed the sandwich, dusted off the ants, and took another bite. Then he turned on a black and white TV and sat on the couch. He patted the cushion next to him. "Come have a seat, Dylan." His tone left no room to argue.

Dylan took a couple of slow, tiny steps forward as he scanned the room. Three heavy-duty locks secured the front door and only one was in Dylan's reach.

Dylan sat on the couch as far away from Todd as possible. "T-T-Todd?"

Todd's head crept around. "What?" he snarled.

"Are you going to hurt me?"

Todd turned back to the TV and took another bite of his sandwich. Dylan was ready to ask again when Todd finally answered, "No."

"W-w-why am I h-h-here?"

Todd groaned and then answered, "I told you this already. I can't be alone at night or they'll come for me while I'm sleeping. You're here to wake me if they try to get in."

"Wh-wh-who tries to get in?"

"The soul snatchers living in the forest."

Dylan gasped.

"They're always watching me, but they only come in when I'm sleeping."

"What do they w-w-want?"

Todd glared at him. "Souls, stupid."

"I don't understand. H-h-how can I stop them?"

"They won't come in if someone's watching."

"But why me?"

"Because children are the only ones other than me who can see them at night. And they don't like to be seen."

Dylan cautiously scanned the room. "W-w-where are they now?"

"Outside. All around us." He shot a furtive glance at a gap in the broken mini blinds. "Shhh. One of them's watchin' me right now."

Dylan leaned forward and looked at the window. "Where?"

Todd nodded subtly. "There. In the gap in the blinds."

"I don't see anyone."

"Right there, damn it." He grabbed both sides of Dylan's face and directed his eyes toward the window. "Do you see him now?"

Dylan didn't see anyone, but he was afraid to say so. "I-I-I think I see something."

Todd shoved his head away. "Yeah. I told you."

"What do I do? I don't know how to stop soul snatchers."

"Your job is to wake me if any of them try to get in. That means there's no sleeping for you tonight. Got it?"

Dylan nodded and tried to sit still, but his bladder was really aching now. "I-I got to pee again, Todd."

Todd pointed to a dark hallway.

Dylan hesitated.

"What're you waiting for?" Todd snapped. "Do it now before I go to sleep, or you'll have to wait until morning."

Dylan looked up at him and then back to the dark hallway. He didn't want to go in there alone, but he really had to pee.

Todd turned the TV to a Western and ignored him. Dylan slowly slid from the couch. With his head on a swivel, he crept to the hallway. He hoped there weren't any soul snatchers in there. He found a light switch on the wall and flipped it up. Nothing happened.

"That light's out," Todd said.

Dylan swallowed hard.

"First door on your left."

Dylan put his hand on the wall and followed it to the first doorway. He reached in and turned on the light. That one worked, but it was dim and flickering and buzzing. Dylan slipped in and pushed the door shut behind him. Then he had to open it again to pull more of his leash through. The floor was sticky and gross. Beside the toilet was a bathtub with the shower curtain pulled closed. Dylan feared one of the snatchers might be hiding behind it. He took a timid step toward the toilet.

Todd shouted from the other room, "Hurry up. I'm getting tired."

Dylan drew in a deep breath, ran to the toilet to do his business with both eyes locked on the shower curtain, and then ran back to the front room without washing his hands. He sat stiffly next to Todd and stared at the gap in the mini blinds.

After a while, Todd's head started to bob and he yawned. A few minutes after that, his head dropped forward and he started to snore.

Dylan was too terrified to move. He scanned the room, imagining monsters or ghosts in every shadow. He still wasn't convinced the furnace wasn't a werewolf in the closet. Or maybe a soul snatcher. Even Todd's coat draped over a chair looked like someone watching him. When the TV programs ended for the night and the screen went to static, it got even scarier. Every creak and groan was another creature coming for him. He almost pissed himself when the furnace werewolf suddenly growled and rumbled again.

Dylan barely blinked until morning, one eye constantly on the gap in the mini blinds. He still didn't see anyone there. Dylan had never been so happy to see daylight than when it finally poked through the gap.

Todd snorted and woke up with a jerk. He looked around, licking his lips. He side-eyed Dylan. "You didn't sleep, did you?"

Dylan frantically shook his head.

"Good." He stretched and groaned. "Did you see any of them?"

Dylan didn't know how to answer that. He thought maybe he should tell Todd about the werewolf and the shadow monsters, but what if Todd got angry? He shook his head instead.

"Good." Todd stood up. "You can get some sleep today while the rest of the kids play."

That was fine with Dylan because he didn't like Todd's version of playing. Games like hide 'n seek and tag were normally fun, but Todd got angry if any of the kids hid too well and sometimes smacked them in the head if they ran too fast. But he said the games were their exercise and they were mandatory.

Todd massaged his knee. "We should probably check on Jessica this morning and see if she's feeling any better." He went to the cupboard and pulled out a Pop Tart package. He tossed it to Dylan "Good job last night. Come eat that over here and I'll get you some orange juice."

Dylan rubbed his tired eyes and slid off the edge of the couch, stumbling a little on numb legs as he went to the kitchen. He wolfed down the Pop Tarts and drank the orange juice before Todd could change his mind. The juice was strong and bitter, but he was too thirsty to care.

After switching Dylan to the shorter leash, Todd marched him back to the barn and tied him to a post at the entrance while he delivered Cheerios to each cage. Then he stopped at Jessica's. She was in the same position as the night before. Todd stared for a minute and then shook his head. He opened the cage and lifted her out.

As he carried her through the barn, he said to the others, "It looks like the soul snatchers got Jessica. You guys have to be more careful. No games today." He untied Dylan from the post and pointed to a shovel on the far wall. "Bring that and come with me."

Dylan couldn't stop looking at Jessica's pale skin and wide-open eyes. She looked like a doll.

Todd flicked the back of his head. "Do what I told you, boy."

Dylan hurried to the shovel with his leash dragging the ground. The shovel was big and heavy and awkward and he had to drag it behind him. Todd led him outside, set Jessica on the ground, and secured the barn doors. Then he grabbed Jessica's bony wrist and dragged her around to the back of the barn.

Dylan followed him with the shovel.

It took Todd most of the morning and plenty of sweat and curse words to dig a hole deep enough for Jessica. He was sweaty and tired by the time he finished, and he still had to fill the hole back in. Once he'd done that, he bowed his head like he was praying. When Dylan didn't immediately bow his head, Todd gave his arm a nasty pinch.

Dylan started crying.

Todd rolled his eyes. "I don't know what *you're* crying about. I'm the one who has to get another kid." He looked at three other mounds of dirt behind the barn and sighed. "When will they get their fill? I'm tired of digging holes."

9
SWAPPER'S DAY
November 12, 1994

Though the swelling had gone down, Jackson still sported a purplish, half-moon bruise under his eye. As much as he would love to forget the beating Brody had given him, his ribs reminded him whenever he tried to get out of bed. The Vicodin he'd taken that morning before he headed out helped make moving bearable.

Jenna was out cold, a rough night at work to blame, and Garrett was at school when he left for the small town of Johnstown thirty minutes away. The closer he got, the worse the traffic grew. The annual Swapper's Day was a popular attraction. He pulled into the line of cars snaking into a field-turned-parking-lot and waited. When he got to the entrance, he paid his five bucks to the farmer-turned-parking-attendant and joined the stop-and-go parade into the field. He didn't remember it being this busy when he'd come as a kid with his stepdad, but it probably had been. He estimated two hundred cars already parked and a hundred more behind him. At five bucks a pop, the farmer looked to make a killing.

Jackson glanced at the "Welcome to Swapper's Day" sign. He must have been seven or eight years old the last time he had seen it. And it looked like the same worn-out, beat-up one. As a kid he had loved Swapper's Day for the toys. You could find anything there, from games like Stratego and Mouse Trap, to old rusty power saws and drills, to G.I. Joe dolls and everything in between. If it was made in the 1960s, '70s, or '80s, it was at Swapper's Day. But that wasn't the main reason Swapper's Day existed. No, Swapper's Day was about trading and buying guns. His dad could show up with a cheap two hundred dollar shotgun, spend all day up-trading for different guns to less informed traders, and then leave at the end of the day with a fifteen hundred dollar semi-automatic rifle which he'd later sell to a friend for a nice profit.

Jackson had no illusions of being able to pull off such a feat. His gun knowledge equaled his astronomy knowledge, which was nonexistent. He'd be happy just leaving with a three hundred dollar Glock for three hundred. He had little idea of what a Glock was other than hearing Dustin talk about how nice they were from time to time. That was enough for him.

Tractors towed passenger cars full of people from the lot to the event a half-mile away. Jackson hopped onto the back of one that was passing by and winced when his ribs complained.

At the entrance of the actual event a young kid was collecting another five dollars for admission. He stamped Jackson's hand with a red smiley face and Jackson made a mental note to scrub it off before he got home. After the entry fees, his wallet was still fat with $350 in cash from his emergency stash.

The fairground stretched as far as he could see and was packed with tent after tent full of venders and customers. Not a person walked by who didn't carry a weapon of some type. Even the children carried knives or BB guns. He had never seen so much camouflage in one place before.

Jackson stopped at the first tent he saw displaying handguns in a glass case.

"Can I help ya, pal?" the cowboy-hat-wearing attendant asked in a Southern drawl.

"Do you have any Glocks?" Jackson asked.

The guy wrinkled his forehead as if sizing him up. "You mean like all them Glocks you're lookin' at in that case?" He tapped a fingernail on the glass.

Jackson nodded. He felt like an idiot.

"Which do you wanna look at? The first or second gen?"

What the hell was he talking about? Jackson pointed to one.

"Ah. A second gen seventeen." He opened the case and retrieved one of the guns. He slid the slidey thing back and looked down the barrel. Then he handed it to Jackson.

Jackson held it like he'd seen cops hold guns in the movies. He studied it on one side and then flipped it over and studied the other. Short of inspecting for scratches, he didn't know what he was looking for. He handed it back. "What's the difference between the first and second gen?"

The vender spat some chew off to the side. He held the gun out and pointed to numbers etched in the steel. "The second gen has serial numbers. You know, for those commie Democrats."

Jackson thought about the implications of serial numbers and then asked, "How much for a first generation?"

The vender grinned and exchanged the gun with another one from the display. "They're a little harder to get nowadays. I can let one go for four hundred smackers."

"Oh. That's more than I intended to spend. Uh ..." *Remember, this is Swapper's Day,* he told himself. "Will you take three hundred?"

"This ain't a garage sale, pal. I can give ya twenty bucks off, but that's it."

"I only have $350 on me."

"Have anything to trade?"

"Uh, no. Not really."

He started to put the gun away, but Jackson stopped him.

"Wait. I'm not trying to low-ball you. I really only have $350. That's it." Jackson fished his wallet out and opened it as proof. "I really need this."

The vendor sighed. "Listen. You're not going to find a gen one Glock for under $380 from any of these vendors. Even at that price, I'm giving up a bit more than I wanted. I can let a second gen go for $350, I guess, but that's the best I can do."

Jackson shook his head. "Thanks, but I'd really like to have a first generation one."

"Okay. I'll tell you what you need to do. You need to find someone walking around selling their Glock. Take a good look at these here so you know what you're looking for. You'll be able to find one, it'll just take some effort. You should be able to get one for what you've got with a little bit of work. You understand?"

Jackson nodded.

The guy wished him luck and moved to the next customer.

Jackson walked away. He still felt like an idiot, but he needed to shake it off. Since everyone seemed to be packing, finding a gun looked to be the easy part. Figuring out who was selling them might be the trick. It was time to engage in one of his wife's favorite pastimes: people watching.

By noon Jackson still hadn't figured out how to initiate a person-to-person exchange. His stomach growled, so he found a hot dog vendor and got in line. With so many people around, all carrying a gun of some type, Jackson was surprised at how safe he actually felt. As a budding crime fighter, he was training himself to spot threats, but this place went against his every natural instinct. Guns and money everywhere, yet everyone seemed so polite and nonthreatening. Almost everyone nodded or said hello if they made eye contact. Anyone not wearing a Bill Clinton T-shirt was welcome, he suspected.

As he waited for the line to move, someone behind him asked, "You sellin'?"

Though the man wasn't speaking to him, Jackson casually looked over his shoulder anyway. The man directly behind him, an older fella wearing an NRA ballcap and holding a toothpick between his lips, turned toward the voice. "Everything's for sale if you name the right price," he said. A rifle straight out of an Arnold Schwarzenegger movie hung from a strap over his shoulder.

The inquirer was a skinny, twenty-something man wearing a bulky Carhartt-style coat unbuttoned to display a vintage Kenny Rogers concert T-shirt. Part of his chin hid behind a patchy goatee. "Is that a—" The kid threw out a combination of letters and numbers that might as well have been the name of a droid in a Star Wars movie.

The older guy said it was indeed an R2-3PO-something-something. He slid the strap from his shoulder and pulled back a lever on the gun's side to look inside. Then he let it snap back with a *ka-clank*. Jackson was catching on. Apparently, the proper etiquette of showing off your gun was to show it wasn't loaded before handing it over. It made sense. The guy handed his rifle to the younger guy.

"How much you want?" the kid asked.

"I'm lookin' to get fifteen."

Thousand? Hundred? Fifteen what? Jackson had no clue.

"I'll git you thirteen-fitty. That's all I got."

Ah. Fifteen hundred. Jackson studied the exchange like the two were carrying out peace negotiations at the UN.

"Sir?" the lady at the hot dog counter said loudly. "I said what can I get you?" Her tone clearly implied she didn't get paid enough to deal with idiots who weren't paying attention.

"Oh, sorry." By the time Jackson paid for his hot dog, bottled water, and salt and vinegar chips, the young guy was walking away with a rifle and the older guy was counting his cash. Jackson would have loved to see how the negotiations had played out. At least now knew what he needed to do to get the ball rolling.

It felt awkward approaching the first two men—one of them wasn't selling and the other didn't even have a Glock—but Jackson was gaining confidence. The third man he approached acted interested.

"How much?" Jackson asked.

The man checked that the gun was empty and passed it to Jackson. "I'd probably let it go for four hundred."

Jackson steeled himself. This was it—the big negotiation. "Will you take …" He paused and counted his money. "… Three hundred and forty-seven dollars and twenty-five cents?"

The guy cocked his head and smirked.

Jackson shrugged. "It's all I got, man."

The man's shoulders deflated and he sighed. "Buddy, you're lucky I'm getting ready to leave and I haven't had any better offers today." He motioned for the cash.

Jackson decided to press his luck. "And an extra clip?"

The man's hands dropped to his sides. "Really, man? You're already getting a killer deal."

"I know. And I appreciate it. But I need an extra clip."

"So, let me get this straight. Your offer is three hundred and forty-seven dollars and twenty-five cents for a first gen Glock *and* an extra *magazine*?"

Jackson wanted to crawl into a hole. "Not called a clip, huh?"

The man shook his head. "Only in the movies."

"Well, that's my offer. Really, it's all I got."

The guy nibbled at his lower lip. After a few seconds of uncomfortable silence, he said, "Throw in that leather wallet and you've got a deal."

Jackson balked for a second, but then nodded and started stuffing his license and credit cards into his pockets. He handed the man the cash and the empty wallet and shook his hand.

The man said, "Just be glad I don't take your shoes, too. You're getting' a helluva deal."

"I know. I appreciate it."

And just like that, Jackson had become a gun owner for the first time. He'd have to buy ammo later.

As Jackson headed for the exit, he passed a booth with kids' Halloween costumes hanging on a makeshift backdrop. One item in particular caught his eye. It was a cheap plastic mask of a Teenage Mutant Ninja Turtle. It wasn't the mask itself that got his attention, but what the turtle wore over his eyes. Jackson smiled and set the mask back on the table, a new idea percolating in his brain.

It was almost 2:00, which gave him forty-five minutes to buy bullets, find somewhere to fire off a few rounds, and still get home before Jenna woke up and wondered where he was. The abandoned Milner's Farm on Outback Road was the perfect out-of-the-way spot. He and Dustin had gone out there a few times as teenagers to drink some Mad Dog 20/20 that Dustin had swiped from his dad.

Tucking the gun in his waistband at the small of his back felt awkward at first, yet he walked a little straighter just knowing it was there. He climbed into his car and left the lot.

He stopped at a Meijer and bought a box of bullets, or "rounds" as the gal behind the counter corrected him. She was a lot nicer about it than the gun's previous owner. She even showed him how to load a magazine before he left.

Halfway between the Meijer and his home was a dirt road leading through a wooded area to Milner's Farm. It was the perfect spot, far away from everyone. With his car parked out of sight from the road, he turned off the ignition and climbed out.

He was confident no one would stumble upon his car, but he locked it anyway. The swinging barrier gate had a chain wrapped around it, but since it didn't have a padlock it wasn't much of a deterrent. The dirt track was mostly covered with weeds, but it was easy enough for Jackson to find his way. After a short walk, he found the perfect spot.

The coated steel of the Glock was warm from being pressed against his body. The grip felt like it had been made for his hand. First, slide the magazine thingy into the bottom. Check. Aim. Check. And fire.

But nothing happened. He held it sideways to examine it. Then he aimed and fired again. Nothing. Did that sneaky bastard sell him a lemon? He tried to pull the trigger again, and still nothing happened. He knew there was a steep hill with a pond at the bottom nearby, and he considered throwing the damn thing into it. Then he remembered what the other gun handlers had done before handing their weapons over. He held the handle firmly and pulled the top of the slide back. It clunked and then snapped forward. He smiled and aimed at a tree twenty feet away with a knot hole at about chest level. Jackson held the grip with both hands like the cops on TV. Then he lined up the site with the knot in the tree.

He inhaled a deep breath, let it out, and then squeezed the trigger. The recoil was more manageable than he had expected. The boom was not. If there was anyone nearby, they now knew a badass with a gun had arrived. He had missed the tree completely, but that didn't matter. Until a man shoots a gun, he can't imagine the power and ferocity it delivers. Some people might be scared away by it. But for Jackson it was a life-changing awakening. It meant never being helpless again. It meant not being beaten to a pulp by a drunk driver named Brody. He aimed his weapon of justice again and squeezed off six more rapid-fire shots. One of the rounds slammed into the tree with the force of a mini atom bomb.

He finished the first magazine and then the second, all the while wearing a smile that could be seen from space. The excitement was even better than when he'd given Spyder a thumping. As he walked back to his car, he pondered new possibilities. Could he actually kill a person if he had to? Probably not, he thought, but simply having the gun would scare most people onto the straight and narrow.

Jackson stopped at the fabric store on his way home and used a credit card to buy black fabric that could be cut into strips. Then he headed home and, with his new weapon snug in his waistband, joined Jenna in the house. He left the fabric in the car for later.

"Where have you been?" she asked.

"Just doing a little Christmas shopping." It wasn't completely a lie—there was nothing he wanted for Christmas more than the ability to protect his family.

"Didn't you tell Dustin at dinner that you already got me something? A Lexus, I believe."

"No. I told him what I was going to get you. Today I actually went shopping for it."

"Nicer than a Lexus?"

"You'll have to wait and see. But if you don't mind living in a Lexus from now on, we can put the house up for sale tomorrow and look into it. Might be cramped for the three of us, though."

She laughed and shooed him off as she tidied up the kitchen counter. He crept upstairs and stuffed the pistol and box of rounds under his bed. He'd find a better place for them later.

That evening he enjoyed dinner with his family even though he was counting the minutes until Jenna left for work. He couldn't wait to get out and prevent some crime.

Once Jenna was finally out the door and Garrett was tucked into bed, Jackson gathered his gear. He put on his black hooded sweatshirt and then retrieved the fabric from his car and cut it into a four-inch-wide strip. Then he cut out eyeholes, grabbed Jenna's sewing kit from the closet, and hemmed the edges with a needle and black thread. He wasn't the greatest of tailors, but a mandatory home-economics class in junior high school had taught him just enough to get the job done. He tied the fabric around his head and took a look in the bathroom mirror. He looked like a badass. He nodded approvingly and then stuffed the mask in his pocket. Then he grabbed his black gloves and his new toy. He was ready. Now all he needed was to find a crime.

Since Pataskala wasn't exactly a hotbed of criminal activity, he decided to head to Columbus, the closest big city. He didn't like the idea of taking his own car, but he still didn't have any workable options. As luck would have it, he backed out of the driveway just as his neighbor stepped out into his front yard with their dog.

Oh no. His neighbor waved. Jackson lowered his window. "Hey, Kevin," he said.

"Hey, Jack. Where you off to so late?"

Jackson's mind raced. "Jenna forgot her work ID. I gotta run it up to her." He immediately wanted to kick himself when he imagined Kevin mentioning it to Jenna the next time he saw her. "Do me a favor. Don't tell Jenna I told you. She likes people to think she's the responsible one in the family."

Kevin chuckled. "Gotcha. Where's Garrett?"

Jackson nodded toward the back seat. "He's sleeping. Didn't even wake up when I put him back there."

Kevin gave him a thumbs up and then called his dog back from the edge of the yard and went into the house.

Jackson sighed. He considered calling off his adventure for tonight, but the feel of the gun pressing against his back was too tempting. But one thing was for certain. He needed a different way of getting around at night other than his own car.

After spending the next three hours driving around the livelier parts of Columbus without any luck, he decided the Kevin incident had been a sign. Still, he enjoyed being out so late at night. There was a certain calmness being alone in a crowded city. It was after two when he finally decided to get back home to Garrett.

10
HELLA DEAL
November 19, 1994

Gary was ten minutes late, which was the Gary that Jackson knew best. Waiting in the corner booth of a mom-and-pop restaurant, Jackson had already dismissed the waiter twice. The next time he came around he was going to order with or without his tardy friend. A black portfolio sat next to him on the bench seat. He didn't want Gary to see it too soon. Jackson doodled a series of interlinked red and blue spirals on the paper tablecloth with the two crayons provided by the restaurant for children and bored vigilantes.

He had requested the corner booth so he could see the whole dining room and keep an eye out for anyone up to shenanigans. Like a would-be robber. Or the woman sitting alone at the table in the center. She looked like she was considering ditching without paying her bill. When her nervous gaze rested on Jackson, he gave her a nod to let her know he was watching. She quickly looked away.

Other than her, no one else seemed suspicious. He made a mental note of the emergency exits and the location of the fire extinguisher just in case.

Just as he was about to give up and flag down the waiter, Gary finally stepped through the door. Gary was a dumpy-looking guy with glasses and terribly crooked front teeth. He was in the habit of combing his few remaining hairs over his otherwise bald head in an attempt to fool the mirror (he obviously wasn't fooling anyone else). In the two years since Jackson had last seen him, Gary's hair situation had become even more dire. He now appeared to have a dead rat flattened across his dome. It was startling to see.

Jackson waved his friend over. "Gary, how the hell are you?" Jackson stood up with his hand outstretched.

Gary grabbed hold. "Jack, you look … Uh." He paused. "*Great.*"

"Me? Look at you. Did you put on ten pounds of muscle or what?"

Gary snorted. "Yeah, muscle. I wish." He rubbed his gut. "The best house McDonald's can build." Then he pulled Jackson in for a hug.

Jackson had met Gary working at the tire shop before Gary left to work at Clyde's Auto Repair about four years ago. He'd always enjoyed Gary's company even if he could be kind of annoying. He was one of those touchy-feely kinds of guys who could grow tiresome fast.

Jackson extricated himself from Gary's embrace. Undeterred, Gary grabbed Jackson by the back of his neck and pulled his head in for a good old fashioned noogie.

"I don't know about the shaved head, though," Gary said as he pushed Jackson away and playfully jabbed at Jackson's gut. "You joining the skinheads?"

Jackson sighed. "You know me better than that."

"Yeah, I know. I'm just teasin'. So, how'd you get that scar, anyway?" Gary asked as they sat across from each other.

Jackson suddenly realized Gary didn't know about the accident. "I was in a pretty bad car wreck earlier this year."

"No kiddin'? I hadn't heard."

"Yeah. Thanks for checking in on me while I was laid up in a hospital bed, by the way. I nearly died."

Concern painted Gary's face. "What? Dude, I had no clue. I'd have—"

Jackson grinned. "Calm down. I'm just kidding. I know you'd have come by if you'd known."

"How'd it happen?"

"Hit by a drunk garbage man."

"I'm sorry to hear that, man. You're all right now, though?"

"Getting there. They had to rebuild my leg and rehab was brutal, but at least I can walk now."

"Aw, man. That sounds awful. I wish I'd known. I'd have stopped by. Maybe brought you and the family some home cooking or something."

Jackson's eyes widened and he grinned. "No, thanks. I'd already survived one nightmare."

Gary paused for a second and then they both laughed.

Gary had just picked up the menu when the waiter arrived with two glasses of water. Jackson ordered grilled cheese, fries, and a pickle.

"Hm." Gary scanned the lunch menu for ages.

"Come on, Gary. It's a front and back. It's not rocket science."

Gary lifted his eyes from the menu, unamused. "You know what?" he finally said. "That sounds good. I'll have the grilled cheese like my impatient friend." He sipped at his water as the waiter gathered the menus and walked away. "I was surprised to get a call from you out of the blue like that, Jack."

"Well, I've been sitting around thinking, who's the ugliest guy I know who I haven't seen in a while?"

"Really? This coming from Scarface?"

"It's not on my face."

"Yeah, that's too bad. It could only help if it were."

Jackson continued to watch the woman at the center table over Gary's shoulder as she paid her bill, gathered her purse, and left. She glanced back as she passed through the door.

Jackson wasn't sure what she had been up to, but whatever it was she'd changed her mind when she saw him watching.

"How's Jenna?" Gary asked.

"She's good. She's working nights at the hospital. How 'bout you? Still married to your cousin Trish?"

Gary grunted and shook his head. "Can't you let that old joke die? You know she's not my cousin."

Jackson didn't even try to hide his amusement. "Sure she is."

"Not like that, she's not. Her uncle happened to marry my aunt."

"Yeah. That makes you cousins."

Gary rolled his eyes and chuckled. "I never shoulda told you in the first place." After a pause, Gary asked, "You still working at the tire shop?"

"Nah. They let me go when I couldn't get back to work after the wreck. They held my job for a bit, but I just wasn't ready yet and they needed to move on."

"We have an opening at Clyde's if you don't mind changing oil all day. I think they'd love to have you there."

Jackson paused, hoping he looked like he was giving the offer some legitimate thought. Then he said, "I appreciate it, Gary, but I'm still not ready to get back to the grind. But I'll keep it in mind if Jenna gets tired of having me at home all the time."

"Then I'll expect a call soon."

The pang of guilt Jackson felt caught him off guard, but he was saved from having to reply by the arrival of their food.

As soon as the waiter set their plates on the table, Jackson grabbed a bottle of ketchup and squirted a pile onto his plate. Gary watched in horror as Jackson dipped his grilled cheese into the ketchup and took a bite.

Jackson caught Gary's stare. "What?" he asked, mid-chew.

"Ketchup on your grilled cheese? What are we, eleven?"

"Some people dip their grilled cheese in tomato soup. I like ketchup. What's the difference?"

Gary rolled his eyes again. "Do you need me to cut the crust off for you, too?"

"Thanks, Mom." The two ate and laughed and reminisced about old times at the tire shop. Gary was as friendly as ever, reminding Jackson of why they had always gotten along so well.

Then Gary reached over the table and smacked Jackson's forearm. "It's good seeing you again, old friend. If there's ever anything I can help you with, you've got my number."

This seemed like as good a time as any to reveal his ulterior motive. "Actually, now that you bring it up, there is something you might be able to help me with."

"Yeah? Name it."

"I was wondering if you still had that old Toyota sitting around. That white Celica?"

"Yeah, I still have it. In fact, I can't get rid of it. Why?"

"I might be interested."

"You don't want it, Jack. Don't you remember how I got it?"

"Yeah, I remember."

"Papers were fake. The sketchy dude who traded it to me disappeared. I'm pretty sure it was stolen."

"Yeah, I know. But it could still do me some good. I bought a car just like it last month and I could use the parts to get it up and running. It was an '86, right?"

"Yep."

"How much you want for it?"

"I don't know, man. The damn thing's been sitting on my property for years now. I'd be happy if I got three hundred bones for it."

The waiter set the bill on the edge of the table and Jackson snatched it before Gary could reach for it. "I got this today," he said.

Gary cocked his head. "How hard did you hit your head in your accident?"

"Very funny. I can cover this. But I don't have three hundred bucks right now for the car. I had another thought, though." Jackson was counting on Gary's penchant for a good barter. In hindsight, Gary would have been the perfect guy to take to Swapper's Day. "Would you be interested in a little trade?"

Gary grinned. "Whachu got?"

Jackson had him right where he wanted him. He held up the portfolio case and placed it on the table.

"I'm intrigued," Gary said, grinning even bigger. Gary would probably trade his own kids for a Pepsi if for no other reason than the thrill of a good negotiation.

Jackson unzipped the end of the portfolio case and slid out a comic book sealed within a clear plastic sleeve.

Gary's smile faded. "Really, Jack? Comic books?"

"Not just any comic book." He passed it to Gary like he was handing over a Ming Dynasty vase. "This is the Incredible Hulk Issue 181."

"That means nothing to me."

"It's the first appearance of Wolverine. You've heard of Wolverine, right?"

"Yeah. He's in that X-Men cartoon my boy watches. He's got kind of a goofy voice."

It was time for the hard sell. "This book is a gem. It's from 1974, and look how good the condition is. You've heard of comic books selling for ungodly amounts of money, haven't you?"

"Yeah."

"This one's worth five hundred all day long in this condition. Hell, it's probably worth a grand if you find the right buyer. And it's only going to continue going up in value. Wolverine's the next Superman or Spiderman in the comic book world. You've heard of them, right?"

"I guess."

"Well, there you go."

Gary cocked his head. "Then why don't *you* sell it?"

"I don't have time. I need that car up and runnin' ASAP. Besides, I don't even know where I'd look to sell it. You're much better at this stuff than me."

Gary stared, stone-faced, at the book. Jackson could see his gears turning.

"You know me, Gary. I'd never screw you over." Jackson wasn't lying. It actually broke his heart to get rid of the prized comic book he'd cherished since he was a kid.

Gary examined the book like it was the Torah. He squinted and held it at different angles as if he knew what the hell he was looking at. The only thing missing was a jeweler's loupe. He finally said, "You know what, Jack? You come out, and if you can get it running it's a deal."

"It doesn't run?"

"Last I tried it did. But it probably needs a jump at the least."

"You've got cables, don't you?"

"Sure. But that'll cost you extra. Do you have any Spiderman pajamas or Star Wars bedsheets to offload?"

"You're a real riot. I'm telling you, it's not junk. In fact, if you keep it, I'll buy it back from you when I get on my feet again for whatever it's worth at that time."

"I guess that sounds okay." He set it on the table dangerously close to a couple of drops of water. Jackson nearly had a heart attack. Gary added, "I probably couldn't let it go for less than a grand though. It's the best comic book I own."

Jackson wiped the table dry with his napkin. "It's the only comic book you own."

"And thereby the best."

Good ol' Gary. Sucker for a trade.

"When do you want to get the car?"

"How 'bout I ride out with you now and pick it up?"

Gary shrugged. "I don't see why not. How're you going to get it back to your house, though? Remember, no papers?"

"Hm. Good point." Jackson rubbed his chin as if in deep thought. Then he smacked the table, giving Gary a jolt. "You know what? Screw it. I'm gonna take a chance and drive the damn thing. Does it have plates?"

"Yeah, I think they're still on it. But like I said, they're probably stolen like the car. I never got my own plates after realizing the car was probably hot. You'll be taking a helluva chance driving it home."

"I'll be all right. I'll drive slow … I'll drive like you."

"You should. You'd get less tickets that way."

"Ha-ha. Very funny. You ready to go?"

"What about your car?"

"I'll leave it here. I live less than five minutes away, so I can have Jenna run me back over later."

"You must really want that car."

"I do."

"Okay, then. Let's go."

Jackson gently replaced the comic book in its portfolio and tried to hand it to Gary, but Gary rebuffed it with a wave.

"I can't take that book, Jack. I got no use for it. Give it to your boy someday. He'll appreciate it more than I will. I'm just happy to get rid of that junker." He aggressively patted Jackson's back. "Plus, my *cousin* has been bitching about that car sitting by the garage for years." He grinned.

Good ol' Gary.

The ride to Gary's property took longer than Jackson remembered. Gary lived deep in the country where the last five or six miles were on dirt and gravel roads that snaked through the woods. Gary sped along the twisty, one-lane road, seemingly unconcerned with the pitter-patter of gravel against the undercarriage.

When they rounded yet another bend, Jackson saw a van approaching in the distance, kicking dirt and debris up behind it like the dust cloud that followed the Roadrunner. The driver appeared to be on a collision course with Gary on the narrow lane. Gary slowed. The van blazed onward without change. Jackson squeezed the armrest a bit tighter. The van's broken grill and cracked windshield indicated a driver who wasn't too concerned with keeping his vehicle accident-free. He hoped Gary was.

Gary hugged the side of the road, almost dropping a tire into the ditch. The white van's rear kicked sideways a tad then straightened and continued its careless course. Jackson winced and held his breath. Gary crowded the ditch even closer before stopping completely. The van blew past, gravel peppering Gary's car. There was barely enough room between their sideview mirrors to pinch a hair.

"Jerk-off," Gary shouted as he pulled back into the center of the road.

"Who was that all the way out here?" Jackson asked.

"That's my dickhead neighbor." Gary owned seven acres of mostly wooded land inherited from his parents, so "neighbor" was a rather loose term.

"Does he hate you or is he just an asshole in general?"

"I've never talked to him. Probably just an asshole. He drives like that all the time."

Jackson sat up straighter. "Turn around, then," he said.

"What?" Gary asked.

Anger built inside. His gun pressed against his back. That guy was a bully, and Jackson wasn't content to simply let it slide. "Turn around. Let's go talk to him. It'll be fun."

"And then what?"

"I'll beat his ass for you."

Gary nearly choked on his own spit. "What?" He snorted. "Are you insane? Is that scar really from an accident or a lobotomy at some windowless hospital?"

"I'm serious."

"Settle down, Steven Seagal. We don't need to beat anyone's asses today. Nobody got hurt. Although, I must admit, he was pretty close this time."

Jackson slouched back in his seat, embarrassed and inwardly cursing himself for his cheesy tough talk. When was he going to learn to shut up? He needed to be more subtle. More Clark Kent, less Superman.

Gary pulled off the dirt and gravel road onto a dirt lane leading to a doublewide trailer. Along the lane were three parked vehicles in varying degrees of deterioration.

The lane ended at the back of Gary's trailer beside a chicken coop. Jackson counted twelve chickens and two roosters. Gary's four-wheeler sat out in the open behind the coop. "Do you keep your quad runner out all the time?" Jackson asked.

"Sometimes."

"Aren't you worried about someone stealing it?"

Gary laughed. "Out here? No, I'm not worried. I don't even lock my door at night."

"What about your neighbor in the van?"

"Just because he's a jerk-off doesn't make him a thief. I've never seen him in my drive, let alone near my house."

The Toyota sat camouflaged within a patch of overgrown weeds near the tree line at the back of Gary's property. There was a two-car detached garage next to it. "Why don't you keep your cars in the garage?" Jackson asked.

"That's my shop. You couldn't fit a car in there if you had a running start." Gary drove through the grass and stopped nose to nose with the Toyota. "Let me grab the battery from my shop. Go ahead and check the fluids before we start it." He tossed a rag from under the quad runner seat to Jackson before walking into the garage.

Jackson pushed through the weeds, opened the driver's door, and popped the hood. Most of the fluids were a little low and the oil was black, but it should hold up for now. Gary returned with the battery and hooked it up. He retrieved the keys from the doublewide, pushed a wider path through the weeds, and climbed in. He gave it a crank and the starter clicked with the turn of the key.

After a jump, the Toyota revved to life. Gary appeared as amazed as he was happy. "Come in for a quick beer while it warms up?" he asked.

Jackson politely waved him off. "I've got to get back, Gary. Jenna's waiting for me. I appreciate it, though."

"Any time." Gary pulled him in for a hug and held on too long for comfort.

Good ol' Gary.

Jackson retrieved his comic book from Gary's car, thanked him again, and then climbed into the Toyota. "You've got my number. Don't be a stranger." He adjusted the seat, closed the door, rolled down the windows, and pulled out of the weed patch. Though it was cold outside, having the windows down was better than marinating in the musty stink.

Jackson crept along the road, partly concerned that the van might come barreling back through, and partly—the part that felt his pistol pressing against the small of his back—hoping it did. Once on the main highway, the steering wheel shook something fierce. New tires were a priority.

He obeyed more traffic laws on the way home than the police probably knew existed. At a strip mall parking lot near the grocery store, he parked the Toyota on the outer edge. He made sure no one was watching before he ducked behind a pick-up truck and scraped the registration sticker off the license plate with his pocketknife. He ripped the sticker a little, but it still looked good enough to keep him from drawing the attention of the police. He hoped it was still sticky enough to hold until he could come back with glue.

With the stolen sticker on the likely stolen plate of the likely stolen car, Jackson crossed the street to where his own car was parked at the diner and drove home. He wouldn't see the Toyota again until Jenna went back to work tomorrow night, but he was excited just knowing it was there.

11
MAKE NEW FRIENDS, BUT KEEP THE OLD
November 19, 1994

Camden was too tired to cry any more. His sobs had turned into occasional gasps and whimpers. The metal floor of the van was hard and cold. The duct tape around his wrists and ankles dug painfully into his flesh. The man who had snatched him from his bed drove along a rough, bumpy road, each turn making Camden slide from one side of the van to the other.

The driver had said his name was Todd and he needed Camden's help, but Camden was pretty sure you didn't tie up people you wanted help from. He'd seemed agitated when Camden told him he was only nine and didn't think he'd be very helpful. Todd hadn't said much since then. Camden lifted his eyes to the back of his kidnapper's head.

Todd constantly dug at his scalp with bloody fingernails. "You ever get the lice," he asked the empty passenger seat. He paused as if listening to someone answer, and added, "Well you're lucky. I get 'em all the time. And there's nothing fun about it." And then he turned the wheel again and Camden slid behind the driver's seat.

"Todd?"

"What?"

"I'm scared. Can I go back home, please?"

Todd didn't answer.

Camden sucked in a breath. He had to be strong. Todd drove for another few minutes before he stopped and turned off the van. He got out with a grunt. The side door slid open and rough hands grabbed Camden's bound ankles and yanked him to the edge. Then Todd slung Camden over his shoulder. As he carried Camden to a barn behind an old trailer, he continued digging at his scalp. He laid Camden on the dirt by the barn doors and fished a small knife from his pocket. He flipped it open and bent over Camden.

Camden panicked, shaking his head frantically. "No, no, no. Please don't hurt me."

Todd jerked Camden onto his belly as the boy continued to beg. He slid the blade between Camden's wrists and sliced through the duct tape. "Quit your crying," he growled. Then he unlocked the barn doors and swung them open. He flipped a switch inside, but nothing happened. He wriggled it up and down, and still nothing. He looked back at Camden.

"A fuse blew. Stay here while I fix it." He stepped into the barn and shouted, "Is everyone okay?"

A little girl's voice answered from the dark, "We're r-r-r-really cold, Todd." Camden could hear her shivering breaths.

"I know, Sam. I'll get the heaters back on in a second."

After Todd disappeared into the dark, Camden started picking at the duct tape around his ankles. He found the end and quietly unwrapped it.

His daddy once told him that if anyone ever tried to hurt him he should run no matter what. Camden looked around and saw a forest at the back of the yard. He and his daddy had played paintball in the woods a few times. He knew if he could get there, he could hide. He was good at hiding.

He rubbed his cold hands together and looked for Todd. The light in the barn flickered to life and Camden could see Todd at the opposite end with his back to him. Camden scrambled up and sprinted for the trees.

He was halfway there when he heard Todd shout, "Blackie. Get him."

Camden glanced over his shoulder. The terror of seeing a vicious dog chasing him almost made his legs stop working. Panic gripped him as he heard Blackie's heavy panting breaths approaching fast. He screamed as he ran.

The next time he looked back, Blackie leaped at him. Horrible pain exploded in Camden's hip and he crashed to the ground. He wailed as Blackie clamped down and shook his head like Camden was his chew toy.

Camden grabbed Blackie's snout to pry him off, but the beast was latched on too tight. Every move was agonizing. Camden cried and screamed as footsteps ran toward him.

Todd shouted, "Let go, Blackie. That's enough." Blackie didn't listen. Once Todd got close enough, he kicked Blackie hard. Blackie yelped and let go, cowering away with his ears tucked and his head low. He showed Todd his teeth and Todd stepped toward him angrily. Blackie turned and ran off.

Camden looked at his leg just below his hip. It was torn wide open and bleeding. Todd dropped to one knee and pressed his palm against the wound. Blood oozed between his fingers.

Todd grabbed Camden's hand and pressed it to the wound. "Keep your hand there," he snapped. Then he cradled the boy and lifted him with a grunt. "And stop being a pussy."

Camden wanted to stop crying, but his leg hurt too much.

Todd carried him back to the barn and laid him on a long wooden crate. He retrieved a dusty rag from a hook on the wall and shook it before shoving it against Camden's wound. He said, "Hold this till I get back. I trust you won't go anywhere this time?"

Camden shook his head and bit his lower lip.

Todd started to leave then turned back. "If you do, I'll let the soul snatchers get you and you'll die in those woods. You understand?"

Camden nodded, though he didn't know what a soul snatcher was. After Todd left, Camden looked around. Several cages full of other children staring back at him sat in a wide circle in the middle of the barn. One of the cages was empty. He winced and tried to sit up. He wiped his eyes with his free hand.

"Hello?" he whispered.

One of the kids said, "Shhh. We're not supposed to talk."

Camden continued looking around until the barn doors swung open again. Todd came in, carrying a blue and white first aid kit. Camden was so tired that he just lay back while the other kids watched in silence.

Todd wet a piece of thread in his mouth and then poked it through the head of a needle. He removed the bloody rag from Camden's wound. Camden lifted his head just enough to see three separate gashes. They weren't bleeding as much as before.

Todd opened a brown bottle and dumped it over the gashes. The liquid started fizzing milliseconds before the sting made Camden bite his lip again to keep from screaming.

Todd held the needle poised over Camden's leg. "Don't you move. This is going to hurt." He leaned his weight against Camden's middle and went to work. This time Camden couldn't keep from screaming. It was like someone was putting fire under his skin. His head swirled like he was going to pass out. It would have been better if he did.

After what seemed like forever, Todd stood straight and admired his work. "Not bad, huh? You got twenty-three stitches."

It felt like a million. Camden looked down at Todd's sloppy work. The lacerations were pinched together with black thread. Pale skin bulged between each stitch. Todd covered the gashes with dressing and tape and then helped Camden to his feet. He pointed to the empty cage.

"That's your new home. Get in." He turned on a heater beside the cage and then grabbed a blanket and tossed it in.

Camden limped to the cage and climbed inside. He wrapped the blanket around his shivering shoulders and pulled it tight.

Todd fed everyone Cheerios before taking them to use the bathroom at the back of the barn, putting a collar on Camden when it was his turn. He put them all back in their cages except for one little girl. He led her to the barn doors before turning out the lights and taking her away. Camden curled up in a ball and cried.

12
ON THE HUNT

November 20, 1994

Since Garrett didn't have school and Jenna didn't work Saturday night, no one set an alarm clock for Sunday morning. Jenna got up around 8:00, waking Jackson in the process. She said she was going to make pancakes before heading downstairs. Jackson tried to go back to sleep but couldn't and finally rolled out of bed around 8:30. He moped around the bathroom a bit longer than usual, feeling weighted down for some reason, like the dark quicksand was creeping in again. And he had another headache, which didn't help his mood. It was almost 9:00 before he found the strength to join his family downstairs. Pancakes were on the table and Garrett was playing Super Metroid on the Super Nintendo.

"Morning, Dad," Garrett said without looking away from his game.

Jackson rubbed Garrett's head. Then he went to the table. It was crucial to go through the motions even if he wasn't feeling it. He kissed Jenna as she hurried by with a bowl of scrambled eggs.

"You want juice?" she asked.

"Sure." Jackson sat down and forked a couple of pancakes onto his plate. He wasn't very hungry, but she'd made the effort, so the least he could do was down a couple.

Jenna set a glass of juice beside his plate and leaned close to his ear. "Terrible story on the news this morning," she whispered.

Jackson looked up. "Yeah? What happened?"

"Another child was kidnapped last night. This time in Heath."

Jackson shook his head. "Damn."

"Jack, that's not far from here."

Jackson lowered his fork. "How many kids does that make now?"

"Ten over the last two years. But this one's the closest to us. The little boy was taken from his bedroom while his parents slept in the next room. Just like the last one. It's so scary, Jack. I feel so sick for the parents."

Jackson seethed at his pancakes. He'd give anything to come face to face with the bastard taking those kids. The things he'd do to him …

"Jack, we need to get a security system. I couldn't live with myself if something happened to Garrett." Her voice wobbled on their son's name.

Jackson didn't answer. His blood was starting to boil.

"Did you hear me, Jack?"

"Yeah. We'll look into it." But his mind wasn't on a security system. It was on justice.

"I mean it, Jack. We need to look into it sooner rather than later."

"Okay, I get it."

As she walked to the sink, she said, "You say the same thing every time. You never call."

"It's fifty bucks a month, Jen. We have to watch our money until I get back to work."

"Like the money you took from your emergency stash? I didn't even ask where that went."

He didn't realize she knew about his stash. "Okay. You've made your point."

"It's important, Jack."

"I know. You're right. I'd like to be working first, but I'll make some calls."

"Speaking of work, are you thinking about getting back at it?"

"I've been looking a little. But there's no good jobs out there right now. At least none *I* could do in my condition."

"You're getting better all the time. You're done with physical therapy. I don't even notice your limp most days. You can't use your accident as an excuse forever. I think you could do something if you wanted. Even part-time."

He rolled his eyes, but not where she could see. He glared down at his pancakes. They looked less appetizing than ever. Thinking it would be better not to offend Jenna more, he managed to get through the first one and half of the second one. When she disappeared into the laundry room, he scraped the rest into the trash. In spite of the difference he knew he could make with his new ability, the news of the latest kidnapping made him feel more impotent than ever before. So many kids missing and he had no idea what to do about it. The cops were obviously worthless.

He needed a win. It had been almost two weeks since Brody had kicked his ass, but it was still doing a number on him. The couch was calling his name again and it was taking everything he had to resist the pull. It was a stark reminder that no matter how good he'd been doing, he was always one bad day away from losing himself in the nothingness again. Maybe he really did need to find his bullet ant ritual to escape the darkness for good.

He had to get out of the house. He told Jenna he was running to the store for deodorant and slipped out. He didn't really need deodorant. What he really needed was a night out patrolling the town. A nice adrenaline rush could do him some good. But first he had work to do on the Celica.

He grabbed his toolbox from the garage and drove to the auto parts store to buy a new car battery, spark plugs, and a quart of oil. At some point he would have to change the oil completely, but that could wait for another day. At the checkout, he noticed some superglue and bought that too. He took his supplies to the strip mall and spent about an hour getting the Celica fit to drive. It was a good thing he'd grabbed the glue because the stolen registration sticker was lying on the ground below the license plate. He glued it back on and then went home. It was just before noon.

With Garrett playing outside and Jenna visiting the neighbors, the couch called his name again. He thought it couldn't hurt to watch the Steelers game. He fell asleep almost immediately and woke up just in time to see the Steelers win against the Miami Dolphins in overtime.

After the game, Jackson moped around for the rest of the day while Jenna went antique shopping with her friend, Janelle. He couldn't wait until she left for work. The quiet day drifted into a quiet evening. Jenna brought Mickey D's home for a late dinner. Then she took a nap before work. Jackson was still on the couch when she came down to leave. When she kissed him goodbye, she paused and asked if everything was all right. She knew him too well.

"It's fine. I'm just not feeling particularly bubbly tonight."

"Is something wrong?"

Yeah. You're still here, he thought. "Nah. Today was just a little rough for some reason. I'm sure I'll be fine tomorrow."

"Do you need me to stay home tonight?"

Panic made his heart thump in his chest. "No, babe. I'll be fine."

"Okay." She kissed his cheek.

No sooner had she pulled out of the driveway than Jackson was in his costume, minus the mask that he kept in his pocket. He tucked the Glock into his waistband, kissed his sleeping son's forehead, and scribbled a note to leave on the table. He crept out the back door and jogged through his neighbors' backyards to the street that led to the strip mall. No Great Dane poop on his shoes this time.

"Thank you, Gary," he whispered as he climbed into the Celica. The car fired up like it was new, though there was a knocking sound coming from the engine that he hadn't noticed before. He'd better change the oil soon.

He wanted to try his luck in downtown Columbus, but an increased police presence after an Earth, Wind & Fire concert at the Ohio Theatre had him looking elsewhere. He needed a plan B. Since the news often reported heavier crime just south of the Ohio State University campus, that's where he headed.

Though the OSU campus had their own security and was a fairly safe place, some of the surrounding areas had fallen on hard times over the years, attracting dirtbags hoping to take advantage of naïve teenagers venturing too far from their dorms. Those vultures were the ones Jackson hoped to meet.

He knew he was in the right place when he started seeing gang graffiti on walls and stop signs, trash piled alongside the road, and boarded-up houses on every block. Despite his budding talent, the place gave him the creeps. Broken streetlights left a lot of the area in darkness. There were plenty of people outside, either drinking on their porches or walking along the sidewalk. Seemingly everyone gave him a dirty look as he drove past, proving he was in the right place. He parked in a carryout lot, climbed out, and locked his doors. He'd be sure to keep his eyes sharp.

Now, all he needed to do was watch for criminals. Within the first five minutes he'd seen two hookers climb into random cars and what might have been a drug deal, though he couldn't be sure. He dismissed the thought of targeting hookers. In his opinion, prostitution shouldn't even be illegal. He figured what someone did for money with their own body should be their business. He didn't see it as any different from a guy with big muscles being paid to work a construction site. Everyone needed to use what they had to get by. He wanted to make more of a difference than stopping some nine-to-fiver from having his willy tugged.

Patience was the key.

Midnight turned to one o'clock. And one drifted into two. He'd already heard two whatchu lookin' ats and three fuck offs, which should have told him it was time to leave, but he pressed on. He was simply more cautious of who he made eye contact with. It wasn't that Jackson couldn't find any criminals—there were plenty of people around who were far from being choir boys—but he wanted someone truly evil that night. A rapist or a murderer would be perfect. Something that would make a real difference to the world. Since the chances of actually witnessing such a crime being committed were remote at best, he'd have to rely on good old-fashioned detective work and a bit of intuition. It was as good a night as any to test his head injury bestowing new abilities theory. He studied each person he passed, waiting to see if they gave him the heebie-jeebies.

He paced the sidewalk, staying close enough to the shadows and alleys to duck away at the first sign of the fuzz. His night was turning into a dud.

At 3:00 he decided it was past time to head home. On his way back to his car, a sedan almost clipped him turning into an alley he was about to cross. The driver continued, oblivious to Jackson's presence.

Jackson shouted, "Fuckin' drunk." Then he stopped and tilted his head. He sure did hate drunk drivers. Maybe the justice gods had just rewarded his patience. It wasn't murder or rape, but drunk driving was drunk driving. It could turn into manslaughter, after all.

The taillights stopped halfway down the alley along the back of a strip mall. The lights went off. Jackson looked around. Was someone setting him up? A drunk driver stopping in a dark alley to wait for Jackson's judgement was too perfect. It was like he'd died and gone to vigilante heaven.

He moved closer. There were two people in the front seat. One of them ducked out of sight. Something was definitely fishy. Another glance at his watch tugged at Jackson's conscience. His first instinct was to get home to Garrett, but his second, stronger instinct was to check things out before he left. It wouldn't take long.

Staying in the shadows, Jackson crept down the alley for a better peek. He tied his mask over his eyes, lifted his hood over his head, and put on his gloves. After a deep, calming breath, he pulled his gun from his waistband.

A fenced-in yard that ran parallel with the alley made the perfect cover for his approach. From there he could see inside the sedan without the occupants noticing him. His heart raced. His gloved finger found the Glock's trigger guard. He felt all-powerful.

He crouched beside the passenger side and held his weapon against his chest with both hands. He almost couldn't catch his breath. *Concentrate. In through your nose. Out through your mouth.* His hands quivered. He just needed another minute to gather himself.

Then the passenger door clunked open, cutting that minute short by fifty-five seconds. A high-heeled foot and a lot of leg swung out.

It was now or never. Retreat or react. Jackson stood up and screamed, "Nobody move." The passenger glanced over like she was used to masked men with guns screaming at her.

She adjusted her fur coat like she hadn't heard him. Who still wore fur? He should shoot her just for that. The driver buckled his pants as if he'd also been through this routine before.

"Don't move, I said," Jackson screamed.

The woman wiped her mouth with her hand. "Honey, I ain't got time for this."

Why wasn't anyone concerned that a gun was pointed at them? "Just shut up."

The driver leaned back to better see Jackson through the rear passenger window. "What do you want, man? Money?"

The woman pulled herself out of the car.

"I said don't move, lady, or I'll … I'll …"

"You'll what? Shoot me?"

"Yeah."

She reached back into the car and retrieved her purse from the floorboard. "Honey, you ain't shootin' nobody."

He chambered a round to scare her. "Bullshit. I'll shoot you. I will."

"Your hands are shaking too much. Now move so I can get back to work. Whatever business you have with this motherfucker is between you and him." She reached out and gently pushed Jackson's gun to the side.

"I'm not messing around here," Jackson shouted. He pointed the gun at the front tire, closed his eyes, and squeezed the trigger. A bomb blast echoed through the alley.

The driver jumped out on the other side. "You shot my fuckin' car, man?"

Now that the man was standing, Jackson could see he was as big as a linebacker. Jackson's stomach clenched. Thank God he had his gun. The man reached for the back door handle, but Jackson waved his gun and shouted, "I said don't move." His voice cracked. He was getting a nasty feeling about this guy. Worse than Doc B and Spyder combined.

The hooker backed against the car. "All right, honey. Calm down. Whatchu want?"

That was a good question. Jackson wanted to punish someone for breaking the law, but nobody deserved to die for a blowjob.

Did they?

"I can't believe you shot my car, man," the guy shouted. "I got no beef with you."

Jackson rolled his eyes. "It's just your tire. Chill out."

The hooker gave him a lopsided grin. "Honey, whatever you want, you'd better hurry. We ain't the only ones that heard the gunshot."

She was right. Jackson had to think fast. "Get over here," he told the guy.

The guy looked in the back seat again and then shook his head in disgust as he took his time strolling around the back of the vehicle. He had a helluva strut for someone with a gun pointed at him. The orange glow of a lit cigarette highlighted his square jaw and sharp cheekbones when he took a drag.

The hairs stood up on the back of Jackson's neck. This guy could be a real problem. "What is this?" Jackson asked, nodding toward the car. "A Beamer?"

"You're a real genius. Seven-series. You like?" The guy flicked his cigarette to the pavement. His smirk infuriated Jackson.

"Stolen?"

"Why? 'Cause I'm black?"

Why did everyone jump right to racism? "I … Wait, no … Stop saying shit like that. I give justice to white people, too."

"Sure you do."

"No, really. I do. There was this one kid who stole some cig—" He shook his head. "You know what, buddy? Just shut up."

"Whatever you say, man. So, if it's not 'cause I'm black, why me?"

"You're breaking the law."

"I'm on a date, man."

"If you're on a date, what's her name?" He nodded at the hooker, who looked bored with the whole situation.

The big guy grinned and gave a knowing nod. "Seriously, though. Are you shitting me here? I ain't done nothin' wrong except wantin' to dip my wick a little. You can understand that, right?"

"We'll see if that's all you've done tonight." Jackson wasn't going to be thrown off this time. He closed the distance between them and shoved his Glock in the smartass's face. The cocky smirk faded. It was funny how a well-placed gun could do that to a person. Blowing his head off would be so satisfying. The guy probably deserved it, too, but shooting him in the face didn't seem right even if the world wouldn't miss him. Without taking his eyes off the man, Jackson said, "You can go, lady. But clean up your act."

"Whatever, honey. You won't see me again." She was probably lying her head off, but at least she was pretending to acknowledge the gravity of the situation. Out of the corner of his eye, he watched her sling her purse over her shoulder and march out of the alley.

"Now you," Jackson growled.

"What are you? Some kind of skinny-ass vigilante or something?"

"Something like that."

"Then why'd you let her go and not me? She committed the same crime I did."

"Because that's not the reason I've got you here. You're drunk."

"I ain't drunk."

"Yes you are."

"No, I'm not."

"Bullshit."

"Listen. Are we going to do this all night? I haven't drank anything tonight."

Jackson studied his face. He didn't actually look drunk. But there had to be something. Maybe he could get the guy to confess to doing drugs or something else. "We both know you're no angel. Just tell me what crimes you've committed and we'll wrap this up."

Please say murder. Please say murder. Please say murder.

The guy wasn't having it. "How 'bout you just let me leave and we'll pretend this never happened? Or even better, you put the gun down and we can throw hands like real men?"

Now that was the stupidest thing Jackson had ever heard. He shook his head. "You tell me what we both know you're up to, and I'll decide how to handle it."

The guy reached into his inside coat pocket and Jackson nearly shit himself.

"What are you doing?" he screamed, his quivering finger moving inside the trigger guard.

"Relax, buddy," the man said as he slowly pulled out a pack of cigarettes and a lighter. "Do you mind?" He nodded at the smokes.

"I guess." Smoking wasn't a crime.

The guy calmly lit a cigarette like he had no idea how close he'd come to his brains painting his Beamer. Jackson removed his finger from the trigger.

"What do you say, buddy? Let me go? Other than tonight, I'm a saint. I promise."

"Yeah, right."

"You've already shot out my tire. I'm gonna have to explain to the po-po why I'm in this alley when they come, and that's no picnic."

Oh, yeah. The police. *Shit.*

"Hell, they're more dangerous to a brother than you anyways."

"Stay right there," Jackson ordered. With his gun trained on the perp, he shuffled to the open passenger door and looked inside. There he saw a small vial half-full of a white substance on the center console. "What's in vial?" Jackson asked.

"Sugar. I'm diabetic."

Jackson snorted. "Whatever."

"Can we get on with this?" the man asked.

Not only was he trafficking in the sex trade, but he had drugs, too. Now Jackson was getting somewhere. He turned his attention to the back seat. Something shiny caught his eye on the floorboard. He looked closer. It was a rifle like something he'd seen at Swapper's Day. His heart sank. That's why the perp had tried to open the back door. Jackson almost threw up. He had been dangerously close to being dramatically outgunned in a shootout and he'd had no idea.

"What's that gun for?" he shouted, his voice shaky again.

"Protection."

"Protection from what?"

"Guys like you."

Jackson had seen and heard enough. He didn't have time to find out the guy's real crimes. He had to dish out some punishment before the police showed up and let the guy go. Jackson shut the passenger door and then shuffled back to the rear of the car. The clock was ticking.

"Gimme your cigarette," he demanded.

"Sure thing, buddy. You can have a new one if you want."

"No. That one's fine." Jackson trained his gun on the guy's chest and reached a timid hand out. The guy gave him the lit cigarette. "Now, get out of here," Jackson said.

"I can't. You flattened my tire. Remember?"

"No, not in your car. On foot." Jackson waved his gun in the same direction the hooker had gone. "Go that way."

"So, all this for a jacking? Are you shittin' me?"

Jackson waved his gun at the man again. "Your car or your life?"

The man held his hands up in front of his chest. "Okay, okay. I'm goin'." He backed away slowly. "This is some straight-up bullshit."

Jackson hurried around to the driver's door, opened it, and pressed the power lock button. He removed the keys from the ignition and tossed them and the cigarette onto the floorboard. Smiling at the guy was probably a dick move. Within seconds, wispy smoke rose from the carpet.

The guy shook his head. "Ah, man, that ain't right." His shoulders slumped. "Can I at least get my gun? It's unloaded. I promise."

Jackson shook his head. "Get moving."

As the guy backed away, he added, "I'm gonna kill you one day, man. I'll find you and I'm gonna run you down."

Jackson flicked the back of his hand at him. "Keep walking, buddy. Be happy that's all I did to you."

"At least tell me who you are, you coward."

Jackson knew he wasn't a coward. Not anymore. But he wasn't stupid enough to give the guy his name, either. He needed a superhero name for his superhero work. Something badass so the criminals knew who to fear.

Without thinking, he blurted out the first name he came up with. "Tell your friends you just met the Spyder Stopper." And then, as if that wasn't cheesy enough, he added, "Make sure to spell it with a 'y'."

The guy snorted and rolled his eyes, and inwardly Jackson was doing the same. He had to stop talking like that.

The guy turned to leave and then paused. "What're you gonna do about the rounds?" he asked over his shoulder.

Jackson tilted his head. "What?"

The guy smiled, flipped him off, and jogged down the alley.

Jackson stood there a moment trying to puzzle it out. And then it hit him. Rounds. Bullets. Fire. *Uh-oh.*

Did he have time to get to the gun? Jackson looked back to the Beamer. The fire had taken hold of the carpet and the wispy smoke had darkened. *Shit. Shit. Shit. Shit.*

He lifted his eyes to the end of the alley where a police cruiser slowed and started to turn in. It was too late to run. He'd already been seen. Jackson ripped off his mask and stuffed it in his pocket. He hid his gun under his shirt and tried to look like an average concerned citizen. He backed away from the car just as the Beamer's window popped from the heat, and then the fire really got going. The cruiser stopped on the opposite side of the Beamer, prevented from getting any closer by the growing flames.

The officer climbed out. "Hey, you," he shouted.

He started to circle around the burning car, but then he glanced up to see the flames impinging on overhead power lines. He stopped short. "Is this your car?" he shouted.

Jackson answered, "Nope. Just happened by and saw it smoking."

"Did you hear a gunshot?"

"Yeah. There must be a gun or something in the car that's going off." As if to give truth to his lie, a gunshot exploded from the car. The officer reflexively ducked and reached for his hip holster before realizing what had happened. He said something into his microphone as he backed toward his cruiser.

"Get out of here," he shouted and waved Jackson away. "I'll meet you on the other end for a statement." He started back toward his cruiser while yelling into his mic for the fire department.

A crowd had formed at Jackson's end of the alley. Not wanting them to see his face, he waved his hands above his head as he ran, shouting, "Get outta here. It's gonna blow." He had no idea if it was indeed going to blow or not, but he needed to cause as much commotion as possible.

Three more gunshots rang out from the alley and the crowd scattered. Jackson joined them as they ran. He was two blocks away before he heard the sirens of firetrucks. The thought of firemen possibly getting hurt pricked his conscience, but he figured they had policies to protect them from things like this. Though, if he was being honest, he might have made that up just to avoid feeling guilty.

He was already feeling the rush of a successful night in the books. Burning the Beamer did a few things for him. First, he knew for sure he wasn't an arsonist by nature because setting the fire didn't give him any kind of thrill. Second, everything from confronting the criminal to the rounds exploding in the fire to escaping the cops gave him a helluva rush. Third—and this was the most important part— it proved the accident had really given him a gift. That gun in the back seat was proof of seedier activity even if Jackson didn't have enough time to get to the bottom of it.

Feeling almost like a god, he climbed into the Celica and headed home. It was 3:17 in the morning.

13

MAKING WRONG THINGS RIGHT

November 21, 1994

Fleeing a crime scene in a likely stolen car with stolen tags while carrying an unregistered gun was ridiculously dangerous, and it felt awesome. On the drive home, Jackson obeyed every speed limit sign and traffic law he could think of. Even turning right on red lights was too risky because he didn't want to be accused of making a rolling stop. Avoiding traffic meant taking the back roads, which also meant taking more time, but he was confident he'd get home long before Garrett woke up.

His hip started aching shortly before a raindrop landed on his windshield. The evening news had said a storm was brewing, but the weatherman was wrong about the time it would arrive. It wasn't waiting until the morning commute. Within a few minutes, the rain was falling in sheets that the wipers couldn't keep up with. He slowed down and squinted through the rain to keep the car within the lines.

Jackson turned onto a two-lane highway coincidentally named Jackson St. He was about four miles from home when a set of headlights appeared in his rearview mirror, coming fast. Too fast. The headlights quickly filled his mirror. The prick's horn blared. At least it wasn't a cop.

It was raining too hard to take any chances with such an aggressive driver on his ass, so Jackson backed off the speed a bit more to let him pass. It had the opposite effect. The car started lunging forward and then braking inches from Jackson's bumper. Jackson figured he should pull over and let the guy pass, but then worried the prick might go on to hurt somebody with his reckless driving. The new Jackson couldn't let that happen. Jackson slowed to about forty MPH, hoping that would force the driver to slow down and annoy the hell out of him at the same time. A win-win. He couldn't help but laugh.

The car's high beams flashed, as if that was going to do any good. The prick swerved side to side and, when Jackson didn't move out of his way, crowded close enough that Jackson couldn't see headlights in the mirror anymore. He decided it was time to end the game before things escalated. As Jackson searched for a place to pull off the road to let him pass, the prick laid on his horn again and swerved over the double yellow line. His engine revved as he sped up and pulled alongside Jackson's car. He leaned toward the passenger seat and made some sort of gesture that Jackson couldn't make out in the darkness and pouring rain. Jackson waved him forward and slowed even more to give him room to get back over. But the prick slowed with him, making sure Jackson saw his extended middle finger this time.

Jackson rolled his eyes and pointed ahead. "Yeah, yeah. Just keep your eyes on the road, jerk-off."

And that's when he recognized the prick's car. It was a Ford Taurus, just like the one that belonged to …

Oh my God.

It was Brody.

The bastard continued driving in the wrong lane, probably too drunk to realize. Jackson fantasized about Brody swerving into a tree and doing the world a favor. But when a set of headlights turned onto the street from a driveway up ahead, Jackson panicked. He whipped his eyes back to Brody's Taurus and screamed, "Get over, asshole," as he slammed on his own brakes. Instead of swerving back into the right lane, Brody gunned it.

Oblivious to the danger, the car pulled right into Brody's path. Jackson's eyes went wide and he laid on the horn.

"Look out," he screamed.

Brody's brake lights didn't even flash. A horrific boom cracked like thunder. Metal twisted and crinkled. Glass exploded. The rear of Brody's Taurus bounced with the impact, the momentum driving the other car rear-first into a ditch.

Jackson pulled off the road. Images of the garbage truck hitting him flashed before his eyes.

One of the car horns blared. White smoke rose from under the Taurus's twisted hood. The passenger side front tire, rim and all, lay next to the front bumper.

Jackson jumped out of his car. The rain was cold, and he was quickly soaked to the bone. He ran to the other car, its crumpled front end jutting upward out of the ditch. There was an unconscious woman slumped against the driver's door behind the wheel. She looked bad. Blood dripped down the window.

Jackson ran around the front of her car, climbed into the ditch, and ripped open the passenger door. He jumped inside. "Ma'am," he shouted. Her face wore a mask of blood, a sliver of white bone showing in a large laceration on her forehead. Her top front teeth were missing. She was young, probably in her twenties. Her chest rose and fell with her strained breaths. It sounded like she was snoring, but she definitely wasn't sleeping peacefully. She wasn't wearing a seatbelt. The windshield above the steering wheel bulged outward, strands of bloody blond hair stuck in the spidered glass.

"I'm going to get you some help, ma'am. Hold on."

Jackson started to climb out, but he was struck by a thought so nasty he immediately felt guilty for having it. Pounding on doors at 3:30 in the morning when he was supposed to be at home wasn't a good idea. Did covering his own ass when someone else needed help so badly make him a bad guy? But to be a true superhero, he needed to be careful and cunning. If that meant looking at all the angles before rushing into action, then that's what he should do. But she really needed help.

He continued to hesitate until porch lights flipped on at the end of a long lane and someone holding an umbrella stepped onto the porch. Jarred out of inaction, Jackson jumped out of the car and ran toward the lane, careful to stay out of the light.

"Bad wreck," he shouted. "Call for help. Hurry."

As soon as the person went back into their house, he ran back to the car. He saw an open billfold next to a purse on the floor and picked it up to read the name on the driver's license. Brody's victim was named Becky M. Shaffer.

"Just hold on, Becky. Help's on the way." He felt useless not knowing the first thing about first aid. He turned to glare at Brody's car and noticed the drunk staggering toward the Celica, which he had left running. Brody stopped in the middle of the street and rubbed his bleeding forehead. His horn continued to blare. "Hold on, Becky. I'll be right back."

He climbed out of the wreck and strode toward Brody.

"You," he shouted over the racket. He wiped the rain from his face in a futile attempt to keep the water out of his eyes. "You caused this."

Ignoring him, Brody staggered toward Jackson's car again and opened the driver's door.

Jackson chased after him. "Stop," he shouted, and kicked the door shut.

Brody turned around and half chuckled. "Hey, man. How's it going?" He pointed to Becky's car. "Did you see that bitch pull out in front of me?"

"What? You did this, Brody. This was your fault."

Brody squinted, the rain running down his face. "How'd ya know my name, buddy?"

Jackson stepped closer and got in his face. Brody belched, and it smelled like a brewery. He looked over Jackson's shoulder to Becky's car. "Is she gonna die?" he asked coldly.

Shock and anger rooted Jackson to the spot. This wreck was his fault as much as Brody's. If he hadn't been so weak when they fought, this might not have happened to poor Becky. Brody was more of an animal than he'd ever imagined.

Brody turned back to Jackson's car and tugged the door open. "Serves her right," he slurred. "Hell, she was probably fixing her makeup or something." He chuckled again.

Jackson planted his foot against the door, slamming it shut again.

Unfazed, Brody released the handle, side-eyed Jackson, and then staggered across the street toward his own car.

Jackson watched in horror as Brody climbed into the driver's seat and cranked the ignition. Luckily, the car didn't start. Jackson raced to the passenger side of Becky's car again and climbed in. He didn't want her to be alone in her most difficult moment. He would be there for her the way Jennifer was for him. Where were the paramedics, anyway? Her breathing had grown more labored and sporadic. She was dying in front of him and he didn't know what to do.

"I'm so sorry, Becky," he whispered. "I could have stopped him before, but I was too weak." And then she gurgled out a breath. Jackson waited on edge for her to take in another, but she didn't. He lifted his gaze from Becky to Brody.

He could hardly breathe, he was so angry. "I did this," he whispered. The horn continued assaulting his senses. He pressed his hands over his ears and screamed, "Shuuut uuuuuup."

Faint sirens wailed over the incessant horn and started Jackson's timer. Brody had given up on restarting his car and now stood by the crinkled hood. He leaned his elbow on it as though he were merely waiting for a bus. Jackson's fists cramped at his sides, reminding him to stop squeezing so hard. Black regret turned to red rage behind his eyes. This wasn't fair. This young woman didn't deserve to die. Jackson gently brushed Becky's blood-soaked hair away from her face as the rain continued to pound the roof.

"I'm sorry, Becky," he whispered. He put his hand over hers and he gave it a gentle squeeze. He wanted to cry.

The sirens grew louder. Jackson thought about his Glock. It was under the seat in his car. He'd have to hurry if he wanted to use it on Brody. As he started to climb out, his eyes fell on the trunk release beneath the glovebox and gave him an idea.

"Goodbye, Becky. I'm sorry I didn't stop Brody before tonight. I won't make that mistake again."

The trunk clunked open with a pull of the lever. He went back out into the rain, lifted the trunk lid, and grabbed a tire iron. He held it at his side, shielded behind his thigh, as he moved toward Brody. Any doubts melted away with a look at Brody's smirk.

"She dead yet?" Brody asked, trying unsuccessfully to light a cigarette in the pouring rain.

Jackson cocked the tire iron back. He wanted to hit the bastard so hard, but he'd never hurt anyone as badly as he was considering hurting Brody at that moment.

Brody's eyes brightened slightly. "Hey, have we met before?"

Jackson closed his eyes and replayed Becky's last breath to remind him what he was doing wasn't for himself. It couldn't end in any other way. All the tension and regret and sadness left his body with a sigh. This was what he was meant to do. Killing Brody could very well be his bullet ant ritual. He couldn't falter now. He opened his eyes to a brand-new world. He smiled.

Without further thought, he swung his arm with all his might. The curved end of the iron bashed Brody's forehead near the spot he had been rubbing. He never saw it coming. The loud *thwack* would have been disgusting if it wasn't so beautiful. Brody's body dropped with a thud. Jackson lowered the tire iron. His breaths quivered with ecstasy. Almost hypnotized, he stared at the blood flowing down Brody's face and mixing with the rain to become the color of watered-down cherry Kool-Aid.

Sirens wailed. Red lights flickered in the distance. Jackson wanted to hit Brody again, but something about the way the bastard had dropped told him one blow was enough. He had actually gone through with it. He watched in fascination as Brody's life left him with a sickening death rattle. If someone had asked Jackson even an hour before how he would feel taking a man's life, he would've answered that it would make him ill. But that's not how he felt now.

The adrenaline was there, as it had been on his other outings, but something else was overwhelming him. It wasn't fear or regret or guilt, or any of the things he would expect. It was more intense than that. It was … power. Power like he'd never felt in his life. It was akin to the feeling of beating up Spyder, but on all the steroids in the world. He took in a quivering breath and gazed into Brody's fading eyes. Then he staggered backward and threw up on the pavement. He had never felt so excited in his life. The rain washed his vomit away as he absorbed what he had just done.

The sirens grew closer and pulled him from his daze. He needed to get it together fast.

He wiped the tire iron on the wet grass and took it to Becky's car, putting it back where he had found it and closing the trunk. Then he wiped his face with his sleeve in case any speckles of blood that might have splattered him hadn't been washed away by the rain. He went back to Brody's corpse and dragged the limp bastard to the Taurus's open door. Empty beer cans littered the floorboard beside the brake pedal.

Brody's car shielded what Jackson was doing from the approaching fire truck, but he had to hurry. He lifted one of Brody's legs onto the floorboard beside one of the cans then stepped back to examine his work. He hoped it looked like the door had jarred open from the impact and Brody had fallen out after hitting his head on the steering wheel.

On the other side of Brody's car, the fire engine's doors clanged shut. "You check that car," one of the firefighters shouted. "I've got this one."

Jackson leaned close to Brody and whispered, "Goodbye, you bastard. The Spyder Stopper has ended your drunken rampaging for good." He didn't care if he sounded like a tool this time. Then he hurried around Brody's car to meet the fireman. The gold lettering on the fireman's coat said Lt. followed by a name with too many letters to try to pronounce. "You gotta help," Jackson cried.

"What happened?" Lieutenant Alphabet asked while the rest of his crew went to work at Becky's car.

Jackson trailed him around the Taurus. "This maniac flew past me in the wrong lane and hit that poor girl." He pointed to Becky's car. "She's hurt bad." Then he pointed at Brody. "That guy looks bad, too. I think he might be dead."

"All right, buddy. You did a good job. Now stand back while we work. There's going to be a lot more trucks arriving soon, so stay outta the way."

The lieutenant started to move past, but Jackson stopped him. "Should I move my car?" he asked, pointing to his Celica.

The lieutenant squinted as though Jackson's car was the last thing on his mind. The rain poured from the brim of his helmet like an overflowing gutter. "Uh, sure. Whatever. Just stay out of our way." He headed toward Brody.

I'll do better than that. "Do you need anything else?" Jackson half-heartedly shouted, already walking to his car.

The lieutenant waved him off without looking back.

A fireman stifled Brody's annoying horn with a clip of the battery cable. Jackson should have thought of that. Two firemen were performing CPR on Becky in the street and the lieutenant was doing the same on Brody when Jackson drove past. Two emergency squads and a police car blew past him. On the drive home, he relived smacking Brody in the head with the tire iron over and over, and each time he felt the thrill anew. The look on Brody's face for that split second before impact was more than priceless. The only thing that dragged him down even a little was the realization that it had felt far too good to be his bullet ant ritual.

Instead of going to sleep after throwing his superhero uniform in the dryer, he sat in his ass groove on the couch and waited for the early edition of the local morning news out of Columbus to begin. As he suspected, breaking news led the newscast.

"Two people are dead after an overnight car accident in Pataskala, east of Columbus," the anchorwoman said with a grave expression. "The details are still rolling in, but police say alcohol is believed to have been a factor. We will have a full report from the scene shortly."

Jackson watched the screen blankly. As far as he was concerned, Becky's death was on his hands, and for that he would never forgive himself. But he now understood that her death had been necessary for him to realize who he was meant to become. There could be no more Beckys losing their lives because of his weakness. His budding gift was the equalizer. He would not be handcuffed like the police. And that was why he would save countless Beckys in the future.

The second story of the morning was a two-alarm fire at a strip mall in the campus area. The fire started in a car in the alley behind the store and quickly spread. The anchor said one fireman was hurt battling the blaze but was expected to recover.

Jackson swallowed hard. He'd have to be more careful in the future. He didn't want to hurt firemen. And then he realized with a grin that he was directly responsible for both breaking news stories of the morning. How often could someone say that?

14
LITTLE SECRETS
November 23, 1994

A loud clang in the dead of night ripped Jackson from a dead sleep. Jenna shot up beside him.

"What was that?" she whispered. "Is someone breaking in?"

"I don't know." Jackson scooped up the clothes he'd left on the floor and slipped on his pants and shirt. Jenna jumped out of bed and threw on her robe.

Jackson hurried to Garrett's room across the hall. Jenna squeezed past him and eased the door open.

"He's asleep," she whispered.

"Wait here." Jackson raced back into their room and returned with his Glock at his side. Though he tried to shield it from her, Jenna's eyes widened.

"What is that?" she snapped.

"Shhh."

She lowered her voice, but not her intensity. "You have a gun?"

"Yeah. It's for protection."

"That's what the police are for. I'm calling them."

"And when they finally get here, I'll have already protected us."

Jenna ran into their room and quickly returned with the portable phone at her ear. Jackson pushed Garrett's door open wider.

"Stay in there with him. I'll check things out."

But she wasn't buying his Dirty Harry routine and shook her head even as he nudged her into Garrett's room.

"It'll be fine," he whispered, and shut the door.

He crept down the stairs step by step until he reached the bottom. There was enough moonlight coming through the kitchen bay window that he could see without turning on the hall light and giving himself away.

Each step down the hall increased his nervous excitement. The old Jackson would have been terrified, but the new Jackson welcomed the thrill. He kind of hoped someone *had* chosen his house to rob. It saved him having to go in search of some crook to take down later. Not a sound came from the other room. Whoever had broken into his house was deathly quiet. Jackson stood with his weapon tucked tight against his chest. His hands trembled, which surprised him after everything he'd done recently. He silently counted to three, placed his finger beside the trigger guard like he'd seen on TV, and then sprang around the corner to his living room with his gun leading the way.

An empty room stared back. His heart fluttered like a hummingbird's. Without taking his eyes off the room, he reached for the wall switch and flicked on the lights. The tension left his shoulders instantly.

A picture frame lay on the ceramic tile in front of the fireplace surrounded by shattered glass. Jackson cleared the rest of the house like he'd seen the cops do on *Homicide: Life on the Street*. After he was satisfied no one else was in the house, he breathed for the first time since he had stood at the bottom of the stairs. He couldn't tell if he was more relieved or disappointed. He shouted, "Everything's okay, honey. It's just a picture frame that fell off the mantle."

He had just started back down the hall when the doorbell gonged, and he nearly shot off his toe.

Jenna came downstairs, still on the phone. "Yes, sir. I believe they're here now. Thank you."

Jackson tucked his gun into his waistband and covered it with his shirt. He met Jenna at the front door. They made eye contact and she glared straight through him, still plenty salty over his gun. He peeked through the dormer windows beside the door before opening it.

An officer stood on the porch. "Is everything all right, sir?"

Jackson recognized him as the one who had pulled him over after the failed Brody Beatdown. "Yes, Officer. A picture frame fell off the mantle and startled us awake."

The officer glanced at Jenna. "Is that what happened, ma'am? Everything's all right?"

She nodded. "We're sorry to bother you, Officer."

Another cruiser pulled up to the curb and the officer at the door used his flashlight to wave him off. Then he reported a "10-39 false alarm" into his shoulder mic.

The officer turned back to Jackson. "Have we met before, Mr. ..."

"Foster. Jackson Foster. I don't think so, Officer ..."

"Davis. Didn't I pull you over one night not too long ago?"

Jackson felt Jenna's eyes boring into him. His hand subconsciously found the back of his neck. "Uh, yeah. I think you did."

"How's the eye?"

Jesus. Whatever happened to confidentiality? "Right as rain, sir," he answered.

"Good. Well, if everything's all right, I'll let you two get back to your night."

"Thank you, Officer. We'll be good now. Thanks for getting here so quickly." The officer turned away and

Jackson pushed the door closed. He dreaded the next two minutes.

"I can't believe you have a gun," Jenna blurted.

"It's cheaper than an alarm system."

"Yeah, and deadlier too."

"Exactly."

"No, I mean deadlier to us."

"How do you figure?"

"Do you have any idea how many people are accidentally shot in their own homes?"

Jackson rolled his eyes. "Those people are idiots."

"I thought we were on the same page about this. No guns in this house while Garrett lives here. That was the rule."

"I know, honey. With all the kids going missing, I decided I'd better have something just in case."

"You know I hate guns."

"That's why I didn't tell you. I didn't set out to hide anything. I was just trying to keep both of our minds at ease."

"Well, you failed. I don't like it, Jack. Not at all. Where'd you get it?"

"I bought it at a flea market."

"When?"

"Last week."

"Why didn't you tell me?"

"Because I knew you'd overreact." He winced, realizing it was a bad choice of words.

Her glare burned through him.

"What if I buy a safe and keep it locked up?"

"You mean it hasn't been locked up?" Her voice got shriller with each syllable.

Uh-oh. "No. But it was well hidden. I promise. Garrett would never find it."

Jenna started for the stairs, but then turned back.

Now what?

She tilted her head. "When did you get pulled over?"

Jackson went into crisis management mode. "I don't know. Last week when I ran to the store."

"What time?"

"Dinnertime?"

"Are you asking me or telling me?"

"Honey, what's the big deal? I ran out to the store around dinnertime, and I got pulled over."

"I don't remember you going anywhere at dinnertime last week."

"Now I've gotta check with you whenever I run an errand? You were in the shower."

"Why don't you just start being straight with me?"

"I am."

She scoffed. "And your eye? Was that when you"— she made air quotes—"fell down the stairs?"

"I think so."

"You *think* so?"

"I mean, of course. It had to be."

She shook her head.

"I didn't think it was a big deal. I didn't even get a ticket."

"What other secrets are you hiding from me?"

He gave her puppy dog eyes. "That I love you?"

Jenna turned away and stormed up the stairs. The bedroom door slammed shut and the lock clicked.

Jackson stood in the foyer. "Damn," he mumbled. Another night on the couch.

15
THE DOWNWARD SPIRAL
November 25, 1994

While Jenna showered and Garrett played in his room, Jackson sat on the couch and watched a rerun of *Three's Company*. It happened to be his favorite episode, "Double Trouble," in which the clumsy Jack Tripper pretended to be his own twin brother in order to date Mr. Furley's pretty niece.

Even though he was back in his ass groove, it was different this time. Jackson wasn't planted on the couch because he couldn't find the will or energy to get up. He was on the couch because he wanted to be there.

Three's Company ended and a paid commercial began. Jackson started to dig between the cushions looking for the remote when a man on the screen caught his eye. He was in his mid-thirties, balding, overweight, and wore a sleeveless blue shirt exposing the saggy flaps of flesh under his arms. A voiceover began to play. "Hi. I'm Jeffrey Callahan, and that used to be me."

The picture cut away to video of what looked like a different person wearing the same sleeveless shirt and riding a jet ski. He was tanned, smiling with brilliant white teeth, and sporting ripped muscles like a boxing champion. If Jackson squinted enough, it looked like it could be the same guy, but the transformation was startling. It was the truest definition of a complete makeover. Jackson wondered how the exercise machine company had had the foresight to get a picture of Mr. Callahan in the same blue shirt while he was fat. He would bet money that Mr. Callahan was probably a gym-rat in the first place and the company had paid him handsomely to do the commercial first and then fatten up like a Thanksgiving turkey.

As Mr. Callahan explained how "you, too," could have a powerful physique for less than a buck a day, Jackson lifted the front of his shirt to expose his puny, hairy chest. Not only was he scrawny, he was soft. Seemingly overnight, youth and energy had given way to Pop Tarts and naps, leaving him the very middle-aged slob he'd swore he'd never become. This would not do if he was going to get serious about crime fighting.

There was no better time than the present to do something about it. He turned off the TV, slipped on a pair of socks and his Nike Air Max 93 sneakers that Jenna had bought him for Christmas last year, and headed to the basement. Pajama pants and a Pearl Jam concert tee may not be the best workout gear, but it would do for a start.

An old weight bench covered by a plastic painter's drape sat in the corner next to an equally old treadmill partially hidden by a towel. Failed New Year's resolution, 1989. Jackson tugged the plastic from the weight bench, engulfing himself in a cloud of dust. The weight bar held the same 135 lbs. as it had the last time he'd used it, probably in February of 1989. With the towel from the treadmill, Jackson wiped off an equally dusty full-body mirror he had mounted to the bare studs of his half-finished basement walls.

Getting in shape starts with the first set, he told himself as he pressed his back to the cold bench. He was winded just thinking about lifting the weights, but he powered through. After a few sets and some lighter curls, he felt like heaving, so he decided that was enough weights for one day. He sat on the end of the bench to wait for the nausea to subside. Then he set the treadmill timer for thirty minutes but quit after fifteen. He was more out of shape than he realized. He used the front of his shirt as a towel for his forehead, and by the end of his run it was drenched. It felt like a good start.

Jenna passed him on the stairs as he headed for the shower. "Did you leave me any hot water?" he asked.

"I think." She side-eyed him. "Were you … working out?"

"Um-hm."

"What's gotten into you today?"

"Tired of being a weakling, I guess."

"Are you tired of being unemployed?" Her ornery grin took a bit of the sting out, though her subtle digs always found their marks.

"I'm working on some things," he lied. A new job would put a damper on his crime fighting, but he still felt guilty for leaving her to pay all the bills. If only superhero vigilante was a paying job.

Chicken and macaroni and cheese were on the table when he returned from his shower, but he was too focused on his approaching night-time patrol to properly enjoy his dinner.

He wasn't sure anything could ever live up to the experience of executing a murderer like Brody, but he was game to try. Maybe a good fist fight would be enough to get his juices flowing.

"You seem to be doing better lately, Jack," Jenna said.

He smiled.

"Do you feel better?"

With his mouth full, he nodded.

After dinner, he played Uno with Garrett. He thought he won, but according to Garrett's rules he lost. When it was time for Garrett to go to bed, Jackson offered to tuck him in.

Jenna feigned a swoon and caught herself on the counter.

"Ha-ha," he said.

She crinkled her nose at him. "I might go in a little early tonight. I've got some paperwork to catch up on."

Jackson pretended to be disappointed. "If you have to, I guess."

When Jenna left for work, Jackson nearly pushed her to the car. He'd been fantasizing about busting crime for hours and he was ready for a scrap.

He raced to the master bedroom and pulled his duffle bag out from under the bed. Inside was his mask, his black hooded sweatshirt, his gloves, and, most importantly, his weapon of justice. The feel of the steel in his hand made him feel like a king. He made sure there wasn't a round in the chamber before he tucked it into his waistband. He was getting comfortable carrying his weapon, but not comfortable enough to trust he wouldn't shoot off his ass cheek by accident. With all his gear assembled, he was ready for action.

He made sure Garrett was sound asleep and left the usual note on the table. A scan of the neighborhood, especially Kevin's front yard, assured no one was watching or having a doggy potty break.

He drove his Celica to 18th Ave in Columbus, an area that was on the news a lot. He parked in an empty lot by an abandoned pawn shop and walked to a brightly lit intersection with a carryout on one corner. Jackson was surprised at how many people were out. Men, women, and even a young child with her mother walked along the sidewalks. Jackson was the only one who waited for the "Don't Walk" sign to change to "Walk" before stepping onto the street.

He eyed everyone, searching for that guilty vibe he was confident he'd recognize, while at the same time being cautious not to make extended eye contact with anyone. When someone bumped him from behind, he grabbed for his wallet and glanced over his shoulder.

"What're you lookin' at?" the man behind him asked.

Jackson snapped his head forward. The man stayed close enough on his heels to make him uncomfortable. Maybe this was just the person he was looking for. *Be prepared for anything,* he told himself. If the guy tried to rob him, he needed to draw his gun and chamber a round quickly.

Stay calm, he reminded himself. If this was where it was going to happen, then so be it. He'd prefer not to have so many witnesses, though. Jackson reached the opposite curb with the perp still tight on his ass. He let his hand drift toward the small of his back. With his other hand he opened the door to the carryout, stepped aside, and held it for the man as a test to see how he reacted. The man passed by, ignoring him. He smelled of booze and body odor and wore three coats, cloth gloves, and a winter hat. He beelined to the Jack Daniels display in the back.

Jackson pretended to shop the candy aisle while he watched the man stumble against the refrigerator, almost dropping his bottle. The man took it to the front and dropped several damp, wadded-up bills on the counter. The clerk handed him change and the man walked out. Jackson grabbed a pack of gum, hurriedly paid for it, and trailed the man from the store.

The man crossed the street against the light, nearly getting taken out by an S-10 pickup truck that barely managed to stop inches away. The driver, a skinny redheaded girl with deep pockmarks on her cheeks, screamed, "Get the fuck outta the street, you drunk-ass bitch." Her voice was a little deeper than Jackson expected from such a frail girl. She laid on the horn. The drunk didn't flinch. Instead, he used her hood to regain his balance.

Jackson followed him from a distance. On the opposite side of the street the drunk sat on the sidewalk with his back against a brick divider that marked the boundary of someone's front yard. He opened his bottle of Jack and took a swig. Whatever he'd been planning to do in the store, he had obviously seen Jackson watching him and decided against it.

Jackson turned his attention to the passing cars, his mind already miles away from the drunk. He still couldn't believe how busy the area was at such a late hour. No wonder it was a hotbed for crime. Standing on the curb, he pushed the limits of what might look suspicious (about ten minutes in the same place) before starting down the sidewalk. He spent the next hour or more trying to find criminals in need of punishment with no luck. This was harder than he expected. He would have to get more creative with his surveillance.

When a car backfired on the next street over, Jackson nearly shit himself and lunged for his weapon. Thankfully, no one seemed to notice his jumpiness.

Eventually he ended up back near the corner store. He'd just started to cross the street when a newer model Chevy Caprice with oversized chrome, five-spoke wheels, and tinted windows pulled up to the intersection. Jackson stopped on the sidewalk next to it. It was fire engine red. The stereo bass was turned up so high that each beat punched Jackson in the chest. A cloud of smoke puffed through the cracked-open passenger window. Jackson strained to see through the tinted glass. The smoke didn't smell like cigarettes. Doping and driving was as bad as drinking and driving, as far as Jackson was concerned.

The driver was a scrawny white guy who looked like Vanilla Ice, and the passenger was a black kid with a fat diamond hiding most of his earlobe.

"I know what you guys are doing," Jackson whispered as they crept by. They appeared oblivious that they'd drawn some heat.

The Caprice pulled into an alley behind the carryout and disappeared. Jackson casually strolled around the store to where he could see it again. Plastic carryout bags had clogged a storm drain beside the alley, creating a dam that flooded part of the road. A glance down the street revealed a flowing fire hydrant as the culprit. He wondered if the fire department knew one of their hydrants was broken. To get closer to the Caprice, Jackson had to go around the large puddle, temporarily exposing himself under a streetlight. He didn't like it, but he had no other choice.

A guy in a hooded sweatshirt and baggy jeans jogged to the Caprice from his hiding spot beside a Dumpster. Jackson ducked beside a telephone pole, making a mental note to keep a better eye on his surroundings.

The Dumpster guy shared some kind of ritual handshake with the passenger and then shoved his hand in his front pocket. They talked for less than thirty seconds, shared another handshake, and then the car started to pull away. Dumpster guy dipped back into the shadows behind the store. When Jackson realized he'd just witnessed a drug deal, he cursed himself for missing the opportunity to burn up another nice car full of drugs.

He checked his watch and winced. He needed to head home soon and didn't want to leave without accomplishing anything. Though he felt weed should be legal as well as prostitution, he figured it wouldn't hurt to rough up a dealer a bit. As for fighting bigger crimes, he could try again tomorrow.

He looked around for witnesses before he sneaked back across the ally to the rear of the store where he could hide in the darkness again. The alley smelled like garbage that had sat in the sun for too long. After a second look around, he slipped on his gloves, tied his mask on, and lifted his hood over his head.

A single floodlight lit part of the alley, but not where the hooded thug crouched beside the Dumpster. As Jackson crept closer, he noticed a second person crouching beside the drug dealer. She was way underdressed for such a chilly night and kept tugging on the hem of her black miniskirt. Her revealing clothes made it obvious what line of business she was in. Their hushed conversation grew heated. The drug dealer poked her in the chest with each angry word. Then he smacked her across the face.

That did it. Jackson stepped from the shadows.

The woman noticed him first. "Who the fuck are you?" she spat, rubbing her cheek.

The dealer cranked his head around.

"The arm of justice," Jackson said, quickly followed by a cringe.

The dealer shoved the woman to the side, almost knocking her down. He was Hispanic and had a dark tribal tattoo covering the left side of his face.

The hooker shouted, "Honey, you loco. I'm outta here, Hector. I'll have your money tomorrow."

"Yeah. You'd better, puta."

The hooker grabbed her bedazzled purse from the ground and gave Jackson the finger before storming off.

"Now, whatchu want?" Hector asked.

Jackson approached, shoulders straight and confident.

Hector stood his ground. "You know who I am? Ain't nobody in some silly mask robbin' me." He lifted the front of his sweatshirt to reveal the ivory grip of a pistol in his waistband. Tattooed letters formed an arch across his six-pack abs, but Jackson couldn't read Spanish.

Jackson's heart pounded harder than the Caprice's bass had. "I don't know who you are, but I know what you are."

"Yeah? What am I?"

"You're a stinking drug dealer and woman beater."

"I'm all kinds of shit, puto. I can be a murderer, too, if you don't turn your ass around and march back the way you came."

Jackson knew better than to say more, but he just couldn't help it. "The Spyder Stopper's about to open a can of whoop-ass on you." Yep, it was as stupid as it sounded in his head.

Hector snorted.

Jackson's gloved fist split Hector's upper lip mid-laugh. Hector stumbled backward. Jackson reached for Hector's gun, but Hector grabbed Jackson's hand before he could pull it free. As they wrestled for it, they fell to the blacktop next to a broken beer bottle. The impact jolted Jackson's spine.

Just don't let go of the gun, he screamed in his head.

Hector punched Jackson in the side of the head with his free hand. Jackson held strong and jerked at the gun again, this time pulling it free. He wrenched it away from Hector's grip and hurled it across the alley. Hector cursed as he flailed at Jackson's face. In his panic, he hit Jackson's shoulder with his first swing and missed completely with the next. Jackson focused on Hector's face and punched again, striking Hector's cheek. He was amazed at how much calmer he was than when he took his beating from Brody. Hector pulled away and scrambled to his feet. Jackson grabbed his ankle to trip him.

Hector yanked his foot free and stumbled backward, landing beside his gun. He looked at it. Jackson followed his eyes. This was bad. Jackson sprang to his feet. Instead of going for the gun right away, Hector landed the luckiest kick in the history of kicks. Fire erupted between Jackson's legs. He doubled over and Hector pushed him away. Jackson landed on his side, both hands firmly pressed to his throbbing balls. Hector dove for the gun.

With one hand still on his junk, Jackson reached behind him for his Glock. Hector grabbed his gun from the pavement and spun around on his knees. Jackson pulled out his own weapon and aimed. He had the jump. He pulled the trigger.

Nothing.

Hector yanked the slide back on his gun, reminding Jackson what he had forgotten. Jackson pried his other hand from his groin and jerked the Glock's slide back, chambering a round. Hector unleashed a deafening boom. Small chunks of blacktop exploded next to Jackson's head. Jackson closed his eyes and squeezed the trigger, creating an equally deafening boom. He heard Hector grunt and opened his eyes. Hector's gun fell to the ground, his wide eyes starkly contrasting his previous mask of bravado. He stumbled backward and dropped to his rear with his back against the store wall.

Jackson rolled to his knees and struggled to get to his feet, increasingly nauseous from the kick to his balls. His hands trembled. With his gun dangling at his side, he limped over to Hector. The dealer stared up at him like a confused child, blood leaking from a tiny hole in his sweatshirt. Jackson kicked the ivory-handled gun out of reach. He knew he should run—that he should be terrified by what he had just done—but curiosity won out over fear. Images of Brody's death blurred his thoughts and it was intoxicating. He knelt before Hector, the dealer's tired eyes following his face.

"Why, man?" Hector whispered. "I ain't never done shit to you."

"Because you're what's wrong with society."

"I don't even know you."

Jackson stared into his eyes. Hector slowly slouched like his bones were melting. His breathing sped up at first and then slowed. Jackson pushed his hood back and lifted his mask enough for Hector to see clearly the eyes of the man who had killed him.

Hector's pupils dilated. Some people didn't believe in souls, but Jackson could swear something left Hector's eyes at that moment. A soul was as good an explanation as anything. A gurgle accompanied Hector's final exhale.

Jackson couldn't look away, transfixed by Hector's dead gaze. In a strange and unexpected way, fighting crime might actually feel better than sex. Like the best orgasm he'd ever had. He never wanted this feeling to end.

Unfortunately, he couldn't stand there all night, as evidenced by the distant wail of a siren. There was a brickyard apartment complex on the other side of the alley. He slipped his mask on, pulled his hood back up, and raced for the parking lot. Blue lights flashed across the brick behind him. He didn't stop running until he reached the pawn shop where his Celica waited. He almost couldn't steady his hand enough to get the key in the lock, but he finally managed. He sped from the lot and made it to the freeway without seeing a single cop. His foot quivered on the gas pedal, and he couldn't get it to stop for most of the way home. His lips started to tingle before he realized he needed to calm his breathing.

It was the scariest and greatest drive ever. Killing Hector felt different than killing Brody. He didn't really have anything against Hector until two minutes before he killed him. But different didn't mean bad.

He pulled into the parking lot of the shopping center near his house and sat behind the wheel for a few minutes. Though he wasn't completely sure how he felt about the whole God thing anymore, he whispered a thank-you to whoever had let him escape without a shootout with the fuzz.

A cold breeze had picked up during the night, but he hardly felt it as he walked home.

The first thing he did when he got in the house, even before taking off his shoes, was race upstairs and check on

Garrett. His boy was sound asleep. He sat next to him and rested his hand on his back. "I love you, Garrett," he whispered. After a few minutes, he kissed his son's forehead and went back downstairs.

There was no use in trying to sleep with this much adrenaline in his system. He ran through every detail a thousand times, always lingering on Hector's final breath. If he felt even a pinch of guilt, he quickly reminded himself that there was one less criminal on the streets because of him.

The morning news reported another shooting in Columbus near Main and 18th. They called it a suspected drug deal gone bad. Jackson didn't realize how big he was smiling at first, but when he did, he didn't try to stifle it.

After Garrett was off to school and Jenna came home from work, Jackson gave her a long, passionate kiss. He felt like a god. When she went to bed Jackson was tempted to join her, but there was still no way he could sleep. He was anxious for Garrett to get home from school so he could play with him like he used to do.

After Garrett got home that afternoon, Jackson threw the football with him outside until Jenna called them in for dinner. At the table, Jackson let out a deep, throaty belch that could wake the gods, and he and Garrett giggled relentlessly despite Jenna giving them *the* look. After dinner, Jackson did his best to play NBA Jam on the Nintendo with Garrett, but he wasn't very good. Garrett seemed to enjoy it just the same and giggled every time he monster-slammed the ball over Jackson's character. After seeing Jenna off to work, Jackson finally went to bed, exhausted. Before he fell asleep, he thought about how good a day he'd had. Just like old times. He was asleep in minutes.

16
CJ'S DANCE CLUB
December 3, 1994

Vanquishing Hector held off the depression demons for a few days, but soon Jackson was itching to get back out. He decided to organize his VHS collection in the TV cabinet to kill some time. In the process he came across an old tape with *Robocop* hand-written on the yellow label. He couldn't resist putting the movie in the player.

He kept working as it played and just happened to look up during the scene where Robocop tracked a perp into a dance club to arrest him. It was especially comical when the bad guy tried to kick Robocop in the metal balls. Though the club scene only lasted a couple of minutes, it gave Jackson an interesting idea. Night clubs were full of people drinking and using drugs, and maybe even rapists trying to use roofies on unsuspecting women. If there was anything Jackson hated worse than drunk drivers, it was predators. Oh, to catch one of those pricks … That prospect made him almost giddy. A quick search of the yellow pages found a place on Columbus's west side called CJ's Dance Club. It could be the perfect destination for his next patrol.

Once Jenna was at work and Garrett tucked safely in bed, Jackson was on his way to the west side of Columbus.

The half-assed pat-down at the entrance would be lucky to find a bazooka, let alone handguns. He had taken a hell of a chance carrying his weapon past the bouncer, but after three quick taps down his sides, he skated through without incident.

He'd never been one for night clubs and they sure weren't worth the ten dollar cover charge, but he figured if he wanted a hunting ground ripe for rapey criminals, he had definitely found it.

It was dark and hazy inside with bright beams of red and green lights dancing across the fog. The bass-heavy music assaulted his ears, pounding thump after rhythmic thump directly into his brain. The DJ played "Closer" by Nine Inch Nails and the crowd was kickin'. Jackson smiled as the crowd screamed "fuck" along with Trent Reznor. It was a poppin' Saturday night.

The overwhelming smell of weed made him reconsider whether the haze was really from fog machines as he'd originally assumed. There was an empty stool at the bar and Jackson made a beeline to it. His sleeve stuck to the grimy bar top when he leaned on it to flag down the bartender. When the bartender finally made eye contact, Jackson ordered a Michelob Ultra.

The bartender seemed to scoff at his choice as he retrieved one from a cooler under the bar. "Seven bucks," he said, and twisted off the cap.

Jackson dug in his wallet and found he only had a ten left after the cover charge. Since he wouldn't dare use his card in the club and leave proof he had been there, he had to make his beer last. "Keep the change," he shouted. He took a swig as he spun around to watch the crowd.

His seat at the bar gave him the perfect vantage point over the sunken dance floor and the tables on the other side. Girls in short skirts with rows of glowing bracelets from their wrists to their elbows packed the dance floor, gyrating for an audience of horny guys hoping to drown them in drinks and phone numbers and maybe roofies.

Jackson admired their confidence to be out there dancing. He'd never get on a dance floor, not even if he was single and Julia Roberts was beckoning him over with a seductive lick of her lips. Despite his eagerness to avoid looking like a fool, he still caught himself bobbing his head to the music and his tapping his wedding ring against his beer bottle.

He kept his head on a swivel, in search of anything that didn't feel right. He repeatedly scanned the bar for drinks left unattended by women to make sure no one dropped in a pill. There were several guys in the crowd that made his Spidey-sense tingle, but no one who stood out as particularly egregious. Then his gaze settled on a group of three men standing in a half-circle on the opposite side of the dance floor. It wasn't that the guys in the group were doing anything obviously criminal, but the way they were ogling and catcalling nearly every woman who passed made them worth keeping an eye on.

After finishing his beer, he asked the bartender for a water and received the same condescending look. Obviously, nothing he ordered was worthy of the bartender's esteem. He sipped at his water as slowly as he had sipped at the beer.

The seat next to him freed up and a young woman plopped onto the stool. Her blond hair was teased straight up in the front with probably two cans of hairspray like she'd climbed out of a time machine from the '80s. She leaned both elbows on the sticky bar and ordered a Long Island. While waiting for the bartender to make her drink, she spun around and leaned back against the bar. Her ear was pierced all the way up with tiny hoop earrings wrapping the tip. She wore a tiny diamond in the side of her nose, which Jackson had always found sexy. He even once suggested it to Jenna, but she had no interest.

She glanced at Jackson. "Hi," she said. Her upper lip glistened with faint beads of sweat.

Jackson smiled and nodded.

"I'm Tuesdae."

Jackson leaned closer. "Excuse me?"

"My name. I'm Tuesdae. Spelled d-a-e, not d-a-y."

Jackson didn't notice her extended hand until she wiggled it. "Oh. I'm sorry." He shook her hand. "That's a very unique name—Tuesdae."

"I know. My mom's kinda weird." She dabbed her forehead with a cocktail napkin. "It's hot out there." She playfully bit her lower lip.

"It's nice to meet you, Tuesdae. I'm Ja—I mean, I'm James."

She cocked her head and smiled. "So, we're doing fake names? Really?"

Jackson grinned. "Well, I mean … Tuesdae?"

She giggled and lightly smacked the inside of his thigh. "Really. That's my name."

"You've been dancin' tonight?" Jackson asked.

"Oh my God, it's insane out there. This DJ's the shit. You been out there yet?"

Jackson cupped his hand around the back of his ear and leaned closer. "What's that?"

She raised her voice. "I said, have you been out there dancing yet?"

"I'm sorry, I can't hear you." He grinned.

She started to ask for a third time, but stopped with another giggle. "Oh. I get it. Not much of a dancer, huh?"

He shook his head. "Not. At. All."

She grabbed his hand and started to pull. "Come on. I'll teach ya."

He panicked and pulled back. "That'd be a nightmare for both of us. Besides." He held up his water glass with his left hand and tapped it with his wedding band.

She shrugged. "So?"

"I'm married."

She looked around. "Is she here?"

"Well, no. Not right now."

"Then let's dance. It can't hurt to dance. This music's bangin'." She touched his leg again with her other hand. For some reason she seemed to be making a lot of sense. She tugged his hand again, and again he pulled back.

"I really can't. I'm sorry."

She let him loose and grabbed her Long Island from the bar. "You're no fun."

He held up his hands and shrugged.

"Who goes to a dance club and doesn't dance?"

"Me, I guess."

After digging cash out of her purse and tossing it on the bar, she gave Jackson a sly grin. "If you change your mind, Ja-James, come find me."

"I surely will. It was a pleasure meeting you, Fridae."

"Ha-ha." She headed back to the dance floor, but her eyes lingered until she reached the stairs. Jackson wanted to wave her back, if for nothing else than the conversation, but that wouldn't be wise. She gave him one more glance and then turned her attention to the dance floor. Jackson watched her for the next ten minutes until she met another guy who *was* willing to dance with her. He watched to make sure the guy wasn't up to anything unscrupulous until he lost sight of them on the dance floor. He didn't see her again for the rest of the night. A small part of him would have liked to run into her again, but the stand-up married guy in him was glad that he didn't.

Over the next hour, he drank glass after glass of water, to the bartender's obvious annoyance, while watching the suspicious group of men still gathered across the room. Finally, when his bladder couldn't hold any more, he climbed down from his stool. He caught the bartender's eye and shouted, "Thanks for the drinks."

The bartender nodded.

"Where's the bathroom?"

The bartender flicked his wrist toward the other side of the dance floor as he started talking to a pretty redhead. The crowd around the dance floor was now shoulder-to-shoulder. If Jackson didn't have to pee so badly, he'd never attempt the journey. He chose the long way around because crossing the dance floor and possibly getting dragged into a Conga-line would be his worst nightmare. Besides, the walk around the dance floor would carry him directly past the group of guys he'd been watching all night.

He must have said "sorry" and "excuse me" twenty times in the first thirty feet before he fell in line behind three other guys headed in the same direction. The man leading the charge to the toilets plowed ahead as though he owned the joint, uninterested in the complaints of anyone he might bump out of the way. He was a big dude, tall, with shoulders as broad as two Jacksons standing side by side, and he strutted like a guy who lived in the gym. He looked like a poor man's Jean Claude Van Damme from behind. As he reached the group of three guys Jackson had been watching, none of them moved. It wasn't that they were trying to be defiant so much as they were more focused on catcalling women than some bear pushing through the crowd.

The fake Van Damme plowed through them. Two of the guys backed away unphased and continued their girl-watching. But the third guy said something, though Jackson couldn't hear what. The muscle-head stopped and turned back. The smaller guy barely came up to the muscle-head's chin. The standoff looked like a regular David versus Goliath. The energy of the room hardened around them.

Without warning, Goliath shoved David against a table, knocking him and the table over. A beer bottle shattered. *Here we go.* It amazed Jackson how situations could go from zero to violence in an instant when two testosterone-filled men got together.

The other two men who had been following Goliath through the crowd backed away. So they weren't with him after all. They were just two guys who had to piss and had the same idea as Jackson.

David bounced up and squared off with Goliath. A space opened up around them as if by magic.

The music continued to blare while the clubbers continued to dance, oblivious to the tension that had just swallowed part of the room. Goliath and David closed the gap between them. Jackson glanced over his shoulder and saw a bouncer fighting through the crowd toward them. When Jackson turned back, David was swinging a beer bottle at Goliath's face. It shattered against his temple, making him stagger backward. Goliath's right hand reached for the small of his back.

Oh shit.

Goliath pulled out a pistol.

Jackson shouted, "No," but Goliath squeezed the trigger without aiming. The boom echoed over the thump of the bass, sending the crowd into instant panic. The bullet struck a light, sending shattered glass flying. The controlled chaos of the dance floor morphed into uncontrolled hysteria in the beat of a hummingbird's wing. Goliath fired off another shot as David dove behind the downed table.

The DJ stopped the music and disappeared from his elevated booth. The crowd scrambled toward the exits, further hampering the bouncer's progress. This was going to be a massacre.

Jackson scanned the crowd. The bouncer would never get there in time. It was up to Jackson to do something. He ducked out of sight of the security camera in the corner and pulled his mask from his coat pocket. He knelt and tied it around his eyes as two more shots rang out. He pulled his hood over his head and assessed the situation.

David scrambled along the floor. Goliath fired three more shots, one striking a fleeing woman in the ankle, and the other two tearing chunks from the wood floor beside David's head.

Jackson pulled out his Glock and chambered a round. When Goliath charged past, too obsessed with murdering David to notice Jackson, Jackson moved the Glock to his left hand, grabbed the back of Goliath's neck, and jammed the pistol into his gut. He squeezed off two shots before Goliath knew what hit him. Goliath froze, his gun clattering to the floor. He turned his head and stared at Jackson with puzzled eyes. Jackson smiled back. Out of the corner of his eye he saw David scramble to his feet and disappear into the fleeing crowd.

Jackson let go of Goliath and stepped back. Goliath dropped to his knees with his hands holding his stomach, stunned. Then he collapsed to his side and drew his knees close to his chest. For being as big and strong as he was, he now looked pathetic and weak. He could have won the fight with David without a gun, yet he chose the coward's way out, injuring innocent people in the process. He deserved to meet Jackson's justice.

Jackson watched the pool of blood spreading around Goliath in an almost euphoric trance. He could have stood there all night if not for the imminent arrival of the cops. He let out a quivering breath.

The bouncer finally made it through the crowd and slid to his knees beside the dying man. He brushed the pistol out of reach and shoved his hands over Goliath's bleeding gut. His eyes lifted to Jackson. Jackson panicked before remembering he still had his mask on.

"You," the bouncer shouted.

Jackson shoved his Glock into his waistband. "You've just witnessed Spyder Stopper justice," he said, pitching his voice low. He groaned almost before the words left his mouth. If he was going to say something, he needed to plan it better. He spun toward the fleeing crowd.

"Wait," the bouncer shouted.

Another approaching bouncer fought against the stampede of panicked clubbers. Jackson didn't want to kill either of them, but he mentally prepared himself just in case. If it was him or them, he knew what his decision would be. He slipped into the crowd, ripped off his hood and mask, and ducked his head. As he neared the approaching bouncer, he put a hand on his Glock just in case he'd been made. The panicked crowd carried him past the oblivious bouncer and eventually through the exit.

Outside the club, people fled in all directions as sirens wailed from around every corner. Jackson blended with the fleeing clubbers and raced toward the parking lot where his Celica waited several blocks away. Whenever he saw approaching emergency lights, he ducked into an alley or a dark entryway until they passed. The adrenaline dump nearly made him cry out in ecstasy. He had stopped a potential mass shooting, brought justice to a trigger-happy criminal, and was currently disappearing without a trace. He ran for two blocks before he felt comfortable enough to slow to a jog. His hip wasn't even aching, though that might have been from the adrenaline.

Since he still had to piss, he relieved himself on the dark steps of a church. It wasn't the most respectful place to take a leak, but he couldn't hold it for another second. When he got to the Celica, he congratulated himself on having the foresight to park so far away from the club. Further proof he was getting better at this. Before long, he was on his way back to Pataskala. It was 2:15 in the morning.

When he got home, he checked on Garrett and then went straight to the basement, too amped up to sleep. He put in work on his bench press. Between every set he shadow-boxed in the mirror like Rocky. The only thing missing was "Eye of the Tiger" playing in the background. Or maybe "Closer" instead. He felt amazing. After finishing his workout, he showered and made toast with peanut butter at five in the morning. He was ready and waiting for the early news.

As expected, breaking news led the telecast. "One dead, multiple injured after an overnight shooting on the city's west side. Police say shortly before 2:00 AM shots were fired at CJ's Dance Club. The gunman was killed by a second shooter who fled the scene. We don't have many details at this time, but police are asking for any information on the identity of the second shooter. At least one eyewitness claims the unidentified man may have called himself the Spider Killer, but CPD has no confirmation on that. We'll have more on this breaking story as details emerge."

"Spyder Stopper," Jackson shouted, and then groaned in frustration.

For not having any training, he was becoming the cause of a lot of breaking stories lately. Though they got his superhero name wrong, he was just glad they didn't make up something generic like Vigilante Kid or J-Dawg. That last one made him chuckle, especially since they didn't know his name started with a J.

That reminded him of Tuesdae. He hoped she had gotten out okay.

17
WALLYBALL
December 5, 1994

The score was fifteen to fifteen in a fifteen-point game where the winning team had to win by two. The front of Jackson's shirt had made a good drying rag for his face at first, but now it was drenched and stuck to his chest and stomach. He swiped his forearm across his brow just as the ball bounced off the wall toward him.

"You got it, Jack," Dustin shouted.

Instinct from years of playing wallyball pushed Jackson's clutched fists into the ball's path. The ball ricocheted off the side wall to Dustin, who cranked his arm back and sent the ball hurtling over the net. Two of the three opponents on the other side dove and missed. The ball hit the ground for a point.

Though Jackson had never been a fan of volleyball when he was younger, something about wallyball had sucked him in from the first time Dustin urged him to try it. There was something about bouncing the ball off the walls like in racquetball that enhanced the fun and removed the boring aspect of volleyball.

As he and his team stood on the verge of a glorious victory, he was glad Dustin had coaxed him out to play for the first time in over a year. Plus, he could use it as a cardio workout and save himself a jog later on the Elliptical. His hip was going to hate him in the morning, but the fun was worth the future suffering.

Dustin, Jackson, and their friend Kelly met in the center for high fives. It was game point in a best of five series. The score was two games to one with Jackson's team, the Tornados, holding the lead against the Dragons.

"Sixteen to fifteen, good guys," Dustin shouted. He grabbed a towel from the back wall and wiped some sweat off the floor so no one would slip. Then he tossed it to the corner.

It was Jackson's serve. He scanned the court, tossed the ball above his head, and slammed it toward the opposing team's wall. It ricocheted toward a gap in their defense for what Jackson thought was a surefire ace, but miraculously one of the Dragons dove for the save. The ball bounced from his fist and sailed toward the net. Jackson took the center back of the court. Another Dragon leapt and spiked the ball, which kissed the top of the net as it zipped past. Jackson and Kelly dove for it. Jackson's fist sent the ball bouncing off the side wall to Dustin.

Kelly's flailing elbow connected with Jackson's left eye, sending lightning across his vision. Dustin jumped and smashed the ball over the net between two diving Dragons for the win. Dustin pumped his fist.

"Did we get it?" Jackson shouted from the floor.

"Hell, yeah," Dustin answered.

The sweet taste of victory was only slightly dampened by Jackson's throbbing eye. He rolled to his back and tried to blink away the pain.

Kelly cried, "I'm so sorry, Jack. You okay?"

Jackson held his hand to his eye. "Kelly, you klutz," he groaned.

Both teams gathered around Jackson to check his injury. "You okay?" one of the Dragons asked.

"Yeah," Jackson answered.

"That was a good score," the Dragon said.

"Yeah, good game, guys," another one added.

All three Dragon's leaned in and shook Jackson's hand, but the third Dragon's grip was weak and limp and he didn't make eye contact. Jackson got a weird vibe from him, and it was more than just being a poor sport.

"Come on, Les," one of the other Dragon's shouted as they headed for the locker room.

Les caught up to them while Jackson stared him down from behind.

Jackson uncovered his throbbing eye and stood up. "How's it look?" he asked.

Dustin leaned around for a better view. "Not bad. You might have a slight shiner, but nothing major."

Kelly patted Jackson's back. "I'm really sorry, Jack."

"No worries, Kell. It felt like I got hit by a child, anyway."

The three of them followed the Dragons to the shower. Les was wrapped in a towel and shutting his locker when Jackson passed him. Les sneered at him. Jackson watched over his shoulder as Les rounded the corner to the shower.

As Jackson started to take off his shirt, he caught a glimpse of the padlock dangling from Les's locker. It wasn't locked. What was Les up to that made him feel so uneasy? After being so right about Hector and Brody and Spyder and probably Doc B, he was curious if his instincts about Les were on point as well. Jackson looked around for witnesses, then quietly removed the padlock and opened the locker.

Les's pants and shirt were hanging on a hook inside and his socks were crammed into his shoes on the bottom. Jackson didn't know what he expected to find. Maybe Les had drugs or something. The pants pockets only held keys, some loose change, and a Velcro wallet. Nothing incriminating.

He started to put the wallet back when another idea came to him. He looked around again and then slowly peeled the

Velcro open, cringing at how loud it was. Les's driver's license stared back through a clear plastic pocket. Caldwell, Lester B. 862 Blacks Rd., Pataskala.

Jackson knew right where that was. He had a new destination for tonight's patrol. If Les was a criminal, Jackson was about to find out. "What are you up to, Lester?" he whispered.

Dustin appeared at the end of the lockers and Jackson nearly jumped out of his skin.

"Hey, Jack?" He adjusted the towel around his waist and cocked his head slightly. "What're you doing?"

Jackson stuffed the wallet back into the pants, closed the locker door, and hooked the padlock on the latch. "Nothin', man."

"Who's locker's that?"

Damn it. Jackson needed to be more careful. He looked around again and whispered, "It's one of the Dragon's lockers."

"Why are you in it?"

Jackson shoved a finger to his lips. "Quiet."

Dustin's eyes narrowed. "What's going on?"

Jackson didn't want to tell him, but if he couldn't trust Dustin, he couldn't trust anyone. "Remember how I told you that I was keeping an eye out for crime?"

"Yeeeeaaahh?"

"I've gone out a few more times since then."

Dustin's eyes bulged. "What?"

Jackson shushed him and looked around again.

"Are you insane?"

"Listen. There's something fishy about this guy."

"So? There's something fishy about you right now, too."

"Stop it. I just mean I know he's up to something."

Dustin shook his head and headed toward the shower. He paused and turned back. "I don't know what's gotten into you, but stay out of other people's lockers. I don't wanna get thrown out of here because you think you're Michael Keaton all of a sudden."

"Michael Keaton?"

"You know. Batman?" Dustin rounded the corner to the showers.

Jackson stripped down and wrapped a towel around his waist. As he was getting in the shower, Les was leaving. They glared at each other again. *I'll see you soon, prick,* Jackson thought. Les shoulder-bumped him as he passed. It took everything Jackson had not to start a fight right then and there.

****

It was two in the morning when Jackson stood beside the mailbox at 862 Blacks Rd., his Glock tucked away at the small of his back. The country road was dead quiet. *Perfect.* From the edge of the driveway, Jackson watched the dark one-story house for a bit to make sure there was nothing going on inside. A red Nissan pickup sat in the short driveway with its front bumper almost touching the attached garage.

The next closest house was at least a couple hundred yards to the west, and all its lights were off too. Jackson had left his car about a quarter-mile away on the side of the road beside a wooded area. After one more look around to make sure the coast was clear, he donned his mask and gloves, pulled up his hood, and sneaked around to the back door. He took his Glock out, chambered a round, and then put it back in his belt. He didn't like having it ready to fire without a safety, but he was getting better with it, and he didn't want any more mistakes like with Hector.

The back porch was pitch-black. He flipped on a small flashlight he had brought along. The door only had a knob with no bolt lock, which should make it easy to kick in. It'd be noisier than he'd like, but he would be ready in case it woke Lester up. Jackson tried the knob to get a feel for how sturdy it was and then froze in disbelief. The crimefighting gods were on his side. It turned freely. The door creaked open into a kitchen area. Jackson slipped inside.

The room was clutter-free with not even a single dirty dish in the sink. The kitchen opened into a living room with an expensive-looking leather couch and ottoman. Guided by his flashlight, he found a short hallway off the living room with three closed doors. He tiptoed to the first. The buffalo he'd felt in his stomach during the Spyder Beatdown made an appearance, only this time he welcomed the nerves. He figured they'd keep him sharp.

The first door opened to a bathroom. The next door opened into what looked like a guest room with a neatly made bed and immaculate dresser beside it. That meant the third door was paydirt.

Jackson took a deep breath, slowly turned the handle, and quietly pushed it open. He pointed his flashlight at the bed where Les slept on his back beneath the covers. Now all he needed was to know what crime Les had committed. Something worthy of capital punishment? Maybe. Maybe not. But he'd soon know one way or another. A glance around the meticulously clean room told him nothing. He was going to have to get the confession straight from the horse's mouth.

There was a folding chair tucked under a desk. Jackson pulled it to the doorway and sat down. He rested his ankle on his knee, took out his Glock, and held it on his lap. Then he cleared his throat.

Les stretched and groaned, but didn't open his eyes.

Jackson cleared his throat again, louder this time.

Les squinted around the room before his eyes blasted wide open when he saw the silhouette of Jackson sitting in the dark. Jackson tried to blind him with the flashlight.

Lester's face went suddenly pale. "Wh-who are you?" He held his left hand up to block the light.

"Justice," Jackson answered in what he was coming to think of as his vigilante voice.

"What do you mean?"

"Let's just say I'm on to you."

"I don't know what you're talking about."

Jackson figured bluffing would be the fastest way to get the information he needed. "Are you going to pretend you didn't do what we both know you did?"

"I-I-I don't know what you mean."

Jackson chuckled. "Yeah. Sure. Don't make me—"

Les jammed his hands under the covers and a sudden boom blew a hole in his blanket. Quilt feathers exploded into the air. The doorframe beside Jackson's head shattered.

Jackson nearly pissed himself. He dove off the chair so recklessly that his chin slammed into the floor and he nearly bit off his tongue.

Les flung the covers off and stood on the bed, aiming a shotgun in Jackson's direction. Quilt feathers fell like snow between them. Jackson blindly shoved his Glock in Lester's direction and squeezed off a shot. Les cowered as the round buried itself in the drywall behind him.

Jackson scrambled into the hall as another deafening boom blew the carpet and plywood flooring to shreds beside him. While hauling balls down the hall in a crouching run, he pointed his gun behind him and fired two blind shots. He heard Les grunt and glanced over his shoulder.

Les held one arm across his bleeding gut and staggered toward him, still carrying the shotgun. Jackson's mouth filled with blood from his terribly stinging tongue, and he swallowed it to keep from leaving DNA behind for the police. It instantly turned his stomach.

He dove out the back door, scrambled to his feet, and ran as fast as he could. He never looked back. When he reached the Celica, he vomited a mixture of blood and his dinner onto the grass. He scraped dirt over it with his foot and then jumped in his car. His quivering hands found the ignition and he started the engine. He threw it into gear and jammed the gas pedal to the floor.

He was two miles away from the strip mall where he kept the Celica before his brain caught up with what had happened. He tried to play out the events, but it had all happened too fast. Who the hell slept with a shotgun and an unlocked back door? It was as if Les *wanted* someone to break into his house.

Jackson parked in the strip mall parking lot. He got out, locked the doors, and headed for home. When he was sure he was out of sight of anyone who might be looking, he ran the rest of the way. Once home, he hurried to the bathroom, dropped to his knees, and vomited again in the toilet. It, too, was bloody. Without looking up from the bowl, he reached for the knob and flushed it. Then he sank to his rear and leaned back against the wall. He gingerly touched his swollen tongue and winced.

It took another half-hour for him to gather his thoughts, though it would take hours to fully come down. He pulled himself to the sink, cupped his hand under the faucet, and gently slurped some cold water to wash away the vomit taste. It stung like hell, but at least the bleeding had stopped. He'd have to tell Jenna his leg gave out again.

Eventually, he made it to the couch. There was no chance he was sleeping, so he watched the blank TV screen instead. His hip began to throb, and he worried he might have reinjured it in his retreat. He limped to the kitchen cabinet where he kept the Vicodin and washed one down with a shot of bourbon.

That helped him fall asleep on the couch around six in the morning. He slept through the time Garrett needed to be ready for school. Jenna didn't say a word when she came home and got Garrett ready to leave. Jackson slept until noon.

That evening, the news reported a home invasion in Pataskala where the owner was shot in the stomach and later died at the hospital. Jackson smiled. That meant a return trip wasn't necessary. He just wished the news had uncovered what Les was up to. A guy who slept with a shotgun under his covers couldn't be a saint, after all.

18
GOING POSTAL
December 7, 1994

After taking down the night club shooter and giving
Lester justice, Jackson figured he should lie low for a few
weeks and let things settle down a bit. But everyday life just
didn't do it for him anymore. He made it two days before he
was climbing the walls. Someone really evil must be out
there for him to be this antsy. Luckily, his hip was feeling
better and it didn't seem as though he'd reinjured it at
Lester's. Even his tongue was healing.

The morning news reported that New York shock jock
Howard Stern had talked a suicidal man out of jumping off
the George Washington Bridge live on his radio program,
and that *really* got Jackson's juices flowing. He couldn't
wait to get out again and do his own bit of good for
humanity.

It was midnight when Jackson left the house. He decided
to take the interstate to Columbus because he couldn't wait
to get started and taking the backroads would take too long.
He had heard the south end had recently been plagued with
gang shootings. He'd already won two shootouts, which was
better than some of the best gunslingers of the Wild West.
Taking out a gangbanger would be a nice feather in his cap.

The CD player in the Toyota didn't work, but the radio
was fine. Well, fine in that only the rear speaker on the
passenger side actually worked. It would have to do. The
rock station played more commercials than music, but
eventually a song came on that he liked. "Roxanne" by Sting,

or maybe it was The Police. When "Roxanne" was over, the DJ droned on about how great Saturday night's Battle of the Bands was going to be and Jackson made a mental note to look into it. Plenty of criminals made trouble at big events like that. He remembered almost getting beaten up at a similar concert in his twenties. The DJ continued talking into the interminable intro of Aldo Nova's "Fantasy."

Jackson was lost in thought with his eyes transfixed on the road when a set of taillights ahead flared and swerved out of the lane. The car slid to a stop half on the berm with its ass end jutting almost back into traffic. Jackson slowed and pulled over several car lengths behind in case someone needed help. Superheroes didn't just fight crime, after all.

Before he could open his door, the other car's door swung open and the driver leaped out. He was an unassuming middle-aged man with round glasses and a full '70s-style bushy mustache. He looked like the kind of guy who would work for a computer company or NASA. Actually, the closer Jackson looked, the more the guy resembled the mugshot of Jeffrey Dahmer that had been all over the news since the serial killer had been murdered in prison last week. After scanning the side of his car, the Dahmer lookalike threw his hands angrily in the air.

From his angle, Jackson couldn't see anything wrong with the car. The guy kicked his own rear tire. Without looking at Jackson, he flicked his hand and shouted, "Move along. Nothing to see here."

There was something off about the way he wouldn't make eye contact. Unsettling, even. The guy undoubtedly had something to hide. Maybe he was drunk. Jackson's heart started beating a little faster and his stomach tickled like the buffalo had woken up again.

He tied his mask over his eyes, pulled up his hood, grabbed the Glock from under his seat, and chambered a round. He climbed out, keeping his weapon hidden by his side. "Hey, buddy?"

The guy still didn't look up. Instead, he leaned into his car as if looking for something in the back seat. Jackson panicked, remembering the assault rifle in the Beamer.

"Freeze," he shouted a split second before realizing he sounded like a cheesy TV cop.

The guy slowly backed out with his head bowed and his eyes looking slightly off to the side. What was he so nervous about?

"What do you want, sir?" the guy said in a soft, almost feminine voice.

The Dahmer vibe grew even stronger. If by some twist of fate this guy was anything like Dahmer, Jackson could have stumbled upon the Holy Grail of vigilantism. He had to investigate further. But he couldn't jump the gun. He needed to play it smart.

"I-I'm just leaving," the guy stammered.

There was no chance Jackson would let that happen, not after Brody had gone on to kill someone because Jackson failed to give him justice the first time they'd met.

"What do you want?" the Dahmer lookalike asked, eyes still fixed on the ground.

Jackson raised his gun.

Catching the movement out of the corner of his eye, the Dahmer lookalike froze and his face paled. "Oh my God. Please, don't shoot."

Jackson advanced, gun trained on the man's chest. Dahmer stumbled backward until he was even with his car's front fender. He dropped to his knees and covered his face with his arms. "Please, don't hurt us."

Jackson stopped at the driver's door, gun still trained on the man's chest. "Why did you swerve like that?" he screamed. "Are you drunk?"

"N-n-no. I-I-I don't drink. I hit an umbrella in the road and it scratched my car. You saw the umbrella, didn't you?" His voice cracked.

"No, I didn't," Jackson snapped. It was a quick-thinking excuse, and it would have been a good one if there actually was an umbrella.

"It was there. I swear. I-I-I was just checking for damage." Without looking up, he pointed toward the side of his car. "See? Look."

Jackson glanced at the rear quarter panel where there was a six-inch long gouge in the paint, but nothing to indicate it was fresh. Something moved in the back seat and Jackson recoiled onto the asphalt. He was lucky there wasn't a car coming. He cut an angle back to the car to look inside without being too exposed. Like a stupid rookie, he hadn't cleared the car. To his relief, instead of an accomplice with an assault rifle, a little girl in a car seat stared back at him.

Maybe this guy was a kidnapper instead of a serial killer. Or maybe both. Jackson's eyes widened as he remembered the kidnappings on the news. What if this was the guy? There was no way Jackson could let him off without knowing for sure. "Who is this girl?" he shouted.

The guy's forehead wrinkled. "What do you mean? She's my daughter."

"I doubt that." Jackson lowered his gun and reached for the door handle.

"Stay away from her," Dahmer shouted, showing the first spark of anger yet.

Jackson lifted the Glock again, which stopped him cold. "Don't move. I'm not going to hurt her. I'm not a monster."

"I don't know what you are."

"I could say the same about you."

Jackson turned back to the little girl, keeping a watchful eye on Dahmer. If the man was a serial kidnapper, he would be cunning and dangerous. "Sweetie," Jackson whispered into the car, hoping his mask wouldn't scare her.

She stared at him with the innocence of an angel.

"It's okay. I won't hurt you. I want to help you. How old are you?"

She held out two fingers and said, "Three."

"You see that man over there?"

She straightened and craned her neck to see out the windshield. She nodded. "Um-hm."

"Who is he?"

"That's my daddy."

Hm. "Okay, sweetie. Your daddy's fine. He'll be right back." Jackson backed away and closed the door. A set of semi-truck headlights approached, so Jackson kept his back to the road and tucked his Glock against his stomach until the semi roared by.

"What's your name?" Jackson asked.

"Steve."

"What do you do, Steve?"

"Why do you want to know?"

"Just answer me." Jackson searched for something—anything—that would confirm what he already felt about this creepy guy. One clue was all he needed. The trigger on his Glock was calling for his finger.

"I work in computer sales."

"Why are you out here so late?"

"Hey, man. Just let us go."

Was he stalling? "Answer me," Jackson barked.

"We went to a movie and then—"

"What movie?"

"You can't be serious."

Jackson shook his Glock at him. "If you went to a movie, then you'd know what was playing."

"*The Santa Clause.*"

Jackson's shoulders slumped. He knew that movie was still in theaters. He had heard Tim Allen talking about it on Letterman and Garrett wanted to see it. "She's too young for that movie."

"It's just a daddy-daughter date. We got candy and popcorn."

"You took a three-year-old to the movies this late?"

"No, but she was still hopped up on sugar so we went to see the Christmas lights at the zoo."

Jackson's wheels spun.

"Look, my ex won't let me have her on Christmas, so I just wanted to make some nice memories. It was a fun night … Until I hit that umbrella and you showed up."

That still didn't explain why Steve was acting so nervous.

"Give me your keys."

"Why?"

"I wanna see what's in your trunk." If there was a shovel, rubber gloves, or even a speck of blood, Steve was toast.

"Then you'll leave us alone?"

"I don't know. Maybe."

Steve pointed to the car. "They're in the ignition."

Jackson leaned through the open driver's door and noticed a trunk release lever. With his eyes still on Steve, he pulled it. Then he backed around to the trunk. Not only was it empty, it was meticulously clean. He had nothing.

He closed the trunk and circled back around the car. He had no choice but to let Steve go, and it was killing him. There had to be something Steve had done that needed punishing, but he just couldn't figure out what it was. He sighed.

"Listen. Against my better judgement, I'm going to leave. I hope like hell that I'm not making a mistake." He gestured with his pistol toward the front of the car. "Get down on your face until I'm gone."

Steve didn't move.

"Now," Jackson screamed. Every fiber in his being told him he was making a mistake letting Steve go, but there was no way he could hurt him in front of his little girl without knowing for certain he was a criminal.

Steve dropped to his knees. "Don't you touch my daughter," he shouted, as if he could dictate what happened next.

"I'm not gonna touch her. Now get down."

Steve kissed the dirt as he was told.

Jackson tucked his weapon in his waistband and tore off his mask before another car zipped past. He backed up to his Toyota and climbed in. The adrenaline and subsequent letdown poured out through his fist as he punched the steering wheel repeatedly and muffled a frustrated scream. If the morning news reported a kidnapped three-year-old girl, he wouldn't be able to live with himself. He memorized Steve's license plate just in case.

He stomped on the gas pedal. Steve was still face down on the berm when Jackson blew past. He sped down I-70, pissed off and more determined than ever to give someone justice. All he had to do was find someone who deserved it.

Between anger, frustration, and second-guessing his decision to let Steve off, his head was spinning. He needed to pull himself together before he did something stupid. A sign for a twenty-four-hour truck stop at the next exit caught his eye. Maybe a cup of coffee would help.

He pulled into the parking lot and sat in his car, replaying what had just happened over and over, hoping like hell that he hadn't missed something. It was always the little clues that police detectives on TV found to crack the case. But what little clues had there been this time? Steve's answers seemed honest. There was a scrape on the side of his car that could have been caused by a discarded umbrella. The little girl answered without distress. The trunk was empty. What could it be?

And then it hit him. The trunk wasn't just empty, it was spotless. Could that be to hide evidence? It was possible. Jackson thought back to the little girl, and his stomach turned at the possibility that his instincts had been right again and he had just left her to a horrible death. It was almost too much to bear. Maybe if he hadn't let Steve off so easily, he might have found something. As his thoughts got darker and darker, he grew more resolute in his mission. He couldn't keep being so naïve if he wanted to catch real criminals.

Angry at himself and full of regret, he went into the diner part of the gas station for his coffee. He swung his leg over the farthest stool and plopped onto the ripped seat. There weren't any other customers in the diner or the convenience store, which surprised him because he'd seen at least four semis in the back lot. Probably sleeping in their rigs, he guessed.

The waitress who approached had strawberry blond hair pulled into a bun. "What can I get y'all tonight, hon?" she drawled.

"Just a coffee."

"Y'all want cream and sugar?"

He held his finger and thumb a millimeter apart and she went on her way. He lost himself in a daze, watching the parking lot through the front glass.

The waitress plunking his coffee in front of him broke him out of his trance. "Sorry 'bout the wait. I made y'all a fresh pot." Her voice was way too loud and bubbly for so late at night.

"Oh. Okay. Thanks."

"Sure thing, hon. Just shout if y'all want anything else. They call me Flo."

He gave her a onceover. "Is that your real name? Flo? Because if it is, you're kind of like a walking cliché."

She giggled. "Nah. They call me that because I sound like Flo from that old TV show, *Alice*."

Jackson nodded.

"Anyways, I'll be in the back havin' a puff."

She set his bill beside the mug and then disappeared into the kitchen.

Jackson sipped at his coffee for the next twenty minutes as he tried unsuccessfully to calm down. It ate at his gut that he might have missed something with Steve. Flo never returned for a refill, which was fine with him. That one cup had already run through him and was pressing on his bladder. He tossed a five on the counter for his ninety-nine-cent coffee and headed reluctantly to the bathroom at the rear of the store.

He opened the door with trepidation. The urinal's rim was caked with dried piss and pubes, and a wad of toilet paper clogged the hole. The entire bathroom stank like someone had a urinary tract infection. This was why he hated public restrooms so much.

He finished his business as quickly as possible and flushed, already forgetting about the wad of toilet paper. The urinal filled to the brim and then overflowed, causing a minor flood on the floor. He cursed and retreated to the sink. The dispenser was out of soap, so all he could do was rinse his hands under the tap, and of course the paper towel dispenser was empty.

He gripped the sides of the sink, pressed his forehead against the grimy mirror, and closed his eyes. "Damn it," he mumbled through clenched teeth. He tapped his head against the glass three times before pulling back to look at his reflection. Staring back was the face of a frustrated but determined vigilante who was about to do great things. All he needed was a chance.

And then the door swung open behind him. A short, stocky man shaped like a fire hydrant walked in. Jackson cocked his head. *Now, what do we have here?*

"Excuse me," the man said. He wore a green John Deere cap over long, greasy hair that covered his ears and neck. The stink of stale sweat temporarily drowned out the smell of rotten piss.

Jackson studied him as he made his way to the urinal. "Long night of driving?" he asked.

"Yep." The trucker stepped into the puddle around the flooded urinal and lifted his foot in disgust. "Are you kidding me?" He looked over his shoulder. "You make this mess?"

Jackson shook his head. He didn't like this truck driver's tone.

The trucker undid his belt. He held his pants up with one hand while leaning almost into the urinal and bracing himself against the graffiti-covered block wall.

"Where you coming from?" Jackson asked.

Without looking back, the trucker answered, "What, do you like men or something? I don't swing that way."

Jackson chuckled. "Relax. I just get tired of my own company on these long drives."

The trucker finished pissing and then shook himself dry. He turned to the sink while fastening his belt and side-eyed Jackson. "You still here? I'm losing patience with you real fast, buddy."

Jackson put up his hands in surrender. In all his weeks of crime fighting, he had never felt so on edge as he did looking into the dark eyes of the man standing before him. His gift was practically screaming at him. *This is it. The big one.*

"It's cool, man. I'm just leaving." Jackson opened the door and stepped out. "See you around."

"What's that supposed to mean?" the trucker called after him.

Jackson glanced back, blank-faced.

The trucker's eyes darkened. "You know what? Forget it. I don't know who you are, but I'd better *not* see you around. I'm just saying."

Jackson nodded politely and closed the door, barely managing to keep a triumphant grin off his face. The only reason the trucker wouldn't want to see someone like Jackson again was because he knew it would be the end of his criminal undertakings. Jackson's hands trembled. He had the urge to go back in and give the trucker a fatal thumping, but he'd left his Glock in the car and this guy was beefy like Brody. Jackson had already learned that lesson the hard way.

Before the trucker could exit the bathroom, Jackson hurried out to the parking lot. The buffalo in his gut started to stir even before he made it to his car. It felt just like that first night with Spyder.

"You'd better not see me later, huh, tough guy?" He didn't have to hide his grin this time.

Sitting behind the wheel waiting for the trucker to come out, he almost rubbed holes in his jeans on the tops of his thighs. It felt like his whole body was vibrating. He glared at the truck stop doors and whispered, "Come on out, you bastard. It's time to reap what you've sewn." He retrieved his Glock from under the seat, set it gently on the center console, and caressed it like a lover. He grew so consumed with nervous excitement that he almost didn't see the fire hydrant man exit the truck stop carrying a coffee.

Once the trucker reached his rig, he flipped an extra step down from the side and climbed into the cab. The truck rumbled to life, jerked forward, and then crept from the parking area toward the onramp.

Jackson knew what he needed to do. He had his criminal. Now he just needed him to confess the crime. He started his car and followed the truck onto the interstate, heading back toward home. Steve the Dahmer lookalike wasn't a kidnapper after all, and the entire incident was meant to lead Jackson to the real monster.

As he reached the same straight-away where he had confronted Steve, he stepped on the gas and swerved into the passing lane. He gunned the engine until he passed the truck's front bumper. Checking his rearview mirror assured him they were the only two vehicles in sight.

Jackson cranked his steering wheel to the right a few feet from the truck's bumper. Then he tapped his brakes just to send the driver into a panic.

The trucker slammed on his brakes and swerved just as Jackson hoped. His trailer went squirrelly and dragged him toward the center divider as he tried to recover. He overcorrected and swerved back toward the berm. The trailer rocked side to side. He swerved again, now completely out of control, before plowing into the grass beside the freeway. Though he tried to pull the cab back onto the road, his trailer slid into a ditch and almost toppled over. His brakes screamed and smoked. The truck bounced and rocked before slamming into the side of the ditch and sending dirt exploding outward. The truck leaned precariously toward the passenger side.

Jackson pulled over to the berm and stopped. He couldn't catch his breath from the excitement. All he needed was to find out exactly what this bastard had done to make his gift go so electric. He couldn't wait for the answer.

He yanked his mask over his eyes, jammed his hands into his gloves, and pulled up his hood. Then he grabbed his Glock. He was the Spyder Stopper and he'd just found the Spyder King. He jumped out and ran to the truck. The driver didn't move inside the cab. Jackson climbed on the barreled diesel container beneath the door and peeked into the driver's window. The trucker was slumped over the passenger side of the bench seat. His forehead was bleeding and his John Deere hat lay upside-down on the floorboard.

The adrenaline was overwhelming. He gripped the assist bar and ripped the door open. "I've caught you now, you bastard."

The trucker looked up, his previous bravado long gone. "What?"

"Tell me what you've done."

"I don't know what you're talking about. Help me out of here." He held his hand out.

Jackson swatted it away. "I know you've done something wrong. What is it?"

The trucker winced and rubbed a knot on his temple. "I didn't do shit. You're the one who cut me off."

Jackson showed him the gun. "Answer me. Confess your crimes and be judged."

"You're crazy, buddy." The trucker squirmed to right himself on the floorboard. "I think I'm hurt, man. Call 9-1—"

In his excitement, Jackson squeezed the trigger without conscious thought. The blast, amplified in the cab, popped his right ear.

The bullet ripped through the trucker's thigh beside his groin. He cried out and grabbed the wound. "What the fuck, man?"

"Tell me." Jackson leaned back to check for approaching traffic. There were headlights in the distance. He'd already taken too long. He held his breath until the car zipped by without slowing.

The trucker started screaming for help.

Jackson scowled. "Confess, damn it."

"Okay. I cheat on my wife with whores," he shouted through gritted teeth. "Is that what you want?"

"No. I want to know your *real* crimes. I know you've done something. What is it?"

The trucker's eyes went wide. "You're the guy from the bathroom."

Shit. "Tell me, Goddammit. Are you a rapist? A murderer?"

"What? No. Come on, man. I'm bleeding to death here. I need some help."

"You diddle little kids? Is that it?"

"No. No way."

"What is it? I know you're guilty of something. Is the trailer full of immigrants?"

"Immigrants? Man, you're crazy. Go look if you want."

"What have you done?"

"Nothing."

"Liar," Jackson screamed. The second boom was somehow louder than the first. The round struck under the trucker's left armpit. It felt amazing.

The trucker grunted and stared at Jackson, confused. He stiffened for a few seconds and then sank to the floorboard. Unable to hold his head up any longer, he rested his cheek against the seat, gazing at nothing with blank eyes. Jackson breathed in the smoke trickling from the Glock's barrel and then let it out with a quivering sigh. He knew he didn't have time to wait for the trucker to die, but he did anyway.

A final gurgling breath signaled the end of the show. Despite not knowing exactly what the trucker had done, Jackson knew it had to be something bad. He soaked in his victory with a smile.

As much as he wanted to stay and revel in his accomplishment even longer, he had already lingered too long. Each second brought him closer to being seen. He backed out of the cab and dropped to the ground.

Another car drove past, but this one slowed and pulled to the berm in front of his car. A freaking do-gooder. For a split second, Jackson considered seeing if this do-gooder triggered his gift too, but then he'd be running the risk of possibly hurting an innocent just to protect his cover. Instead, he ran to his car, jumped in, and gunned it before the Good Samaritan climbed out of his vehicle. He felt so alive.

19
MAD CLOSE
December 8, 1994

Jackson slept until 10:00 the next morning. He didn't even notice when Jenna climbed into bed after work. He assumed she got home in time to get Garrett off to school because she didn't wake him to complain. Though he felt rested, he lounged around the house for most of the morning. He had already played through last night's patrol a hundred times or more, and each time he was more resolved in the righteousness of his actions than the time before. The number of crimes he had likely prevented was endless.

Eventually, he got motivated enough to get a late afternoon workout in. After he was good and sweaty, he cooked a cheeseburger and fries for a late lunch and waited for Garrett to get home from school.

Garrett popped in from the garage as Jackson was scraping the hardened grease from the skillet and loading the dishwasher. "Dad?" he called.

"What's up, kid?"

"I'm home."

"I see that." Jackson had always made it a point to hug Garrett when he came home from school. The habit had fallen by the wayside during the dark days of his recovery, but a few days ago he'd made it a priority again and hadn't missed one since.

"Dad, did you know that man?"

Jackson wiped down the stove. "What man, bud?"

"That nice man who said hi to me after I got off the bus."

Jackson paused. "Who was he?"

"I don't know. He walked with me to the driveway. He said he was a friend of yours. He gave me this." Garrett held out a Troll doll with wild pink hair that stood up like Don King's.

Jackson set down the rag and took the doll to examine it. "That's weird. Was it Dustin?" he asked as he made his way to the front porch.

Garrett shook his head and giggled. "No, silly. I know Dustin."

Jackson looked up and down the street and didn't see anyone out of the ordinary. "Do you see him now?"

Garrett shook his head.

"What else did he say?"

"He asked me my name."

"Did you tell him?"

"Yes."

"Was it the mailman?"

Garrett shook his head again.

"And you've never seen him before?"

"Uh-uh."

Hm. Jackson scanned the neighborhood again before turning back to Garrett. He put on his stern dad voice to get his message across when he said, "Listen to me, okay?"

Garrett nodded.

"You never walk with strangers. We've talked about this before. If a stranger tries to walk with you or hold your hand or something, you're allowed to run from him. You can even yell for help if he doesn't leave you alone. Okay?"

"I know, Dad."

"From now on, I don't even want you getting off the bus unless me or your mom are waiting for you. Is that understood?"

"I have to get off the bus, Dad."

Jackson gently grabbed Garrett's shoulders and knelt so they'd be face to face. "Listen. There are bad men in the world. Sometimes they seem nice, but they're not. We will be at the bus stop from now on every day, but if me or your mom aren't there for some reason, you tell the bus driver you don't feel safe and ask her to watch you all the way to our door. I'll call and tell the school about it too. Okay?"

Garrett nodded.

"All right. Run inside." Jackson followed him into the house. He waited until Garrett was out of earshot to call the school. After he talked to the principal, he decided to call the police as well. They said they'd send someone out for a report.

Jenna came downstairs and joined Jackson where he was waiting on the porch. "Whatcha doin'?" she asked.

He didn't want to tell her because he knew she would flip out, but he had no choice. "I have a police officer coming to fill out a report."

She cocked her head. "Why? What's going on?"

"It's nothing, babe. Some guy talked to Garrett when he got off the bus and I figured I'd play it safe."

Her eyes widened. "What do you mean? Who?"

"I don't know. I'm sure it's nothing."

"Where's Garrett now?"

"He's fine. He's playing in his room."

Her face filled with panic. "What are we going to do?" she cried.

"Exactly what we're doing, honey. We stay calm and tell the authorities." He tried to hug her, but she pulled away.

"Don't tell me to be calm," she snapped.

"You're right. I'm sorry. We won't let him off the bus without us being there from now on. Okay? I've already told him. And I called the school. They said they'd step up their precautions and alert all the bus drivers."

Her eyes darted everywhere, and Jackson could practically hear her mind racing. "We need to get that security system. No more putting it off."

"I know. I'll call first thing in the morning."

"You promise?"

"Yes."

A cruiser pulled into the driveway. Jackson and Jenna met Officer G Davis on the sidewalk.

"I'm seeing you a lot lately," the officer said.

Jackson grinned. "I guess so. That's never a good thing to hear from a cop, though, is it?"

"I wouldn't think so."

Jackson invited him in and they all took seats at the kitchen table. Garrett poked his head around the corner. Officer Davis gave him a smile. "Hey, buddy. Come on out."

Garrett looked to Jackson for confirmation before climbing on one of the chairs.

"Could you describe the man who talked to you?" Officer Davis asked.

"He was tall and skinny, like my dad," Garrett answered.

"What color was his skin?"

"White."

"Did you see his hair? What color was it?"

Garrett squinted in thought. "I couldn't see it. He was wearing a shirt with a hood."

"Like a sweatshirt?"

Garrett nodded.

"Was there anything else you can remember? Did he have any tattoos that you could see?"

Garrett shook his head. Then his eyes brightened and he said, "He was missing a tooth."

Davis's eyes brightened too. "Oh? Which one?"

Garrett opened his mouth wide and pointed.

Davis continued to ask questions and write down everything Garrett said. Then he asked, "Could you look at something for me?"

Garrett nodded.

Davis pulled a laminated picture from his clipboard and slid it across the table to Garrett. "Have you seen a car like this in your neighborhood recently?"

Garrett looked at it and shook his head. Jenna looked over his shoulder. She shook her head too.

When Jackson glanced down, his polite smile faded and a lump filled his throat. He took a closer look. The picture was a grainy black and white security camera photo from outside a parking garage. It showed the unmistakable image of an older model Toyota Celica. *His* Celica.

Jackson's heart dropped into his foot. It took everything he had to keep from falling off his chair. He could barely hear Officer Davis saying, "We want to talk to the owner."

Jackson struggled to catch his breath. His panicked thoughts went to the parking lot where his car currently sat out in the open. He wiped sweaty palms on his jeans under the table. He felt the blood draining from his face and feared Officer Davis would notice. "Can I get you a drink?" he blurted as he stood up.

"Sure," Officer Davis answered without looking up from his report. "If you've got a bottle of water, that'd be great."

Jackson went to the fridge, his hands trembling.

Officer Davis put the picture back in his folder while Jackson pretended to search for the bottled water that was right in front of him. He needed to get his nerves under control fast.

Jenna said, "I don't understand. What's this car have to do with the man who talked to Garrett?"

Officer Davis answered, "You're aware of the string of kidnappings recently?" He waited for Jenna's nod before he continued. "After one of the children went missing, a school bus driver reported seeing a stranger near the bus stop around the time of the disappearance. Her description of the man matches Garrett's: a tall, thin white male in a hooded sweatshirt."

Jenna asked, "Aaand …?"

"Columbus police are investigating a string of shootings. A tall, thin white man in a hooded sweatshirt was seen fleeing the scene and climbing into that car after one of those shootings."

Jackson's mind scrambled. *This is not good.*

"Did you hear on the news that the shooter calls himself the Spider Killer for some reason?" Officer Davis chuckled.

Jackson groaned inwardly. *Spyder Stopper, damn it.* He needed Officer Davis gone ASAP, but Jenna wouldn't let it rest.

She leaned forward and regarded Officer Davis intently. "What makes you think that Spider guy has anything to do with the kidnappings or the guy who talked to Garrett today? I mean, everywhere you go there are tall white guys in hooded sweatshirts."

Jackson swallowed hard. He wished his wife would stop talking, but he also desperately needed to hear the answer. Where had he gone wrong?

Officer Davis smiled. "Fair enough. We don't know that there *is* a connection, but it seems pretty coincidental that someone suspected of multiple murders just so happens to operate in the same general area and share the same description with a suspected serial kidnapper, wouldn't you say?"

Jenna nodded. "I suppose."

Jackson cleared his throat. "I don't know. Seems a bit far-fetched to think somebody shooting people would also be kidnapping kids, don't you think? I mean, they're very different crimes." Even as he said it, his stomach turned.

Officer Davis shrugged. "Just the same, we'd really like to talk to the driver of that car. We follow up on all possibilities, including and especially coincidences. Unfortunately, no one's gotten a good look at the guy's face. This is the first we've heard about a missing tooth. That'll help a lot as we move forward. And we should get more information after this picture goes out on the eleven o'clock news tonight."

Jackson's eyes shot to the clock above the stove. Then he glared at the back of Officer Davis's head, picturing his car—covered in fingerprints and hair follicles and all sorts of DNA—waiting in a parking lot less than a mile away. When he passed the water bottle over Officer Davis's shoulder, he briefly considered snapping the man's neck and hiding the body. But of course he couldn't do anything that drastic. Especially not in front of his family. He needed to play it cool.

Officer Davis guzzled the water and then handed the empty bottle back to Jackson. Jackson automatically tossed it in the recycling bin, his body on autopilot while his head continued to spin.

Officer Davis stood up and shook Jenna's hand. "In the meantime, folks, keep a close eye out and let us know if you see anything suspicious. I'll check with your neighbors and see if anyone saw this car in the neighborhood today. I'll get the detective to check with Garrett's bus driver, too. And we'll step up patrols in the neighborhood in the mornings and afternoons."

Jackson knew by the look on Jenna's face that she wasn't reassured.

Officer Davis extended his hand toward Jackson, but Jackson pretended not to see it, afraid his hands were too clammy. Instead, Jackson patted Davis on the shoulder. "Thanks, Officer. We'll keep our eyes peeled." He walked the officer to the door, his mind still racing. He still didn't know how the police had connected the shootings. Maybe some careful fishing would get some answers.

"Hey, Officer?" he said as Davis stepped off the porch.

Davis turned back.

"Police work is so fascinating to me. I love all of those Law and Order shows. I mean, how the hell do you guys do it? Like those shootings in Columbus that you were talking about. How in the world could you ever narrow it down to one shooter? That seems impossible."

"I don't know how CPD linked these particular shootings, but I'd guess they used the bullets."

"Bullets?"

"Yeah. Forensics can tell by the marks on the bullets if they've come from the same gun. We send every bullet from a crime scene to the lab for evaluation."

Right. Ballistics. Just like in every damn cop show I've ever seen. I'm such an idiot. Jackson nodded absently. He was already planning what he was going to do after Jenna went to work. "That makes sense. Thanks for your time, Officer."

Officer Davis climbed into his cruiser and backed out before pulling into the neighbor's driveway next door.

Jackson rushed inside and looked at the clock again. It was 5:15. Five hours to go before he could clean up his mess.

He wasn't the only one with nerves strung tight. When Garrett asked to play outside before dinner, Jenna nearly took off his head. She apologized, but Jackson could tell she was on edge. But not nearly as on edge as he was. Each passing minute felt like hours. While Jenna reheated leftover lasagna for dinner, Jackson went to the basement and pounded his knuckles raw against his heavy bag. Anything to get his mind off his colossal screw-up. Nothing he did helped.

He ate dinner that evening like a starving dog. At one point, Jenna asked him to slow down before he choked to death. He smiled, downed the rest of his food at a slightly less frantic pace, and then excused himself for a shower. It was 6:35. His incriminating Celica consumed his thoughts, yet there was nothing he could do about it until after Jenna left. If he left right after, he'd have less than an hour to get rid of it before it made the news.

While shower water poured down his face, he ran through all the possibilities. What if they were already watching his car and waiting for him to show up? Or what if a cop saw him driving it to where he wanted to dump it? Both were valid concerns, but they were nothing compared to the risk of leaving it in the open and letting the cops go over it with a fine-toothed comb.

The shower water ran cold before he finally climbed out and got dressed. It was almost 8:30.

He spent an hour on the couch with Jenna pretending to watch *Friends* and *Seinfeld* reruns. Then Jenna kissed him and went upstairs to get ready for work while some show called *Madman of the People* played. He hoped Jenna didn't ask him if it was any good. He wouldn't even be able to tell her what it was about.

Jenna was out the door by 10:15. Her car was barely out of the driveway when Jackson bolted upstairs for his bag of supplies, including his Glock, gloves, mask, and sweatshirt. He grabbed a bottle of bleach and some rags from the laundry room and shoved them into his vigilante bag. Then he grabbed a bottle of lighter fluid from the garage and some matches from the junk drawer by the phone. With everything waiting by the front door, he ran upstairs to check on Garrett.

Garrett was lying on his side facing the window. Jackson started to close the door, but Garrett called out, "Dad?"

Jackson sighed and checked the time. It was 10:33. "What is it, son?"

"I'm scared." He rolled over to face the door.

Jackson sat on the bed next to him. "What are you scared about, bud?"

"Was that man I talked to really bad?"

"Maybe. But there's nothing to be afraid of. We were just taking precautions. Do you know what precautions means?"

Garrett shook his head.

"It means we were just making sure you stay safe. Officer Davis is going to help Mommy and me keep an eye out for that man. And you just can't talk to him or any strangers anymore. Okay?"

Garrett nodded. "Will you sit with me until I go to sleep?"

Jackson reluctantly agreed. As much as he needed to get rid of his car before everyone saw it on the news, he didn't dare leave Garrett while his son was still awake. Jenna would skin him. Then she'd probably call the cops herself. Garrett rolled back over. When he finally fell asleep, Jackson crept from his room and raced down the stairs to the front door. It was 11:13. He put on his shoes, grabbed his bag, and yanked the door open.

Dustin stood on the porch with his fist raised and ready to knock. Jackson's heart skipped a beat and Dustin nearly tumbled from the porch.

Jackson shouted, "Jesus. You scared the hell outta me. What are you doing here?"

Dustin's face was flushed. Somberly, he asked, "Is it you, Jack?"

"Is what me?"

"On the news. Columbus detectives are looking for a 'vigilante' who's been killing people. It's you, isn't it?"

"I don't know. I didn't see the report."

"Stop with the games."

"Why would you think it's me?"

"Because you're the only one I've had to come get in the middle of the night after getting a butt-whupping while trying to, how did you put it? Fight crime. You're the one who was suddenly super interested in guns a few weeks ago. You're—"

"Okay, okay. I get it. I mean, I have gone out a few times and helped people, but—"

"Were you at that dance club in Columbus the other night?"

Jackson didn't answer.

"You know we've been friends since elementary school, right?"

"Dustin ..."

"You know I'd help you in any way I could?"

Jackson nodded.

"I need to ask you something, and you'd better be deadly honest with me."

He nodded again.

Dustin's fist tightened at his side. "Are you kidnapping children?"

Jackson was taken aback by the question. "God, no. Are you insane? That's someone else. The cops have their stories crossed. You know I would never hurt a kid."

"It's just ... They think—"

"I know what they think, but they're wrong. My God, Dustin. That's not me. You know that. You believe me, right?"

Dustin didn't agree so much as he didn't argue. After a few seconds he said, "Then talk to me. We can get you help for what you *have* done."

Jackson didn't need help. At least, not the kind of help Dustin was talking about. A ride home after ditching the Celica, on the other hand, would be great.

"I'll tell you what, Dustin. I'll tell you everything you want to know if you give me a ride. I have one last thing to do before I quit for good. I'll never do this again if you help me, but I need to do this one last thing tonight and I can't do it alone."

Dustin hesitated. Jackson saw in his eyes that he was wavering. Dustin looked away for a moment. Then he nodded.

"Yeah, I'll help you tonight as long as you promise to let me get you a different kind of help tomorrow." They both knew what he meant. "They said you've killed some people?"

Jackson bit his tongue for a second. Then he answered in the only way he could. Honestly. "I have."

"Jesus, Jack." Dustin turned away.

"Only people who deserved it. I swear. I'll tell you all about it on the way home. But we need to go now."

"Where?"

"Did the news show a picture of the suspect's car?"

Dustin nodded.

"It's mine. I've gotta get rid of it. And I mean fast."

Dustin looked like he was going to ask more questions, but then he shook his head and led the way to his truck. At the strip mall, Jackson had him circle the lot three times to make sure no pigs were watching.

"Where are we taking it?"

"Out past Milner's Farm. I'm gonna burn it. You remember where the Milner's pond is, don't ya?"

"Yeah."

"Follow me close so no cops get on my ass."

"Okay."

Jackson didn't breathe as he climbed into the Celica and turned the ignition. He expected to be swarmed by cops at any moment. With his bag on his lap and the Glock's handle poking out, he decided no cops were taking him in that night. Not alive, anyway.

As long as he could still trust his friend, he'd be in the clear within the hour. He just needed to get to Milner's without being seen. With each mile closer, his shaky knees slowly stilled. So far, so good.

He only passed a couple of cars during the last two or three miles. The Milners had died a few years back in a biplane accident. Everyone in town had always thought that Mr. Milner wasn't much of a pilot and his wife was insane to ride with him. In the end, everyone was proven right. They had no designated heirs and no one had ever claimed their property.

Jackson stopped at the rusted gate, got out, unwrapped the chain, and swung the gate open. Instead of walking into the woods like last time, he drove along a single-lane dirt road mostly overgrown with weeds. Dustin followed. They rounded a bend and continued another two hundred yards before reaching the pond.

Jackson hopped out and ran back to Dustin's window. "Go park behind the barn. I'll be over there." He pointed to the other side of the pond.

Dustin nodded and backed up to the dirt drive that led to the barn. After his taillights disappeared, Jackson drove to the far side of the pond to the edge of a drop-off. He immediately went to work with the bleach, scrubbing the steering wheel, gear shifter, dash, seats, and center console. He hit the door handles and the gas cap next.

He removed his Glock, the matches, and the lighter fluid from his bag and then tossed the bag into the back seat. He knew he'd have to get rid of the gun, too, but he didn't want to do that until he could get a replacement.

The moon gave off enough light that he could see Dustin approaching from the barn. Jackson squirted the lighter fluid over the dash and seats and floorboards. He reached in and slipped the gear shifter into neutral and then turned the wheels toward the drop-off.

He struck a match and tossed it into the open driver's side window. The lighter fluid took off like a wildfire.

"Now what, Jack?" Dustin asked with his hands on his knees, panting like a marathon runner.

"We gotta push this over the hill before it really gets going."

Like a good soldier, Dustin placed his hands on the trunk and Jackson did the same. They pushed the car forward.

The car careened down the steep drop-off and crashed into a tree. Jackson prayed the recent rain was enough to keep the tree from bursting into flame and starting a forest fire.

Dustin put his arm around him. "We're gonna get you help."

Jackson sighed. "Please stop saying that. We need to talk first."

They started walking toward the barn, but Dustin kept looking back over his shoulder. "Damn, that's a lot of smoke. Do you think someone might see it from the road?"

"I don't know. But I don't wanna find out. Go get your truck. I'm going to start for the road to make sure no one's coming. Pick me up on your way out."

Dustin headed toward the barn while Jackson jogged down the long lane toward the road. He stopped near the gate.

To his horror, a set of headlights turned into the lane. He ducked into the brush beside the lane, praying it wasn't the fuzz. As the headlights crept forward, he saw his worst nightmare come true. There was a set of strobe lights on the roof.

He glanced back down the lane and saw Dustin's headlights staring back. The headlights bounced as Dustin's truck jerked to a stop.

"Oh no," Jackson breathed.

The cruiser stopped and the side spotlight flared to life. The officer directed the beam toward Dustin's distant truck and then opened the cruiser's door.

The officer stepped in front of his cruiser and motioned for Dustin's truck to come closer. He rested one hand on his gun belt and reached for his shoulder mic with the other.

Jackson needed to act fast He burst from the brush with his gun raised. He stayed in the shadows away from the spotlight. "Don't key that mic," he shouted.

The officer flinched and reached for his weapon.

Jackson fired off a flurry of three panicked shots. One shattered the spotlight, one popped a tire, and one hit the officer's chest. The officer grunted and sprawled face-first across the cruiser's hood before tumbling to the ground, his head striking a rock with a dull thump.

Jackson ran to his side and rolled him over so he could see the officer's face. Blood trickled from a cut above the cop's left eye. It was Officer G Davis. He was unconscious but still breathing.

Dustin's truck engine revved and he raced down the lane, stopping less than ten feet away. He jumped out. "What did you do?" he cried as he ran to Jackson. When he saw Davis lying in the dirt and weeds, he shouted, "You shot him."

"Shut up. Help me move him outta the way so we can get his car off the road." Jackson took Officer Davis's handcuffs, careful to cover his fingers with his sleeve. He rolled Davis back over, cuffed his hands behind his back, grabbed his ankles, and dragged him to the ditch beside the road.

He pulled out his Glock again and pressed the barrel to Officer Davis's head. It wasn't what he wanted to do, but Davis was probably a dirty cop anyway and deserved what he was getting.

Dustin grabbed Jackson's arm and yanked it back. "What are you doing?" he screamed.

"He's probably crooked," Jackson said, and corrected his aim.

"Probably?" Dustin bear hugged Jackson from behind and spun him away from Davis, putting himself between the two men. "I'm not going to let you kill him."

Jackson broke out of his hold, whirled around, and pointed the Glock at Dustin.

Dustin's head tilted and surprise filled his face. "You're really going to point that at me?"

Jackson winced and lowered the gun. He groaned and shook his head. "Damn it. All right. At least help me get his car out of the way?"

Dustin nodded.

Jackson ran to the driver's door, his eyes still fixed on Officer Davis in case he woke up. If the cop even glanced his way for a second, he would be forced to kill him. Pulling his sleeve back over his hand, Jackson reached into the cruiser and popped the trunk release. He searched inside, knowing cops always had flares. He brushed a blanket aside. *Jackpot.* He grabbed a flare and the blanket and closed the trunk. He hurried to Officer Davis and covered his head with the blanket. Then he struck the top of the flare against the rough cap to ignite it. The air filled with a sulfur stink. Jackson tossed the flare on the carpeted floorboard of the cruiser. He turned the steering wheel toward the ditch and dropped the shifter into drive. When the car lurched forward, he saw Dustin kneeling beside Officer Davis.

"What are you doing?" he barked.

Dustin stood up with a start. "Nothing."

Officer Davis groaned and started to move under the blanket.

"Get in the fucking truck," Jackson shouted. He climbed into Dustin's truck and Dustin climbed into the driver's seat. Before closing his door, Jackson popped off another round near Davis just to keep his head down. The tires threw rocks and dirt in their wake.

"What were you doing with the cop?" Jackson shouted.

"Nothing."

"Goddammit, Dustin. Tell me what you were doing." Jackson made sure Dustin saw the gun still in his hand.

"I was just checking to see if he was breathing."

"Did you tell him anything?" Jackson screamed.

"No."

"Did you tell him who I was?"

"No, man. Of course not."

"You better not have. You have to be smarter than that."

Dustin didn't look at Jackson, his eyes locked on the road. His jaw clenched and he didn't say anything else.

"So, we're not speaking now?" Jackson asked.

"It's just … I mean … I can't believe you shot a cop."

"He had a vest on. He's fine."

"You still shot him."

"I had no choice."

"You mean no choice except not shooting him?"

"That cop's name is Officer Davis. I know he's crooked, man."

"What? How?"

"I don't know. I just had a feeling."

"A feeling?"

"If he wants to bring *me* down, he must be crooked. Why else would he want to stop me from fighting crime?"

"You're crazy, Jack. You've lost some marbles. You need *help*."

"There you go with the help again. Don't you understand yet? I don't need that kind of help." He shook his head. "You can't tell anyone about any of this. It's like Clark Kent. No one can know."

"You're not fuckin' Superman."

Jackson smirked and looked away. After a few seconds of silence, he said, "You know, you're in this now, too."

"What?"

"You've helped me destroy evidence and shoot a cop. That makes you my accomplice. We're both in this deep now. My secret is your secret."

"No, Jack. I didn't have anything to do with shooting that cop. That was all you."

"Just the same."

"No. It's not just the same. It's pretty fucking different."

"So, this is where you turn on me?"

"What? No. I'm not turning on you. But I'm not taking the fall for shooting a cop if you get caught, either."

"I'll never get caught. I'm too good at this now." He looked out the window. "I think it's time we had that talk."

"I think so, too."

"Head to the rest stop on I-70 and we'll have some coffee. Maybe calm down a bit. You'll understand after you hear my entire story."

"I don't know, Jack. Maybe we should go home and get some sleep. We can talk tomorrow."

"Just give me twenty minutes." Jackson gave him his best puppy dog eyes and softened his tone. "Okay?"

Dustin hesitated before turning toward the freeway.

20
BULLET ANTS
December 9, 1994

Dustin and Jackson sat in one of the booths at the truck stop, eyes locked on each other, both waiting for the other to say something first. Dustin broke the ice after Flo delivered their coffee.

"You've changed, Jack."

"I know."

"It's bad, buddy."

Jackson shook his head.

"You just don't see it."

"You're wrong. I do see it. But it's not bad. It's exactly what needed to happen. What I've gone through, what I'm still going through, is helping me."

"I don't understand."

"I've been weak for my entire life. You know that. You've always known that."

Dustin shrugged. "That's why I always took up for you in high school. But you're way past high school now."

"In a way, I've never escaped high school. My accident proved how weak I still am. I mean, Christ, Dustin. I couldn't even pull myself from the couch to save my family. I was dying a little every day. But you know what? The accident also awakened something inside me."

"I think it broke your brain."

"No," Jackson snapped. He looked around to see if he'd drawn anyone's attention. A trucker at the counter was the only other patron, and he didn't look up from his paper.

Jackson took a calming breath. "No," he said again, a little softer this time. "It helped me get to here."

Dustin gave him a blank look.

"I haven't finished growing yet, Dustin. I'm getting stronger with every mission I accomplish, but I haven't found my bullet ant ritual."

Dustin's forehead crinkled. "Your bullet what?"

"Bullet ant ritual."

"I've got no idea what you're talking about."

"There's a tribe in the Amazon called the Sataré-Mawé that makes boys go through a painful ritual to become men."

Dustin sipped from his coffee. "I'm listening."

"They have to wear bamboo gloves full of bullet ants."

"So, what's a bullet ant?"

"A type of ant with the most painful bite in the insect world. There's no worse pain known to man."

Dustin scowled. "I don't know. I've had kidney stones."

"Bullet ant bites make kidney stones feel like massages. The pain is excruciating, but the boys can't take the gloves off or they fail. And do you know what they do for the pain?"

"Beat up criminals?"

Jackson gave him a withering look. "Funny. No. They endure it. That's the point. They willingly endure the worst pain imaginable."

"Sucks to be them." Dustin slouched in his chair. "What's this have to do with you going off the deep end?"

"Just listen to me. This ritual is their rite of passage. It's their transformation. The tribe believes the boys can't grow without pain. And do you know what? They're right."

"So, you're going to the Amazon and shoving your hands into ant gloves to become a man?"

"No. You're still not listening."

"You're not making sense. Explain it to me without the crazy."

"Remember when you were fifteen and those three kids beat you up?"

"Of course."

"That's when you went through your bullet ant ritual. I remember when you came out of the hospital. You were different. Stronger. You didn't take shit from anyone after that."

"That was a long time ago."

Jackson pinched the bridge of his nose. Dustin still wasn't hearing him. "Have you ever wanted to die, Dustin?"

"No."

"I have. Almost every day since my accident."

"I'm sorry, man. I know it's been rough for you, but what's this have to do with ..." Dustin looked around then leaned closer and whispered, "... shooting cops?"

"It's part of my ritual. I'm trying to find my bullet ant gloves."

Dustin leaned in again and whispered, "And you thought killing a cop would help you grow somehow? That's insane, man."

Jackson looked away. Maybe a different approach would work. "The accident gave me the tools to help me find my bullet ants."

"What do you mean?"

"It gave me the ability to sense when people are criminals."

Dustin shook his head and fell back against his seat. "Jesus, Jack. I've heard you spout this kind of shit before, but you're even further gone than I thought. I can't believe I have to say this to my best friend, but you're not a superhero with superpowers."

Jackson bowed his head. As painful as it was to realize, Dustin refused to understand. "I knew you wouldn't believe me."

"I think you've lost your mind." Dustin studied his face, no doubt hoping to see a smile. But it was no joke. Jackson returned a stone-cold stare. Dustin sighed. "When's this going to end? When you're dead? When you're in prison?"

"I don't know. The boys of the Sataré-Mawé go through the bullet ant ritual twenty times before they're considered men."

"Enough with the fucking whatever tribe."

"I will complete my ritual."

"And how will you know when you're done?"

"I guess I'll just know."

Dustin stared at him stoically. "This ain't right, Jack. This ain't the Jackson I know. So, what happens now? Where do we go from here?"

Jackson didn't know how to answer that. Dustin was the only person in the world he had ever trusted with his deepest secrets, and he was starting to regret trusting him now. "We should go home."

"Yeah, I think so. You can get some sleep and we'll talk again tomorrow when we're both not so tired."

Jackson watched his friend with sad eyes. He felt bad for him because Dustin didn't understand how important his work was. And he had so much more to do.

Dustin reached across the table and patted his shoulder. "Hey, man, it's all right. You've done some stuff that maybe you shouldn't have, but I'm sure you did it for the right reasons. I think you just need some professional help. What do you say to laying off the crime fighting for a little while until we can think clearer?"

Jackson wished it was that easy. There was a heart carved into the top of the table and he traced the gouges with his fingernail. "Yeah. Maybe."

Dustin held out his hand in a gesture of truce. "You know I'm your best friend. You can trust me."

Jackson reached into his back pocket and took out his wallet. "Yeah. I'll get the coffee," he said, and tossed six bucks on the table.

21
TODD'S WORK
December 9, 1994

Garrett woke up, his belly hurting from sneaking some leftover Halloween candy from the pantry before bed. His mom always said he'd have a tummy ache if he ate candy before going to sleep, and she was right.

"Dad?" he called.

No one answered. The pain squeezed his stomach again. He let loose a whopper of a toot. It made his belly feel a little better for a few seconds, but the cramps quickly returned. He slid out of bed and cracked his door open. The hallway light was off.

"Dad?" he called again.

There was still no answer. His dad was probably downstairs sleeping on the couch. Garrett scampered to the hall bathroom, flipped on the lights, and closed the door. He saw the KitKat bar he'd stashed on the towel shelf and decided it wasn't worth it. He didn't want the cramps to get worse.

Other than a few more toots, not much happened on the pot. But eventually the toots did their job and he felt good enough to go back to bed.

He was reaching for the toilet handle when a loud crash from downstairs startled him. It sounded like glass breaking. Garrett tiptoed to the door. He opened it slightly and heard someone fumbling with the lock on the front door. Garrett ran to his parent's bedroom to see if his dad was sleeping. The bed was still made. He grabbed the portable phone from the nightstand and hurried back to the hall. He stood near the top of the stairs and listened. Whoever was downstairs was getting something in the refrigerator.

Garrett dialed Jenna's work number.

"Two North," a woman answered.

Garrett was relieved someone he knew had picked up. He whispered, "Valerie, it's Garrett. Is my mom there?"

"She's working, honey. Why are you whispering? What's wrong?"

"Someone's downstairs and I can't find Dad."

"Hold on, hon. I'll get your mom."

"Val, wai—" There was a click and then hold music started playing. The footsteps downstairs marched back down the hall toward the staircase. Garrett didn't know if he should hang up and call the police or wait for his mom to answer. He tiptoed into his bedroom and crawled under the bed. The hold music continued to play. He laid the phone next to his ear as he watched the open doorway.

Two dirty boots stopped in the hall outside his room.

Please answer, Mom, he silently begged.

The boots stepped into his room. The music continued playing on the phone. Garrett worried it was too loud, so he pressed the down volume button, forgetting that it chimed when pressed. He froze, his eyes bulging.

The feet stopped beside the bed.

Garrett held his breath.

A deep, scary voice said, "You under there, kid?" Then the man dropped to one knee and jammed his hand under the bed. Garrett scrambled toward the other side, but the man caught his ankle. Garrett kicked madly while the man pulled him out. He stood and hoisted Garrett up beside the bed.

Garrett got a good enough look at him in the glow of the nightlight to recognize him as the man from the bus stop. He had the start of a straggly beard and buzzed hair just like

Garrett's and his dad's. His head was covered in scabbed-over scratches. This time he wasn't friendly at all and his eyes looked mean. He snatched the phone and held it to his ear. Then he smiled and Garrett saw his missing front tooth. He pressed "End" on the receiver.

Garrett kicked the man as hard as he could in the knee then bolted past him for the door. The man grabbed Garrett's pajama collar, yanking him back. He rubbed his knee with one hand and tossed Garrett against the bed with the other.

Terrified, Garrett watched him.

The man snarled, "You little shit," and backhanded Garrett on the cheek.

Garrett saw stars as he sprawled across his bed. His cheek burned like fire. The man held Garrett's hands together and wrapped his wrists in duct tape. Then he did the same with his feet. Last, he stretched a piece over Garrett's mouth.

Winded, the man sat on the bed and worked his knee. He wiped sweat from his face on a pair of shorts from the floor and then tossed them in the hamper beside the closet.

"You're gonna live with me now, Garrett. My name's Todd."

Then he grabbed Garrett's arms and slung him over his shoulder.

22
EZEKIEL 25:17
December 9, 1994

During the drive to Jackson's house, neither he nor Dustin spoke another word. It was uncomfortable and affirming at the same time. When they turned into the neighborhood, a white van with a broken grill nearly sideswiped them as the driver plowed through a stop sign. Dustin swerved.

"Look out, asshole," he shouted.

Jackson figured the driver was probably another drunk. If he didn't already have so much on his plate, he'd tell Dustin to follow him so he could teach the driver a lesson.

Dustin pulled into Jackson's driveway and Jackson climbed out. Dustin leaned across the passenger seat and lowered the window.

"Hey, buddy. We'll talk tomorrow, okay?"

Jackson turned back and nodded.

Dustin backed out of the driveway as Jackson walked up to his porch. He froze and his heart seized. The dormer window by the door was broken and shattered glass covered the floor inside.

"Oh my God," he whispered.

Dustin pulled his truck back into the driveway and stopped.

"What's going on, Jack?" he shouted.

Jackson ignored him and plowed through his unlocked front door. The phone was ringing. He ignored it and charged up the stairs to Garrett's room. He swung Garrett's door open to an empty bed. His knees weakened. He gagged and choked back a mouthful of coffee-flavored vomit.

"Garrett?" he shouted, and raced through the upstairs, searching each room. As he passed the stairs, he saw Dustin standing at the bottom.

"Jack?" he called up.

Jackson stared back with terrified eyes. "He's gone, Dustin."

"What do you mean?"

"Garrett. Someone's taken Garrett."

"What? Are you sure?"

"Look for him down there. Please find him, Dustin." Panic blurred his sight.

While Dustin searched the main floor, Jackson searched the upstairs again, shouting for Garrett over and over. A knot replaced his stomach. Jackson returned to the top of the stairs, devastated.

Dustin appeared at the bottom again. He solemnly shook his head.

"Check the basement," Jackson cried.

"I did, Jack. He's not there either."

Jackson slumped against Garrett's bedroom and his back rode the doorframe to the ground. He thought he might vomit again. He buried his wet eyes in his palms.

"What have I done?" he sobbed. "Oh God. Garrett."

The phone on Garrett's bed stopped ringing and then started ringing again two seconds later. He looked up from his hands to find Dustin standing in the hall, his face pale and one hand over his mouth.

"He's gone," Jackson moaned.

Dustin crowded past, grabbed the ringing phone, and handed it to him. "Answer it."

The caller ID said it was Jenna's work.

He took a deep breath and held it to his ear. "Hey," he said, trying to sound calm despite the quiver in his voice.

Jenna was frantic. "Jack, where have you been?" she screamed.

"Here," he lied. "Why?"

"I've been calling nonstop for the last ten minutes."

"I was sleeping."

"Val said Garrett told her someone was in the house and he couldn't find you. He wasn't on the phone when I got to it. Is he all right?"

"Yeah. He's fine. He's sleeping."

"Let me talk to him."

"What? He's asleep. I'm not waking him up."

Dustin gave him a look that said, "What the hell are you doing?"

"Wake him up," Jenna shouted.

"No. You're being ri—"

"The police are on their way. I already called them."

"You called the police?"

"Of course I did. You weren't answering."

His mind raced. What could he tell her? What would he tell the police? How could he find his son? Where—

And then an image of the speeding van leaving the neighborhood hit him. He had seen it before. It was too much to be a coincidence. He lowered the phone from his ear.

"Jack. *Jack*," Jenna shouted.

"Dustin, I know where that van came from," he whispered.

Dustin cocked his head. "What van?"

"The one that almost hit us when we were pulling in."

Dustin grabbed the phone. "Jenna, it's Dustin."

Jackson staggered from the room as if Evander Holyfield had punched him in the face.

"I don't know, Jenna. He's been acting strange all evening … What's that …? No … I don't know.

Jackson mumbled, "I gotta go."

Dustin side-eyed him. "Yeah, I think coming home's a good idea … Okay … Yeah. See you in a few. Be careful." He hung up.

Jackson shot toward the stairs.

"Where you going?"

"I know where Garrett is."

"What do you mean?"

Jackson paused halfway down. "I know where the guy driving that van lives."

"Then wait for the cops and tell them."

"They can't save Garrett like I can." Jackson barreled the rest of the way down the stairs.

Dustin chased him, still holding the phone. "Jack, wait. You need to be here when the police come. They'll be here any second."

Jackson turned back and gave him an ashen stare. Every second he waited further risked his son's life. Besides, whoever took Garrett deserved real justice, not some lifetime in the courts only to get a slap on the wrist. "Listen to me, Dustin. The police will waste time asking a thousand questions while that bastard is hurting my boy."

Dustin looked down at the phone. "Let me just call them—"

Jackson grabbed the phone and threw it against the wall. "You're not listening. I'm going." He ran outside to his car with Dustin trailing him.

"You can't leave, Jack," Dustin shouted. Jackson ignored him and climbed into the driver's seat. He pulled the door closed as Dustin reached his window. "Jack, stop. Don't do anything stupid. You're going to get yourself killed."

Jackson slammed the car into reverse and backed past Dustin's truck, almost taking off the side mirror. Dustin stepped back to avoid getting hit. Jackson backed into the street and stomped on the gas pedal. He glanced in his rearview mirror and saw Dustin backing out of the driveway to give chase. The only thing Jackson could do was try to lose him, but that would be difficult without drawing the attention of the cops.

On the next straightaway, Dustin gunned his engine and pulled alongside Jackson's car. Jackson kept his eyes forward as if ignoring his friend would make him go away. Out of the corner of his eye, he saw Dustin frantically waving for him to pull over. His stupid friend was going to get someone killed like Brody had.

When he couldn't ignore Dustin any longer, he lowered his window and shouted, "Go home, Dustin."

Dustin shouted back, "You gotta stop, Jack. This is crazy." Luckily, Dustin wasn't as reckless as Brody. At the first sign of headlights, he let off the gas and pulled back into the proper lane behind Jackson.

Dustin continued following, occasionally flashing his lights and beeping his horn all the way to the road that led to Gary's place. The pavement turned to gravel, and still Dustin stayed on Jackson's ass. They drove another quarter mile or so past Gary's before the gravel turned to a dirt track that had probably looked more like a road before the weeds took over. Jackson wondered if he had missed a turn. With Dustin's truck headlights blazing through his back window, he knew couldn't turn around without his friend putting a stop to the whole thing. And he was so close now—he could feel it in his bones. His only option was to keep going and hope.

And then Jackson's car hit a slight bump. By the time he realized he was driving on four rims, Dustin had already crossed the same bump. Jackson slowed to a stop and got out.

Furious, Dustin jumped out and slammed his door. "What the hell's wrong with you, Jack?" he shouted. When he saw his tires actively deflating, he kicked the side of his truck.

Jackson hadn't seen him so mad in a long time. For a brief second, Jackson worried his friend might give him a beating and drag him back to his house on foot.

Dustin stopped a couple feet short. "You're insane, Jack. We are going back to your house and talking to the police. This shit has to stop now. I can't believe you drove all the way out here on some harebrained wild goose chase while the only people who can help your boy are at your house wasting time trying to figure out where the hell you are."

"That's exactly why I drove out here. I know where my boy is."

Dustin groaned and rolled his eyes. "This is enough. I'm done." He looked around at the surrounding woods. "I don't even know where the fuck we are. Listen. We're going to find a phone and get back to your house with Jenna so we can do whatever the police need us to do to help Garrett."

Jackson angrily pointed behind the truck to a set of spike strips that crossed the dirt road. "Look, Dustin. Why would someone put down spike strips all the way out here?"

"I don't know, but we'll tell the police. We'll let them handle this. That's what they do." Dustin stormed back to his truck, grabbed a flashlight from the glovebox, and started walking, angrily bumping Jackson's shoulder as he passed. Then he paused and without looking back asked, "Coming?"

Jackson took a calming breath and followed. At least Dustin was going in the direction Jackson wanted to go.

"I'm sorry, Jack, but we gotta tell the cops about all this shit you've been doing. You need to stop with this crazy superhero fantasy and get some help."

Jackson glared at the back of his friend's head while they walked. He bit his lower lip. Was this his bullet ant ritual? He brushed his hand against his Glock and then jerked it away and shook his head. There was no way he could do *that*. Not to Dustin.

And it was at that moment that he realized he was still the same pitiful wimp he had always been. Without the bullet ant gloves, he would always be the guy who stood by and did nothing while criminals like Spyder stole all the cigarettes. He was still the same weakling who couldn't stop some drunk driver from killing an innocent woman. After everything he'd done, he was still the guy he had grown to despise after his accident. He might as well go back to his ass grove on the couch and waste away to nothing.

That is, unless he found his bullet ant gloves and the balls to put them on. Since he'd rather be dead than still be that guy, he had no other choice. The bullet ant gloves had to hurt or they'd be pointless.

He closed his eyes. It was time to put them on and take the pain.

He swallowed hard and drew his Glock from his waistband. He pictured pouring ants into the bamboo gloves as he lifted his weapon and aimed at the back of Dustin's head. The Beckys of the world needed him to be strong. *Garrett* needed him to be strong. A tear blurred his sight and he wiped it away with the back of his hand. He wanted to vomit. His gun hand trembled around the grip.

"I can't believe I followed you all the way out here, man," Dustin grumbled without looking back. "I must be as insane as you. We should be with Jenna helping the cops, not trouncing through some godforsaken forest."

Jackson winced. The pain had already started and it was only going to get worse. Almost unable to breathe, he lowered the gun and wiped his eyes again with his free hand.

He couldn't believe how painful it was. Then he pictured those brave kids of the Sataré-Mawé and brought his weapon back up with a sense of purpose. *Just do it already.* His tears flowed freely as he shoved the barrel to within inches of Dustin's head. He sucked in an unsteady breath and moved his finger from the trigger guard to the trigger. "I'm so sorry, Dustin," he whispered.

Dustin didn't hear him.

Jackson held his breath, closed his eyes, and squeezed. But his trigger finger didn't obey. He tried again. Nothing. He banged the gun against his forehead then aimed it again. He had no choice. He *had* to put on the gloves. But again, his trigger finger wouldn't squeeze the goddamn trigger. His hand shook. It was so simple. *Just pull the fucking trigger already.*

But it wouldn't work. It was like he'd had a stroke or something.

And then Dustin stopped.

Jackson summoned all his strength. *Put. On. The. Gloves.*

Dustin said, "I think I see a house up ahead. There's a light on in the window."

It was now or never.

Dustin started to turn around.

Jackson gritted his teeth and yanked his gun back to his side. *Damn it.* He turned away so Dustin wouldn't see his tears as the bullet ant gloves crashed to the ground. He had failed. He was weak.

"What's wrong, Jack?" Dustin asked.

Jackson wiped his eyes with his sleeve. "Nothing, man. I'm just worried about Garrett."

Dustin touched his shoulder. "I know, brother. We're both worried about him. Let's go to that trailer and call for help."

Jackson nodded and lowered his head. He needed to shake off his failure if he wanted any chance of finding his son. As they got closer, they saw an old barn behind the trailer. In front of the trailer was the white van Jackson had seen leaving his neighborhood.

Dustin glanced at him. "Is that the …?"

Jackson nodded. "Same one. Do you believe me now?"

"I don't know. But I'm willing to take a closer look."

Jackson steeled himself and put his weakness behind him. "Turn off the light. We need to get the drop on this bastard." He pushed past Dustin.

Dustin grabbed his shoulder. "Hold up, man. Don't go jumping to conclusions. We still don't know what's going on."

How much more did he need? Jackson shook off Dustin's hand and marched toward the trailer.

"What are you gonna do?" Dustin whispered.

"I'm going to go into that trailer and kill whoever's in there."

Dustin hurried to catch up and grabbed his shoulder again, his eyes wide. "You can't just go in and kill someone without knowing for sure."

"You're really getting on my nerves, Dustin. What more do you need to see so we can stop fucking around?"

Dustin nodded toward the barn. "That trailer is tiny. If this guy's kidnapping kids, he might keep them in there … don't you think?"

"And if we search the barn that'll satisfy you so I can do what needs to be done?"

"If Garrett's in there, you bet."

Jackson sighed. "Okay. Let's go have a look."

The two jogged to the barn and examined the padlock and chain that secured the double doors. The padlock was old and rusty and wouldn't take much effort to pick. While Dustin kept watch, Jackson used the screwdriver in his keyring pocketknife to probe the mechanism. The padlock popped open. Quietly, he unwound the chain, eased the door open, and slipped inside.

Dustin followed and pulled the door closed. He turned on the flashlight again. Then he stumbled and caught himself on the barn wall.

Jackson's knees went weak too. *Oh. My. God.* Staring back from six cages were six sets of terrified little eyes. Beside each cage was the red-orange glow of a space heater. Dustin traced the wall to find a light switch, but Jackson stopped him.

"We can't let him know we're here until we get these kids to safety." Jackson turned back to the cages. "Garrett? Garrett, are you here?"

From the farthest cage, a tired little boy's voice answered, "Dad?"

Jackson started crying and ran to him. He dropped to his knees and shoved his fingers between the wires. Garrett touched his hand. Jackson leaned his forehead against the cage and openly sobbed. "You're safe now, buddy." He grabbed the padlock and shook it in frustration. It was too new and high quality to pick with his little screwdriver.

Dustin went from cage to cage, reassuring each child that they would be free soon. Garrett leaned his forehead against Jackson's with the cold steel of the cage between them. Relief and hate boiled in Jackson at the same time. "I'm going to kill everyone who had anything to do with this, Garrett. I swear. But I'm so sorry. You have to stay here for a few more minutes until I can get the keys."

"No, Dad. I'm scared. I wanna go with you."

Jackson used his heartbreak to fuel his rage. "I know, son. But you have to be strong."

"Please, Dad. Don't go."

Jackson stood up. It was like tearing off his own arm. "I love you, son." With Garrett begging him not to go, he turned away and left part of his heart on the floor.

The kids knew the stakes, as evidenced by their continued silence in the face of potential rescue. Jackson met Dustin in the center of the barn. "We have to find the keys. That bastard with the van will have them."

Dustin nodded, his eyes locked on Jackson's. There was new resolve in them. "Okay, Jack. This is it. I'm all in. How do you wanna do this?"

Jackson scanned the barn. "We gotta get him away from the trailer in case it's full of weapons."

"And then what?"

"And then I'll blow his fuckin' head off."

"How will we get him to come out?"

Jackson looked around again. "I don't know. We need a distraction or something."

One of the little boys from the cages whispered, "Sir?"

Jackson turned to him. "Yeah, buddy."

"Todd'll be out here soon to get one of us."

"What do you mean?"

"Every night he takes one of us inside to watch out for the soul snatchers while he sleeps."

"Soul snatchers?"

"Yeah. If we don't watch for them, they'll kill us too."

Jackson squeezed a fist at his side. Then he knelt beside the cage. "Listen to me, buddy. There's no such thing as soul snatchers. This Todd guy is crazy. Do you hear me?"

The little boy nodded.

"We're going to get you out of here, okay?"

He nodded again.

"How many people are in the trailer?"

"Just Todd."

"Perfect. We'll be back to take you to your parents real soon. I promise."

The little boy gave him a hopeful yet reserved smile.

Jackson and Dustin crept out of the barn, replaced the lock and chain, and hurried around the side out of sight from the trailer. Dustin peeked around the corner while Jackson checked that his Glock was locked and loaded.

Though it was only a few minutes, it felt like an eternity before Dustin said, "The trailer's back door just opened."

Jackson mentally prepared for violence.

Dustin whispered, "He's coming. And he's got a big stick."

Jackson white-knuckled the grip of his Glock. "Tell me when he's almost to the door."

"Okaaaay … He's almost there."

Jackson stepped around the side of the barn like the Terminator. "Hey, Todd," he shouted, and lifted his gun. Dustin stepped out beside him.

Todd froze and tilted his head. "Are you them?"

"Them who?" Jackson parried.

"The soul snatchers."

Jackson shook his head.

"Then who are you?"

"The end of your evil reign."

Dustin side-eyed him again. Jackson shrugged, embarrassed. He stepped forward, gun trained on Todd.

Todd smiled. He was missing a tooth, just like Garrett had said. He had such evil in his eyes that Jackson had not yet seen. "What are you gonna do with that?" he asked in a deep and menacing voice.

"Stop your deadly game," Jackson answered. Okay, it was official. He was an idiot.

Todd shook his head, put his fingers in the corners of his mouth, and whistled. "Blackie," he shouted.

A dog tore from the other side of the barn on a laser-straight path toward Jackson. Jackson popped off a shot that struck the dirt beside the beast. Blackie leaped and latched on to Jackson's shoulder with a vice made of razors. His weight and momentum slammed Jackson to the ground. Jackson's gun flew from his hand. Blackie shook his head and tore the flesh and muscle of Jackson's shoulder. From his back, Jackson saw Todd closing the space between them with an axe handle dragging the ground behind him.

Dustin rushed to Blackie. "I'll get him, Jack." He kicked the dog, but Blackie didn't let loose. Todd charged. Dustin shouted, "Hold on, Jack."

Jackson pushed and punched and ripped at Blackie's fur, but his weak efforts were useless against the ferocity of the blood-thirsty beast. Blackie shook his head again, paused to clamp down tighter, and then shook even harder. His razor teeth tore deeper into Jackson's muscle with every agonizing shake.

Jackson caught a glimpse of Dustin as his friend ducked Todd's swinging axe handle and clobbered the psychopath in the face. Todd stumbled backward.

Blackie dragged Jackson in a circle as Jackson flailed uselessly at him. When Jackson finally got another glimpse at Dustin, his friend was sprawled unconscious on the ground with Todd standing over him. Todd rubbed his jaw and turned to Jackson.

Jackson redoubled his efforts to get Blackie off him. Todd marched up as Blackie twisted and snarled. Todd's sick grin was almost worse than the pain.

"Get 'em, Blackie," he crowed, and laughed. "Hold him there."

Blackie froze, teeth still embedded in Jackson's flesh. Todd drew his axe handle back like a golf club aimed at Jackson's head. He was deliberate in dragging it out to savor the moment. Jackson twisted and thrashed beneath Blackie, trying to keep his head out of Todd's path, but Todd was content to wait until he saw his shot.

Jackson pushed away the pain in his shoulder and focused on Todd. He only had one chance. Todd swung at Jackson's head like Jack Nicklaus at the Masters. Jackson closed his fist around fur and flesh and yanked with all his might as he rolled to the side. Todd's axe handle struck Blackie's skull with a muffled thump. The mutt instantly went limp and his jaws loosened. Jackson yanked his mangled shoulder from Blackie's mouth.

Todd screamed, "Goddamnit, Blackie. You got in the way."

Jackson scrambled to his knees out of Todd's reach. He pressed his hand against his jagged wound as he struggled to his feet.

Todd knelt beside Blackie and put a hand on the dog's chest. Then he stood up and turned to Jackson. "You killed my dog," he said.

Despite the pain, Jackson managed a smile. "Good."

He tried to lift his right hand, but Blackie had done too much damage to his shoulder. Every movement sent pain ripping down his arm. This fight, which wasn't fair to start with, had just gotten infinitely harder. But Jackson hoped his rage and skills would even the odds.

Todd pounced, swinging his axe handle with a grunt. Jackson ducked at the last second. The axe handle soared over the top of his head. Jackson drew back and slammed his foot into Todd's crotch with all his strength. It was the luckiest of lucky kicks, even better than Hector's. It landed hard enough to hurt his foot.

Todd stumbled backward. It seemed to take a moment for his brain to register the pain. Then he doubled over, his axe handle falling to the dirt. He dropped to his knees and dry heaved.

Jackson retrieved the axe handle with his good arm and used it to get to his feet. It was heavy. Solid. It took everything he had to lift it to his shoulder with only one hand, but he got it there.

On his knees with his hands glued to his balls, Todd lifted his eyes. He wanted to get up, Jackson could see that, but sometimes a man's will couldn't overcome the weaknesses of his body. Fear had replaced Todd's confidence. He must have known then what was going to happen. In the end, he was nothing more than a coward.

"Where are the keys?" Jackson growled.

"What keys?"

Jackson stepped closer and raised the axe handle higher. Todd cowered.

"The keys to the cages. Now."

Todd fished in his pocket and pulled out a keyring full of keys. "Here," he said, and held them out.

Jackson snatched them and crammed them into his pocket.

"Now, leave me alone. Take those stupid kids and go."

Jackson shook his head. "Is there anything you want to say before I bash in your skull?"

"Please don't?"

Jackson met Todd's evil eyes with his own righteous glare and then brought the axe handle down like a sledgehammer on a railroad spike. Todd's eyes filled with panic for the briefest of seconds before the handle split his forehead. Somehow, the monster stayed on his knees. The blow would have killed him if Jackson had use of both arms. Todd looked up with glassy eyes.

Jackson jerked the handle back for another blow, this time striking above Todd's right ear. Todd collapsed to his side. Jackson hit him again and again until his body convulsed and quivered on the ground. And then Jackson hit him some more. Todd's face quickly became unrecognizable. He stopped breathing several blows before Jackson stopped hitting him.

Jackson dropped the axe handle and gasped for air. As exhausted as he was, it was worth the pain and effort. He retrieved his gun from the ground behind Todd and heard Dustin groan. He glanced over his shoulder and saw Dustin shaking his head as he pushed himself up to his knees.

"Is he dead, Jack?" he asked, rubbing a bloody knot on his forehead.

Jackson bowed his head and nodded.

Dustin got to his feet. "You did it, Jack. You saved these kids."

Jackson nodded again.

"It's over, brother."

No, it wasn't. There was one more thing that needed to be done. He turned to face his friend. His eyes were completely blurred with tears.

"What's wrong, Jack? We've won. You did it. It's all going to be all right now."

Jackson shoved his hands all the way into the bullet ant gloves and squeezed the trigger. The recoil felt like a jolt to his heart. He didn't hear the gunshot so much as see the round strike Dustin's chest with the force of a baseball bat.

Dustin's eyes widened. A dime-sized circle of blood appeared around the hole in his sweatshirt and quickly spread outward, reminding Jackson absurdly of Sir Meatball of the House of Marciano's.

"I'm so sorry, Dustin. I had to do this. I had to wear the gloves." Tears streaked his face, but this time he embraced them. The gloves felt horrible and amazing at the same time. He was as strong as the Sataré-Mawé kids after all.

Dustin dropped to his knees. The look of shock on his face was devastating. Jackson watched as the color drained from Dustin's cheeks. It was a strange feeling to watch the life drain out of a friend knowing he was the cause. Dustin collapsed on his face.

The bullet ant bites were more painful than he ever could have imagined. He dropped to his knees, crawled to Dustin, and hugged him with his good arm. Dustin choked and coughed up blood.

"I'm sorry it had to end like this," Jackson whispered. He wondered if he could ever accept what he had been forced to do. When Dustin's last breath left him, Jackson didn't feel any of the joy he had after Hector or Brody or the others. He felt nothing but unimaginable pain. Though the children were waiting, he couldn't leave his friend to die alone.

He sat holding Dustin's head in his lap and rocked back and forth. If any doubts tried to creep in about whether he had made the right decision, he pushed them away. He had to stay strong, like the boys of the Sataré-Mawé. He only hoped he didn't have to wear the bullet ant gloves nineteen more times. But if that was what he had to do, he would find the strength. His work was too important. He couldn't give up on himself again.

He held Dustin until long after his tear ducts had run dry. Eventually, he found the strength to lower his friend to the ground. He stood up, gazing at his dead friend. Dustin stared blankly back at him. He reached down and gently closed Dustin's eyes, letting his hand linger on Dustin's cheek. "I love you, Dustin."

It was time to go.

23
RIGHTEOUS
December 9, 1994

As Jackson turned toward the barn, he glanced at Todd's body and tilted his head in thought. A brilliant idea formed. If the cops were looking to connect the kidnapper and the Spyder Stopper, maybe Jackson could give them the evidence they needed.

He went to Todd and knelt beside him. Using his own shirt, he scrubbed the Glock clean of his fingerprints. With his hand still wrapped in the fabric, he placed the gun in Todd's hand and folded his fingers around the grip. He moved it around a bit to leave multiple prints, and then grabbed Todd's left hand to put more prints on the slide. Then he placed Todd's trigger finger on the trigger, aimed in Dustin's general direction, and emptied the magazine into the trailer as if they were errant shots. Then he tossed the gun aside.

With his wounded arm dangling at his side, he let himself into the barn and flipped on the lights. Six sets of hopeful eyes in cages stared back.

"It's okay, guys. You're safe now. Todd can never hurt you again." His eyes found Garrett and he smiled. Garrett smiled back.

Jackson took out Todd's keys and freed each of the children as quickly as he could. When he opened Garrett's cage, Garrett threw his arms around his neck and squeezed. Jackson never wanted to let go.

Before taking the children outside, he needed to make sure they didn't see the bloody carnage. Todd's corpse was a grizzly sight, and Garrett would be inconsolable if he saw Dustin. He knelt in front of the doors and had the children gather around.

"My name's Jackson. What are your names?"

Camden answered first, followed by Samantha, Dylan, Frederick, and finally Drew. Jackson found it difficult to look at a couple of them. They were so thin their bones pressed against their pale skin. It made him want to bring Todd back to life just to kill him all over again.

Samantha pointed to his shoulder. "Does it hurt?"

Jackson nodded. "Very much." At least the bleeding had stopped.

"Did Blackie do it?"

"Yes."

"He's a meany dog."

"Yes, he was."

Jackson looked closer at Samantha's neck. "Is that a dog collar?"

"Um-hm."

"Take those off. All of you." The children removed their collars and threw them as far away as they could. "Are you ready to go home?"

They answered with smiles and nods. Samantha hugged Jackson. He muffled his groan so she wouldn't know how badly it hurt. He stood up and took Garrett's hand. "Everyone hold hands. It's going to be dark where we're going, but I promise you'll be safe. Do you trust me?"

"Yes," they chorused.

He pointed to where Dustin's and Todd's bodies lay on the other side of the wall. "Don't look over there. Okay?"

They nodded.

"I mean it. Look at Todd's trailer and don't turn back."

He led them from the barn to Todd's van. Dylan stopped short and the line staggered to a halt.

"What is it?" Jackson asked. The answer was painted on their faces. "Oh. Not getting in the van, huh?"

They shook their heads.

"I get it." Jackson looked around for another car, but they were in the middle of nowhere. He thought about his car and Dustin's truck, but they'd never get more than ten feet driving on rims in the dirt. He'd have to go into the trailer for a phone, and he was pretty confident the children would refuse to join him. He gathered them around. "I'm so proud of you kids, but I need you to be strong one more time. Can you do that?"

They nodded.

"I'm going to go into Todd's trailer for a phone. I want you all to stay right here and hold hands. Okay?"

They nodded again. They were so brave.

Jackson smiled. "I'll be back before you can count to twenty."

The trailer was a cluttered mess. There was a Pop Tart wrapper on the counter surrounded by ants. The plywood floor was covered in dark stains and Jackson feared they might be bloodstains from other children. Just the thought of it made him sick to his stomach. He searched for a phone, but the only phone jack he found on the wall was empty.

The only way those kids were getting out of there was to walk straight out of hell. Gary's home was a couple of miles away. He hoped the kids were up for it.

"Did you find a phone?" Drew asked when Jackson returned.

Jackson shook his head.

Drew's shoulders fell. "Oh."

"Hey, hey. It's okay, buddy. We're just gonna have to walk for a little bit. That's all. And you'll be fine because I'll be with you. And I'm going to protect you. All right?"

The only ones he was really worried about were Samantha and Dylan. They were the thinnest. Jackson offered to carry one of them with his good arm, but they both refused. They were all so much stronger than children should have to be. Maybe their ordeal with Todd had been their bullet ant ritual. They walked hand in hand and never faltered or complained all the way to Gary's house.

24
WHAT'S THE 411
December 9, 1994

Jackson gazed blankly at the hospital curtain as doctors and nurses cleaned his shoulder wound and stitched it up. The shots of local anesthetic were the worse part. Each time the curtain opened he hoped it would be Jenna, but it was always another nurse or doctor stopping in to meet the man who'd saved all the kids. Everyone loved him. Well, everyone except his wife. He wondered why he hadn't heard from her yet, though he suspected he already knew the answer.

The doctor advised him to see an orthopedic surgeon in the coming weeks, finished sewing up his shoulder, and then shook his hand before stepping out.

"Nurse?" Jackson called as someone passed his curtain.

She peeked in. "Yes?"

"Did someone get ahold of my wife?"

Her forehead wrinkled. "About two hours ago. I'm surprised she's not here yet. Do you want me to call her again?"

"No. That's all right. Thanks." Jenna must have really been pissed.

Jackson was dozing off when another set of footsteps approached the curtain. An unfamiliar man's voice said, "Knock, knock. May I come in?"

"Sure," Jackson answered.

Like every detective in every show he'd ever seen, this guy wore a tan overcoat over a button-down shirt and a loose tie.

"I'm Detective Smits. I need to get a statement if you're feeling up to it."

Jackson nodded, one eye still on the curtain behind him, hoping for Jenna to appear.

The detective produced a small notepad and a nubby pencil. A set of bifocals rested on the tip of his nose. "Can you tell me how you ended up at Todd Skelton's property this evening?"

"Do you know if my wife has arrived yet?" He was hoping to learn if she had talked to the police and, if so, what she'd said.

Detective Smits looked over the top of his glasses. "She hasn't come in yet?"

Jackson shook his head.

"Yeah. I talked to her."

"She's pretty pissed, huh?"

"I'd say yes. Not the brightest plan to leave Garrett home alone tonight to have coffee with Dustin, was it?"

"I don't suppose so. What else did she say?"

Detective Smits grinned. "We talked a bit."

It looked like that was all Jackson was going to get. He'd better not press. "Was Garrett with her?"

"Yeah."

"Is he okay?"

"Seems to be coping. He'll definitely need some long-term therapy, though."

Jackson groaned inwardly. He knew all about head shrinks.

"So?" Smits continued. "Tell me what happened tonight."

Jackson bit his lower lip. "As you know, I went to the truck stop with Dustin for a coffee. I—"

Detective Smits interrupted, "Do you leave Garrett home alone at night often?"

Jackson hesitated. It was important to only lie about the most damning parts of the story. Lying about anything else just to make his situation less uncomfortable would be too risky. "I have in the past, yes. I've gone through a bit of depression since I had a car accident earlier this year."

"I'm aware."

"Yeah. Anyway, I found getting out of the house helped break the monotony of the long, lonely nights since I struggle with sleeping. Sometimes I'd go to that diner and sometimes I'd run to the store just to get out. I knew I shouldn't, but …"

"And Todd Skelton's house?"

Jackson explained seeing the white van hauling ass from the neighborhood and recognizing it from his visit with Gary. "I just put two and two together," he said.

"Your wife said you knew she had called the police. Why didn't you wait for them?"

"I don't know. My mind was all over the place when I saw Garrett was gone. I remember thinking I had nothing to lose. I mean, what were you guys going to do differently than you have with the other missing children? They were still missing, weren't they?"

Smits nodded. He flipped the page in his notepad. "About your friend, Gary. He said you called him out of the blue a couple weeks ago."

Oh shit. The car. What did Gary tell him? Play it cool. "Yeah, I thought seeing some of my old friends might help with my depression."

"And you two drove out to Gary's house?"

"Yeah, that's right."

"And that was because he was going to give you a …" He flipped through his notebook again.

If Jackson had been standing, his knees would have betrayed him. He swallowed hard.

"… comic book or something? A Superman book?"

Jackson relaxed. Gary, that wonderful bastard, hadn't said anything about the car. Good ol' Gary. "Actually, it was an Incredible Hulk and Wolverine book. Very rare."

The detective scratched the side of his head. "Oh yeah, right. That was it."

"Gary thought Garrett might like it one day. He told me about it while we were having lunch and I just had to see it."

"So, what happened when you got to Skelton's?"

Jackson had been working on this part of the story since the paramedics had loaded him into the ambulance. He described everything more or less as it had happened up to the point where he put on his bullet ant gloves and killed his best friend, claiming Todd had pulled the trigger while Jackson fought with Blackie.

"It looks like you hit Skelton quite a few times. More than necessary?"

"I think I blacked out after I saw him shoot Dustin. I knew no one else was coming to help, and if Todd got up again, I might be lying next to Dustin right now."

"I understand. I'll have to present all the evidence to the DA, but I don't think he'll pursue that aspect. We can all understand what you went through."

Jackson nodded gratefully.

"Okay, Mr. Foster. That's all I need for now. We'll probably talk again when you're up and about. You don't mind, do you?"

"Not at all." Why would he mind? They were buying everything, and he was basically a hero.

Detective Smits handed him a card. "Call me if you think of anything that might be pertinent."

Jackson shook his hand. The detective had a strong, confident, honest grip.

Smits paused before leaving. "You know, it's a real good thing what you did for those kids."

"How are they doing, by the way?"

"They're being reunited with their families as we speak. Other than a couple of them being malnourished and all of them needing a lifetime of therapy, they're doing okay. Kids are resilient. Because of you, they didn't meet the same fate as Skelton's other victims."

"What do you mean?"

"We've begun excavating behind the barn. So far, we've found three shallow graves. We expect to find more."

"Oh my God. That's horrible."

"Yes. Yes, it is. I hope you and your wife work things out soon. It's none of my business, but if I were you, I'd apologize and beg for forgiveness."

"You must be married, Detective."

He held up his left hand and wriggled his wedding band with his thumb. "Twenty-three years next month."

As Jackson made small talk with the very person who could put him away for the rest of his life, he couldn't believe he was pulling it off. The world seemed so thankful for what he had done, he could shoot someone in front of the hospital on national TV and they'd probably give him a mulligan. Too bad his wife didn't buy into the hype. He watched the curtain for her until the nurse finally came in to discharge him.

He took a cab home. No one was there. The first thing he did was call his in-laws.

"Hello?" his father-in-law answered.

"Bob?"

"What do you want?"

"Is Jenna and Garrett there?"

The other end was quiet.

"Please, Bob. Just tell me they're there so I know they're safe."

Another quiet few seconds followed. Then Bob said, "They're safe."

"Can I talk to them?"

"Not right now."

"Okay. Will you tell Jenna I'm sorr—"

The line went dead.

Jackson replaced the receiver. He covered the broken dormer window with some cardboard and duct tape and ripped down the yellow crime scene tape covering it. It wasn't a secure fix, but it would have to do for now. He was exhausted. He went to the fridge and grabbed a beer and a Vicodin. He felt a headache coming on. Then he plopped into his ass groove on the couch and flipped on the TV.

Infomercials.

25
KEYS TO THE CITY

December 16, 1994

It was a typical chilly December morning in Ohio as the crowd began to gather in the parking lot outside city hall. A stage had been erected at the front of the building where various local dignitaries were gathering. Even the governor was there. Jackson waited offstage while city council members addressed issues about zoning and the coming Christmas parade activities.

Under a coat draped over his shoulders, Jackson's left arm rested in a sling. Sixty stitches, a tetanus shot, and a future surgery on the ligaments aside, he was as good as he could be.

The ceremony was scheduled to start at 10:00 AM and it was already 9:45 with no sign of Jenna or Garrett. He hadn't seen or spoken to them in a week. He scanned the growing crowd, recognizing Drew and Samantha with their families. They looked different and he realized it was because they had regained some of the weight they had lost during their ordeal. He hoped all the children would be there, but he understood if the event was too much for them. He also saw Dustin's widow, Karen, and Gary, and Officer Davis.

By 10:00 the ceremony began, and there was still no sign of Jenna. The police chief stepped up to the podium to say a few words about Officer Davis and his "outstanding record as a law enforcement officer," blah, blah, blah. The chief described Davis's encounter with Todd Skelton at Milner's Farm, praising his bravery. Jackson hid a smile. He knew the truth on that matter. The chief went on to say how thankful he was that Davis survived getting shot in the line of duty. Officer Davis crossed the stage and humbly received a handshake and a round of applause.

After Officer Davis waved and left the stage, he stopped in front of Jackson and held out his hand.

"You did real good finding those kids. We're lucky to have men like you in our community."

Jackson awkwardly took the man's hand with his left and shook it. Then Officer Davis joined his wife and newborn baby while Jackson seared a hole in his back with a glare. He just couldn't shake the nagging feeling that he should have taken care of the "outstanding" officer when he'd had the chance.

Jackson scanned the crowd again and still saw no sign of Jenna and Garrett. The police chief introduced the mayor next, who began by offering a prayer.

"Hey, Dad?"

Jackson spun around to see Garrett standing next to Jenna beside the stage. Jackson ran to them, knelt, and wrapped his good arm around his son. He never wanted to let go.

Garrett eventually pushed away. "Okay, Dad," he said.

Jackson stood up and leaned in for a kiss from Jenna, but she gave him her cheek. "Thanks for coming," he said.

"We needed to be here."

Behind him on the stage, the mayor read off a list of his own political accomplishments while the crowd fidgeted to keep warm.

Jackson said, "I'd like to see you guys again. I've missed you both."

"I know. I'll make sure you see Garrett soon."

"And you?"

She didn't answer.

Remembering Detective Smit's sage advice, he added, "I'm sorry for everything."

She looked past him to the stage. "I think they're getting ready for you. You should head over."

"Can Garrett go with me?"

"Of course."

Mayor Blackstone wrapped up his political speech. "And this brings me to why we're here this morning." He called up Karen from the crowd and waved Jackson to the stage. Jackson took Garrett's hand and walked with him to the podium. Karen was crying, so he hugged her.

Mayor Blackstone repeated Jackson's bullshit story of how he and Dustin had gone out for coffee to discuss life in general and ended up killing a kidnapper and saving six children. He presented Karen a posthumous medal for Dustin and hugged her as her tears flowed. Though it was hard for Jackson to watch, he took solace in knowing Dustin would forever be remembered as a hero.

Then it was Jackson's turn. The crowd applauded for several minutes nonstop. Once the applause died down, the mayor presented Jackson with the keys to the city. The crowd gave another rousing round of applause. The mayor extended his hand and Jackson shook it while locking eyes with him. It was a weak grip, not befitting a politician. He got a funny feeling about him.

Mayor Blackstone leaned in and said, "Good work, young man. You've saved a lot of lives. Our city and the country as a whole are indebted to you."

In return, Jackson whispered under his breath, "Does the city need saving from *you*?"

Mayor Blackstone smiled awkwardly. "What's that? I didn't quite hear you."

Jackson smiled. "Nothing. Just making a bad joke."

The mayor gave him a politician's grin and turned back to the crowd.

Jackson sighed. His work wasn't done after all.

EPILOGUE

February 7, 2005

Jackson pulled into a parking space outside Garrett's new apartment and waited. He and Garrett had a lunch date scheduled. Though he didn't get to see his son nearly enough, he'd seriously considered canceling after having a bad morning. Jenna had called to say she was getting remarried. He'd been expecting it considering how close she was getting to that Carter douchebag, but it still hurt to hear. Jackson didn't completely trust the guy. He was good to Jenna, but he had a weak handshake. Jackson wouldn't be surprised if he had to pay him a visit some night.

He tapped his fingers impatiently on the steering wheel and kept glancing at his watch. He'd been on edge since Jenna's call. As much as he loved spending time with his son, what he really needed now was another night of hunting bad guys.

After Todd had posthumously taken the fall for the real Spyder Stopper, Jackson had been forced to change things up a bit. Those changes meant a whole new set of inconveniences. It was a complicated process now, involving a lot of travel and taking time off from his job at the tire shop. It was usually worth the effort, but he couldn't do it often. It was so tempting to throw caution to the wind and patrol his home turf, but in all these years he'd only done it once and he couldn't do it again. He couldn't risk the cops figuring out that the Spyder Stopper was still in action.

Garrett opened the passenger door and climbed in. "Hey, Dad."

"Hey," Jackson answered, unable to hide his sour mood. He backed out of the parking spot and headed for the restaurant.

"Watch the Superbowl last night?" Garrett asked.

"Some."

"Pretty good game, huh?"

"I guess. If you're a Patriot's fan."

"I was rooting for the Eagles, actually. But I think that Tom Brady's gonna be a pretty good quarterback, don't you?"

"I guess."

Green Day's "Boulevard of Broken Dreams" played on the radio. Jackson thought it was especially fitting today. Talk about a lonely road.

"I really like this song, Dad. You heard it before?"

"Yeah. I've heard it."

"And?"

"It's fine."

An awkward silence fell between them.

The song ended and a local DJ came on, his tone way too cheery for a Monday. Jackson barely listened, already drafting preliminary plans for his next night out. Then something the DJ said caught his attention.

"In local news, today marks the tenth anniversary of the unsolved murder of former Pataskala Mayor Timothy Blackstone. The Blackstone family is holding a candlelight vigil in his memory at City Hall and is once again asking for anyone with any information regarding the murder to come forwar—"

Jackson turned off the radio. He couldn't believe it had been ten years already. Just thinking of it made him furious. After all the trouble he went through to take out the corrupt politician, the public still didn't know what a monster he'd saved them from. At first he couldn't understand how the police hadn't discovered all the mayor's crimes, but then he realized they must be complicit. Officer G Davis wasn't the only crooked cop in Pataskala. And what enraged him the most was that he couldn't risk doing anything about it.

The awkward silence continued until Garrett broke it. "What's wrong, Dad?"

Jackson shook his head, pulling to a stop at a red light.

"She told you, didn't she?"

Jackson hesitated and then nodded.

"When?"

"This morning."

"I figured you wouldn't be happy. I know it sucks, but Carter is a nice guy."

Jackson groaned.

"I'm sorry, Dad, but it's been ten years. You should really start dating, too. At some point, you have to move on."

"I know. I'm just too busy to date. Besides, I don't know if I could make it through another—"

A loud crash swallowed his words and his car jolted forward. His head snapped back against the headrest.

"What the …" A glance in the rearview mirror showed an SUV with a smashed front end and steam pouring from its radiator. "Are you kidding me?" Jackson groaned. The day just kept getting worse. He looked over at Garrett. "You okay?"

Garrett rubbed the back of his neck. "I think so."

Jackson slammed the gear shift into park and cursed under his breath, "Fuckin' asshole."

Garrett leaned around to see through the back window. Then he touched Jackson's shoulder. "Hey, Dad. Calm down. It was just an accident. We're all right."

But Jackson wasn't having it. He kicked open his door and marched toward the SUV. "What the hell are you doing?" he shouted as the driver started to open his door.

It was a kid, probably no older than Garrett. When he saw how angry Jackson was, he pulled his door closed.

Furious, Jackson shouted, "Get the hell out here and talk to me like a man."

"I-I'm sorry, man," the kid shouted through the closed window.

Jackson rattled the handle, but it was locked. "How in the hell could you hit me?"

"I-I-I wasn't paying attention."

Garrett ran to the front of the SUV and stopped. "Dad, what are you doing? Calm down."

Jackson ignored him. "What's your name, kid?"

"Arnold, sir. I didn't mean to hit you."

Jackson glanced at the damage to the back of his car and it infuriated him more. He'd just paid the damn thing off. Enough playing around. "You got insurance, kid? You'd better."

Arnold nodded.

"Get out here and show me."

"Let me get my—" Arnold lunged for his center console.

Jackson panicked, memories of Lester and his shotgun under the covers bombarding him. If Arnold was going for a gun, Jackson couldn't let him get the drop. He stepped back and drew his 9mm from his concealed shoulder holster. Arnold didn't see him and continued to fumble with his center console.

Garrett shouted, "Dad, stop."

Jackson saw the gloss black of a gun grip. "Don't do this," he shouted.

The kid started to turn toward him, the gun in his hand. Jackson squeezed the trigger. Just like cops are taught, he fired three shots as he fell away to avoid return fire. The first one shattered the SUV's window. All three thudded into Arnold's chest and side. Jackson landed on his back, gun still trained on the SUV. He could just see Garrett ducking beside his car.

The *whoop-whoop* of a police siren startled him as a cruiser whipped around the corner, almost as if it had been lying in wait. The cop bounced out and drew his weapon.

"Drop the gun," he screamed.

Jackson tossed his gun onto the pavement and threw his hands above his head. The cop had the drop on him, and he'd be a fool to shoot it out in the middle of the day with witnesses everywhere. Besides, it was obviously self-defense. Once the officer saw Arnold's gun, he'd have to clear Jackson of wrongdoing.

"Get on your face," the cop shouted.

Jackson did as ordered. The pavement was cold. "This isn't necessary, officer," he said.

The cop pinned him in place with his knee and cuffed Jackson's hands behind his back. He was going to feel like such a fool when he realized the shooting was justified. The cop patted him down before looking into Arnold's car.

"Oh shit," he shouted. He called for medics with his shoulder mic as he yanked Jackson up and slammed him against the back door. "Hey, kid. Hold on. I've got the paramedics coming."

Jackson shook his head. "Be careful, officer. He's got a gun in his right hand."

"Shut up," the officer snapped. "He doesn't have a gun. He's holding a cell phone."

Jackson's eyes went wide. "What?"

"You stupid son of a bitch. You shot some kid holding a cellphone."

Jackson shook his head. "No, no, no. That's impossible. Look again. He pulled a gun on me after he hit my car from behind."

"I don't see any guns, man. You just shot some kid." He grabbed Jackson's shoulder and jerked him over to the cruiser. While he checked Jackson for weapons a second time, Jackson saw Garrett standing off to the side. His eyes were red and his face was twisted with pain. The officer shoved Jackson into the back seat and slammed the door shut. Then he ran back to Arnold's car.

Jackson watched as more cops arrived, along with a fire truck and an ambulance. The paramedics pulled Arnold onto a cot and started CPR as they rolled him to their truck. Jackson would have been more concerned if he wasn't so sure they would find the gun any minute now.

From the back of the cruiser, he watched the detectives go to work, taping off the scene and placing small cones over each of the three shell casings. Then they talked to Garrett. Eventually, the arresting officer returned to the cruiser to transport Jackson to the station. Garrett looked devastated as the cruiser pulled away.

During the ride, Jackson asked, "Well, did you find the gun? Did Garrett tell you about it?" He already knew the answer. There were no other possibilities.

The officer ignored him. Jackson got a bad feeling he was part of some elaborate setup, only he didn't know why. They couldn't know who he was. To his shock, the police booked him and charged him with second degree murder with an illegal firearm. One of the detectives took great pleasure in telling him he was going away for a long time. Jackson would be sure to remember the pig's name.

Jackson sat through his trial in utter disbelief of what was happening to him. He knew he'd seen a gun and he knew he had done what was necessary, but no one seemed to believe him. The entire trial was a farce. Everyone was on the take. But the thing that hurt the most was when Garrett testified through crocodile tears about how angry Jackson had gotten. His own son lying and saying Arnold never had a gun was the deepest knife in his back imaginable. That hurt him with the jury more than anything else. Jackson couldn't understand how his own son could betray him so. Jenna, maybe. But not Garrett.

When the detectives insisted there were no weapons found in Arnold's car, Jackson knew they were lying, too. When the jury found him guilty and the judge sentenced him to twenty-five years in prison with the possibility of parole after eighteen, Jackson nearly vomited. And when the prison cell door slammed shut on the first day of his sentence, he lost what little faith he had left in the justice system.

That was also the day he realized he had more bullet ant rituals to endure. One wasn't enough. He was still too weak. If he'd been stronger and bolder, he would have cleaned out the whole Pataskala police department years ago. Then he wouldn't be in prison on trumped up charges while everyone, including his family, turned against him.

Eighteen years was a long time to wait. But Jackson's justice didn't wear a watch. He would get through his sentence because killing Dustin had made him stronger than he could have ever imagined. If he was patient and jumped through every hoop they put before him, he would one day get his chance. And when he got that chance, a lot of people were going to meet his justice. First he would put on the bullet ant gloves, and then he would go to work. No one who had wronged him would be safe.

The legendary Spyder Stopper would return.

ABOUT THE AUTHOR

Douglas R. Brown is an author living in Pataskala, Ohio. He began writing as a cathartic way of dealing with the day-to-day stresses of life as a firefighter/paramedic in Columbus, Ohio. He has been married since 1996 and has a son and some dogs. His catalogue includes a werewolf tale with a twist (*Tamed*), an epic fantasy trilogy (*The Light of Epertase*), a dystopian fantasy adventure (*Death of the Grinderfish*), and a creepy short story collection (*A Firefighter Christmas Carol and Other Stories*). Visit Douglas at www.epertasepublishing.com or email him your thoughts at epertase@gmail.com.

OTHER BOOKS BY THE AUTHOR

A FIREFIGHTER CHRISTMAS CAROL

DEATH OF THE GRINDERFISH

TAMED

THE LIGHT OF EPERTASE
TRILOGY INCLUDING
LEGENDS REBORN
A KINGDOM'S FALL
THE RISE OF CRIDON

www.ingramcontent.com/pod-product-compliance
Lightning Source LLC
Chambersburg PA
CBHW060523260626
47161CB00003B/739